The Children

The Children

CHARLOTTE WOOD

First published in 2007

Copyright © Charlotte Wood 2007

All rights reserved. No part of this book may be reproduced or transmitted in any form or by any means, electronic or mechanical, including photocopying, recording or by any information storage and retrieval system, without prior permission in writing from the publisher. The *Australian Copyright Act 1968* (the Act) allows a maximum of one chapter or 10 per cent of this book, whichever is the greater, to be photocopied by any educational institution for its educational purposes provided that the educational institution (or body that administers it) has given a remuneration notice to Copyright Agency Limited (CAL) under the Act.

This project has been assisted by the Commonwealth Government through the Australia Council, its arts funding and advisory board.

Allen & Unwin
83 Alexander Street
Crows Nest NSW 2065
Australia
Phone: (61 2) 8425 0100
Fax: (61 2) 9906 2218
Email: info@allenandunwin.com
Web: www.allenandunwin.com

National Library of Australia
Cataloguing-in-Publication entry:
    Wood, Charlotte, 1965– .
    The children.

    ISBN 978 1 74175 335 6 (pbk.).

    I. Title.

    A823.3

Internal design by Greendot Design
Set in 13.5/16 pt MrsEaves by Midland Typesetters, Australia
Printed in Australia by McPherson's Printing Group

10 9 8 7 6 5 4 3

For sisters and little brothers, especially mine
and
always,
for Sean

Who said *Happiness is the light shining on the water.
The water is cold and dark and deep . . .*

WILLIAM MAXWELL, 'Over by the River', *All the Days and Nights*

CHAPTER ONE

February, 2006

GEOFF SHOVES the ladder—*thunk*—against the house, and kicks hard at the bottom rung to dig its heels more solidly into the soil of the garden bed. Then he picks up the plastic shopping bag of newspaper-wrapped tiles and begins to climb, the bag heavy in the crook of his elbow as he moves.

He bought the tiles from Macquarie Hardware this morning. He stood in the queue in the cavernous building, as he does most Saturdays, holding the one or two things he needs for the weekend's domestic repairs—a packet of wall plugs, or a couple of star pickets. This morning after he bought the tiles he walked out into the bright glare of the car park. He put the bag of tiles into the boot of the Falcon and then walked back across the car park to the half-case supermarket, pulling from his pocket the shopping list in Margaret's looped blue handwriting. Although it was early, already the car park was busy with slow cars, with shopping trolleys tinging over the bitumen. Rundle was coming slowly alive for its Saturday.

He emerged from the gloomy little arcade carrying Margaret's extra-large bag of flour against his chest. He shifted the bag to his hip as he bent to unlock the boot again—and as he did a sudden, shocked recognition sprang up at him: the bag was the exact soft weight of a sleeping baby. He was surprised by the physicality of this memory, its strength. He hasn't held a baby in more than thirty years.

Now, as he climbs the ladder, he is puzzled in a pleasing way again at the mysterious and intricate workings of the human brain. He pictures it, a mass of tiny, coloured electrical wires the thickness of hairs. As he climbs, the plastic bag slides forward, its handles cutting into the skin of his forearm; he shrugs his shoulder to shift it down his arm. Near the top of the ladder he steadies himself, pressing his hips forward against the last several rungs, and then lifts the bag carefully into the guttering, making sure the tiles cannot slide away.

Geoff knows the brain doesn't look like electrical wiring, but all the same he likes the image: an old, corroded thread of wire, deep in the tangle, suddenly sending out a hot white spark of memory.

He climbs the last few rungs, hunching, tilting himself forward, and crawls up onto the roof. He is too aware of his ageing body, of the anticipatory decisions he must always make now about its movement. He steadies himself for a moment, kneeling there on all fours on the sloping tiled surface. He glances about at the bright roofs of his neighbours, the fresco of red and orange tiles, of telephone wires and television aerials and sky. A mynah bird perches on the Collins' aerial, frowning out of its dark yellow-rimmed eye for a moment before flying off. The aerial quivers, an echo of flight.

Geoff crawls a little further onto the roof and then, when it is safe to do so, turns to sit on the slanting tiles, his bony knees apart, hands dangling between them. From here he can see off into the distance outside town, the flat plains, the painted striations of river and hill and horizon. He draws his gaze closer then, to the furze of trees lining the river, nearer again, to the bright metallic sheet of the fire station roof over on Fitzroy Street, then the few houses beyond his, then to the Collins' next door, and his own backyard. From here the view of his yard is spacious, surprising, making the place where he has lived for more than thirty-five years suddenly unfamiliar. He stares down over his garage roof, his barbecue, his pergola. His intimacy with it is in this instant scrubbed away, and he is struck by a light, strange feeling that there might yet be things to discover down there, in his yard, in his life.

Just nearby, in the guttering, he catches sight of a mottled, ancient tennis ball. Again there is the little *zzzt* of memory, to do with the children, to do with the weight of a baby in his arms all those years ago.

When he falls a moment later, what he sees is the colourless flap of a bird's wing and a rushing, tilted sky.

MARGARET STANDS on her tiptoes, peering into the back of the pantry, reaching out her hand to a green-lidded bottle of paprika among others in the blue plastic ice-cream container, when she hears the noise. Something sudden and heavy on the roof above her head. She stands there in her kitchen looking up to the ceiling with a cylindrical little spice bottle held aloft in her fist. She stares upward, listening for more sound.

CATHY FISHES the ringing mobile telephone from her shoulder bag, pushing the groceries along the supermarket's stalled conveyor belt with her free hand. She looks at the screen and puts it to her ear. 'Hi, Mum,' she says into the phone.

'Oh, Cathy,' says her mother's voice, in a surprised way. It is not her usual message-delivering telephone voice, but high, and bewildered.

The checkout girl presses the conveyor button and the last of the groceries jolt, then slide forward. The girl drops a box of tissues and a tube of toothpaste into a pale green bag, unhooks it to sling it alongside the others, and waits. Cathy is hungry. She casts a look along the queue behind her, wondering if it is too late to run back for bananas. But there are people waiting; a man behind is glaring at her.

'Did you ring me accidentally,' says Cathy to her mother, frowning, tucking the phone between her neck and ear as she opens her wallet and passes a fifty-dollar note to the girl.

Her mother's voice, its disbelief: 'Dad's fallen down.'

HE LIES in the new hospital ward, the dark purple mess of his face obscene in the whiteness of the bed. All around him is white. Stainless steel and white, slivers of blue-and-white, mint-green-and-white. Nurses stride around in the quiet, twirling keys on lanyards, or holding things in their gloved hands. Their rubber-soled shoes on the new linoleum, *squidge*, *squidge*.

Tony Warren, the wardsman, kneels to check that the brakes on the bed's rubber wheels are properly engaged. Then he straightens and puts his hands into the pockets of his blue overalls. He steps to the head of the bed to look at the man's slack, unconscious face. He moves his own head this way and that, to better view the particular gruesome flowerings of colour and swelling. The ventilator tube coils out from the old man's mouth, then up over the ear and his bald, bandaged head, on the opposite side to the mashed temple. Hands still in his pockets, the wardsman leans in to inspect the dark, pulpy edge of the large wound, which is visible despite the dressing and the sticking plaster holding the ventilator tube in place.

As he inspects the edges of the wound the wardsman winces, showing his teeth and inhaling a quick, quiet breath.

Tony Warren is unnoticed as he stands there by the bed, the large ward empty but for a couple of murmuring nurses and two other unconscious patients at the end.

There are no visitors, yet. They will soon gather, as they always do, rushing into the ward with their eyes wide, glancing around them at their shocking new world. But for now the patient is untended, a mechanically breathing corpse.

The wardsman looks up to read the card taped to the wall above the bed, the name in black texta capitals: GEOFFREY CONNOLLY. The wardsman stops, his gaze fixed on the card. Then he leans in again, removing his hands from his pockets and resting his forearms on the bars of the bed, staring once again for several long seconds at Geoff's damaged, horrible face.

Eventually he sticks his hands back into his blue overalls pockets, pivots around and without looking up, walks back along the wide lane between the beds. At the door he stops and whacks the oversized red button on a panel on the wall, and the wide laminate door swings slowly open with a hydraulic sound.

He leaves the ward, and the door closes, *pssshh*, behind him.

 CHAPTER TWO

TO BE adult is to be alone. Mandy sees this line, an epigraph, just before she bends back the cover of the novel and shoves it, pages splayed, into the seat pocket in front of her. She moves her head to look out of the window, past the women in the seats beside her. But beyond the women's profiled faces the plastic shutter is pulled down, and she can see nothing but a crack of light beneath it.

A French biologist said the thing about being alone. Mandy wriggles in her seat, pulling at the knees of her trousers to stop their tight bunching at her crotch. She longs for the needling hot jet of shower water on her bare back, for clean underwear. There are still three hours to go. A child's sleepy wail rises from the back of the plane.

Mandy's mother's dazed and careful telephone voice comes into her mind. Her father had made a strange high shriek, flailing in the gravel, she said. Mandy does not want to picture this, her father's fallen body and this impossibility of sound. She moves her jaw, pushes the image away. It is replaced by the boy again.

The woman next to Mandy is still asleep, her brow creased, frowning at the light. Mandy can see dried white spit at a corner of the woman's mouth. She touches a thumb and third finger to the dry corners of her own lips.

He was a boy she had seen daily, but to whom she had barely spoken. Once, in the hot chaos of the street outside the Al Hamra she gave him a fake silver biro, and he shouted, *'Tanks!'* in an American voice, and grinned at her in a sly way that could have meant either, and equally, that he liked her or hated her.

Over the months she saw him everywhere in the streets near the house, wearing his high-waisted bright blue tracksuit pants and a tan polo shirt—the kind her father wore in photos from the fifties, with its caramel-allsorts stripes on the collar. On the boy's bare feet the dusty vinyl sandals all the children wear. She has seen him giggling in the street, hanging around a couple of soldiers; the Americans heavy with gear looking dumbly down at him.

Whenever she went out with Graham, the cameraman, the boy would run around in front of them with his friends, a gaggle of tall and little ones, all skinny and perfect-skinned, their black feathery hair neatly cut over their heads. They would push and jostle each other before the camera, holding up both hands, making two-fingered 'V' symbols, shouting *'Hello! Hello!'* and *'I like Spiderman!'*

The boy—named Ahmer, she learned later—had a big nose, perfectly arched thick brows above his big eyes, and two oversized white front teeth. They reminded her of her brother Stephen's teeth as a child, and the boy had the same sticking-out ears. She had seen him playing marbles with his friends next to a pile of burning rubbish; or on the main roads with the other children, waving as a tank passed, the soldiers' guns aimed straight above the children's heads. Occasionally Mandy has felt a dull surprise at how quickly she became accustomed to these scenes, these things: that children played with the burnt, street-flung doors of exploded cars; that they leapt to catch the tense gaze of a soldier with a machine gun; that in Baghdad's gritty dust this boy could remind her so much of her own little brother in their long-gone Australian childhood.

And then the day she saw him sitting alone in the street, oddly bent in the wild powdery air and the terrible noise, and the lower half of his body gone. The blood laced over his face, and the boy silent and motionless in that strange sitting, still alive, just watching her as she ran with her arms hugging her head; recognising her.

The woman next to Mandy suddenly inhales loudly through her nose, blinking and staring in the stunned way people do when they are woken. The gloom is beginning to lighten, and the air in the plane shifts with people waking and stretching in their seats.

In a Baghdad morgue, Ahmer's father Ibrahim stood speechless, dressed entirely in white, one large clean hand clutching the other behind his back. He watched, as Mandy and the photographer watched with him, an attendant from the morgue washing his son's body on a concrete slab. The pale walls of the square room, the rectangles of light from the high windows. Grey cement, galvanised-iron buckets. The gentle white lather of soap covering what was left of Ahmer's body. The attendant wore a grey t-shirt and black trousers, a neatly trimmed beard. Ibrahim wore a white overshirt, white trousers, and a white kaffiyeh with two black coils wound around his head.

The blood was dark as mud on the boy now, a slick patina over his neck and forearms—why specially his arms?—as if he had plunged them over and over into a deep, sticky pool of it. His chest and ribs and stomach were clean, where his jumper had been, and here on this skin was only a single small, sweet bruise of boyhood, from a slingshot, or a table corner. In the middle of all that blood this space of clean skin was miraculous. Mandy wondered how Ibrahim could stop himself from falling upon it.

The boy's face had been cleaned of its nets of dried black blood, but somehow a new bright red pool gathered beneath his body on the slab as the attendant gently turned him. This bright red was almost the only colour in the room—the red and, Mandy saw with a different shock, the pink-and-green striped towel which the attendant had folded with neat tenderness over the pulpy dark mess below Ahmer's hips. The towel, threadbare and stiffly clean, was straight from Mandy's childhood, identical to the two her mother still keeps folded in her linen cupboard behind the new, fluffy, plain ones. The candy-striped towel and the flash of bright blood in the monochromatic room. The photographer moved his body soundlessly—wishing, Mandy could tell, that he could silence the callous whizzes and clicks of his camera.

When Ibrahim turned to look at Mandy, his neat, trimmed beard seemed whiter than it had the day before. Behind his thick chemist's glasses with their slightly bent frames, his eyes were swollen and rheumy. He stared at her for a long second before turning back again, gripping his hands together more tightly behind his back as he watched a stranger lifting and turning and soaping his ten-year-old boy's beautiful, destroyed body.

In the stale recycled air of the plane, above the rows of seats the television screens flicker into life. The plane icons on the screens creep across the bright blue ocean towards the orange coastal frill of Australia.

Her father has fallen off the roof. In three hours she will be at Sydney airport, and Chris will be there waiting.

To be adult is to be alone.

CHAPTER THREE

Day one

MARGARET LEANS into Geoff's doughy, swollen face.

'The girls and Christopher are coming today,' she says in a low voice. She pauses. '*Mandy* is coming home.'

Geoff lies there, unchanged. It feels futile to be talking to him, but all the nurses and the doctors have told her she should, so she does. It is three days since the accident. She supposes he still looks shocking, but she can't tell anymore. Perhaps he looks much better. It seems she cannot now remember his face as it used to be—unblotched, unswollen, bare of the tubes, without the dreadful purple wound spreading its bruises across his face. She can stare at Geoff now without flinching, or crying. His eyelids are still the shiny, dark purple puffy slits, no lashes visible, but perhaps they are a little less swollen, less glossily tender, than yesterday? Margaret looks up for a nurse to ask, but the only two she can see are at the desk, bent together over the back of a computer, holding electrical cords in their hands.

There is the mechanical sound of Geoff's breathing, the sound of the oxygen hissing gently around them. She takes off her jacket and fits it carefully over the back of the visitor's chair, taking her time. Then she sits down, crossing her legs. She thinks now she should not have said that about Mandy coming home. In ordinary times it would mean something very special; someone's wedding, a rare Christmas.

She doesn't say anything about Stephen. There is nothing to say. She sees a nub of thread in her stocking and leans forward to run her fingertip over it, wondering if she will be able to nip it off with her fingernails, or whether that will only pull it and cause a ladder. She decides not to risk it. She remembers the varicose vein scalloping her thigh and uncrosses her legs. She sits back in the chair and watches Geoff breathing, being forced to breathe, by the ventilator. The machines around the ward bip and sing their lopsided notes. There is so much time in here.

One of the nurses has left the computer and stands holding a telephone receiver to her ear, still watching the other girl fiddling with the cords. 'Well, how long will *that* take,' the first one says into the phone, rolling her eyes at the other nurse.

The new ward, this Intensive Care Unit, has been opened only a week. Some of the machines are still covered in plastic wrapping, or have delivery stickers on them. The first day Margaret went to the bathroom, the toilet was covered in fine cement dust and there were plastic covers over the drains of the sinks. She is grateful that Geoff was not quite the first patient in the intensive care unit; the young man a few beds away appeared in a picture in the local newspaper, thin and groggy. He has had his leg amputated from diabetes. Margaret heard the doctor telling him the same thing she herself has been told, how lucky they are. That this unit has been opened, that the specialists are happy to come now, that the patients have not had to travel all the way to Sydney in an air ambulance.

She stands up and lifts the crumpled sheet, holding it above Geoff's chest covered in its wires and white medical sticking tape. She lets the sheet billow down softly, and then spreads it lightly across his shoulders, stepping around to the other side of the bed to straighten it. She wonders if it might hurt him, this weight of the sheet. She wonders if he can feel. If he were conscious, would he feel the pain still? The sound he had made, the weird scuffling in the gravel and that terrible sound, a baby's grizzling coming out of the man she had never heard cry. That sound she never wants to hear again.

She watches his face, all day, every day, for signs of the pain, or of waking. But there has been nothing. The nurses and the doctor say that the stillness is good, that he needs to be kept still, even though they take him off each day for some new test, some scan. The wardsman comes and wheels the bed away for a time, then wheels it back. She doesn't go with them.

There is so much time.

At home in the mornings she finds herself rushing, guiltily, to get ready. When she wakes up—usually after a long, urgent dream about some mundane, unfinished task like clearing out the laundry cupboard, but over which she must nevertheless face some brutal public judgement—she lies there in the bed, so *tired*. Then she turns over and sees the clock and it is already seven. How can it be so late when the last time she looked, just a minute ago, it was five-thirty? So she sits up, panic rising in her, and then scurries to the shower, the breakfast table, ironing board. Ticking off lists and remembering to stuff into a plastic shopping bag the cards that have begun to arrive, and some magazines, and the library books she must return, and then clopping in her good shoes down the driveway.

But once she has arrived, at nine o'clock at the latest, and set down her bag of things and taken off her jacket, the day yawns ahead, each hour a long ribbon into the future. And she is suddenly so heavily tired again, sunk there in the squishy wide chair with its new vinyl smell, a magazine resting on her stomach.

At the far end of the ward a twosome of doctors is doing the rounds. The nurse from the computer has left the desk and follows the doctors, slinging the stark blue curtains closed along their railings around each bed, cloaking the patient and the doctors inside. Margaret pictures them in there, arms folded, asking questions of the person in the bed, waiting for answers, nodding. When they get to Geoff, will they have anything to say? She tries to think of questions of her own to ask. The children will ask her things, and she must be able to answer them. But there is only one question. After her first irritated moment of confusion on the phone—'*What do you mean, Mum?*'—Cathy had made Margaret repeat what she had said. She could not believe her own words. Then Cathy had said, the same disbelief in her voice, 'Well—is he going to be all *right*?'

Margaret keeps returning to the moment, three days ago, that she heard the scuffling thunder of Geoff's falling body overhead. It seems like three years ago. And now it has begun to seem to her that at the moment Geoff fell, she fell too, began spinning back through her marriage. It is as if his skidding boot, his body as he tumbled, has knocked loose a stone in a wall and made a small irregular gap through which her life comes pouring, dry as sand. She cannot stop it. The pouring sand is made of decades-old glimpses of memory—of her mother folding an unopened letter into a small concertina and pushing it deep into the darkness of a hedge. It is herself, an exhausted young mother, lying on her back in a garden. It is standing with an axe held above her head, too scared to kill a snake even to protect her children. And then the sand is more recent: her eldest daughter sending her weary-sounding postcards from godforsaken places in the world never heard of except on the news, and Margaret's knowing that between the front of the postcard and the back lies the truth—that these are places Mandy knows her parents will never go; that she has chosen a life in which her mother can't come after her.

In the dry, almost silent rustle of the pouring sand, Margaret thinks, *I was going to be an air hostess*. When she was nineteen she wrote away to Ansett from Brisbane, saying nothing to her parents. But she never got a reply, so she married Geoff instead. Except that years later, as she lay in hospital with a new baby in her arms, her father told her what he had spied one day while clipping the hedge, the glimpse of mouldy folded envelope, long after she'd written away. 'Good thing your mother hid that letter from Ansett, after all!' He'd said it almost by accident, grinning and googling into the baby's tiny face.

Margaret remembered the moment, all the hurtling shock and hatred. She'd gathered the baby's, Mandy's, little knitted jacket around her and held her close, away from the proud grandfather. The room had begun breathing and swelling. Years later Cathy took her to an art exhibition, and there was a big tunnel thing that made Margaret sick to walk through, the walls pressing in. She understood that thing, never mind what the notices said on the gallery wall. That white breathing corridor was a missed life, and you clinging to a tiny, hungry baby for protection, and being shown your other future, pushed deep into the dark of the hedge, speckled with bird dirt and mildew.

Sometimes when the children were small she had let herself daydream about the air hostess she would have been. She daydreamed herself in Monaco, or lying on her back on perfect green grass, staring up at the vast struts of the Eiffel Tower—that would be on a day off— or just handing out those little parcels of neat dinners and simply a slot to put the trays back into. No sinks, no nappies. Only little squares of food and drink with their neat covers on little trays, and quiet people sitting belted into their seats while she would stroll up and down, and sometimes go and check her lipstick and stockings and re-pin her chignon.

Margaret had always known that this was stupid.

She knew it would not really have been like that, but she liked to think of it that way all the same. It is the same now, when every so often she makes a visit to the 'clairvoyant' in Armidale that her friend Yvonne told her about. She knows it is stupid, but she only goes these days when there is something bad in the news about a place where Mandy is, and when she has not been in contact. But that happens nearly every day now, and Margaret only goes to the psychic—Marilyn—a few times a year now. Psychics are only pocket-emptiers, she knows, and anyway the woman never tells her anything really, except *'Mandy knows you're with her, and she loves you.'* It is stupid, but Marilyn's certainty is comforting; like when a doctor tells you firmly, *You will get better.* So it is enough to be told that her daughter loves her, by a complete stranger wearing too much eye makeup, and who has a yappy little pug dog that she pushes by the face into a tiny cage with a blue plastic door whenever Margaret arrives. The room always smells of dog, and she can see its angry little eyes from behind the plastic net of its cage whenever she lets her gaze wander from Marilyn's eye shadow. At tennis, she doesn't mention going to see Marilyn, even when Yvonne talks about her own 'readings', and Yvonne doesn't seem to know. At least Marilyn is clairvoyant enough to keep her mouth shut.

Margaret sniffs now at her own joke. The doctors are standing at the far bed of the young woman with a scarf wrapped around her head. The young woman's face is pale as the sheet, and she stares up at the doctors out of her sunken eyes, answering their questions only with a slow blink, or a tiny shift of her head.

Margaret looks at her watch. Mandy should be getting off the plane now. Chris said he would take her home for a shower and breakfast, and then they would leave at noon at the latest, collecting Cathy on the way. He said that nobody has yet heard from Stephen, but that they would keep trying.

Sometimes Margaret realises it is a little strange that it is her daughter's husband, not Mandy herself, who rings her up, who organises things. Who says, in a tender voice, *'You take it easy, Marg.'* But men are different now than they used to be. Some men.

She is aware, too, that in the back of her mind she has begun to think of Geoff as if he is back at work again, or off on a Rotary trip. Not this ruined mess before her. When she looks at that face again now she feels the shock forcing breath into her lungs once more, and she must breathe it out, in two hard pushes, to stop herself from crying. 'Just *calm bloody down*,' that's what he would say to her now. If he could speak. He would say it kindly, she thinks. But with a firm hand on her shoulder. She breathes out again, more steadily this time.

After she was married and they moved to Rundle, Geoff would go off to work and Margaret would sit on a rug in the garden with the children. Sometimes she would lie down there in the sun and let the children wander about. Sometimes she fell asleep, out of tiredness, out of boredom. Nobody said anything about depression back then. She wonders if that's what it has been, her whole adult life. *Depression.* Or *anxiety*, the way everything is explained now, on the radio, on the television. Politicians even, having *bipolar disorder*. Names for everything.

Margaret was never given Valium like her friends, although once a doctor offered it to her when she went to him with an itchy scalp. In the seventies. 'Isn't Valium a dirty word these days?' she'd said without thinking, smiling a little. The doctor had stared at her for a second then, and put his pen down, and said coolly that perhaps she needed to change her shampoo instead, and stood up for her to leave the room. Afterwards she wished she had kept quiet, let him write it down for her. Perhaps it would be nice to live for a while in the glazed, pretty world that her friend Judy seemed to inhabit. Geoff said that dancing with Judy at the P&F ball was like dancing with a tin can. Plenty of tinkling noise and light as a feather. Margaret thought at first he meant it as an insult, but later she wasn't sure.

Looking over at him in the bed, she is suddenly seized by a thought—*Where are his hands?* She jumps up, leans over and searches for his left hand under the sheet. She finds it and peels away the sheet so she can lift it out, hold its cool weight in both her hands for a moment. She strokes her thumb over the familiar sun-blotched, veiny skin. She lowers her face for a second, holds her cheek against the soft skin of his hand. Then she lifts the sheet and lays his hand back down, carefully, on the narrow strip of mattress at his side. She strokes his forearm and then leans over to find his other arm; it is there, straight by his side, plastered and tubed. She lowers the sheet again and tucks it back in.

She sees across the beds that the doctors have disappeared again. They are not coming to speak to her after all. It is always like this: the waiting, the expectation, then nothing. Then they will suddenly appear and blurt things at her when she's not ready, and then take him away, then reappear. She smooths her trousers beneath her bottom and sits down again. She tries not to feel relieved that the doctors have gone.

In a moment she hears a noise. The tea lady is coming with her trolley. The trolley is old, battered stainless steel, out of place among all the muted new colours and spotless surfaces. The tea lady's murky green uniform looks old and out of place too. She wheels her trolley along the speckled linoleum, raising her eyebrows at Margaret as she approaches. Margaret smiles and shakes her head; later she will walk to Sidewalks on the corner for a proper cup of tea.

She sees the tea lady make a brief, furtive glance at Geoff's leaden face before she moves away. And Margaret understands suddenly, like a heavy punch to the stomach, that it is clear to strangers that Geoff will soon be dead.

THESE PAST few days, driving to and from the hospital, Margaret has had the odd feeling that there's a small animal somewhere inside her car. She catches glimpses sometimes, at the corner of her vision, of something dark and quick. She has cleaned out the car, poking the vacuum hose as far under the seats as possible. But tiny creatures—like mice, or big cockroaches, little birds even—can flatten themselves against surfaces, and lurk there, undetected.

When the children were small they bought a kitten at a school fête, and it escaped in the car. All the children's little hands grasping at it, and it screeched and yowled and in the rear-vision mirror Margaret saw the furry thing backflipping and then the children all diving for it. They could hear it miaowing all the way home, hidden somewhere beneath the seats. When they pulled into the driveway, though, and the children were all standing on the grass, Margaret could not find the kitten under any seat. They pulled everything from the car—jumpers, old exercise books, soft-drink bottles, cricket pads and a cordial-stained picnic blanket. Eventually they opened all the car doors and went inside, hoping the kitten would sneak out when they weren't there. Early the next morning Margaret stole out to the car to listen. Still the kitten was faintly miaowing. Eventually, with the children all banned from coming out of the house, Geoff tracked the sound to the door. The animal had somehow squashed itself in between the inner and outer panels of the door. It took a crowbar to jimmy the upholstered vinyl panel off, and the exhausted kitten fell, wet and heavy, to the ground on the driveway.

Margaret thinks of this now, as she drives home from the hospital. She knows there can be no animal. There is no sound. With the kitten they could hear it crying. But now, stopped here at Rundle's one set of traffic lights outside the supermarket, there it is again, this time at the shoulder of the passenger seat near the window: a tiny grey darting.

The kitten, all those years ago, had lasted a few months in her family's care before it shot across the road to escape a tennis ball, and was run over.

She knows there is no kitten; that there is probably nothing at all. She must ask Geoff about it. And then for the umpteenth time she feels the stab, as if she has just been woken by a loud noise and for an instant doesn't recognise the room she has slept in for forty years.

Outside Woolworths, Pauline Newberry is standing

at the corner, talking to a woman Margaret doesn't recognise, wearing a green dress. The woman has her hand up, shielding her eyes from the sun.

Margaret knows she must somehow accommodate herself to this recurring bolt of understanding. And to these strange thoughts that have come tumbling in since Geoff fell down—the creature in the car, the futile remembrances of old hurts that her own parents inflicted—things long-ago accepted, now suddenly lurching. The air hostess she might have been. Wondering, again, why she has no grandchildren.

She must gather herself before Chris and the girls arrive. She flicks the indicator, listens to its slow tick. There is no creature in the car. *Be rational*. That's what Geoff would say.

The traffic light turns green, and she waits for a space between the oncoming cars to turn right.

But she has been rational. For years she has been on the watch, for both of them: bowel cancer, Alzheimer's, heart attack, glaucoma, stroke. She has listened to the warnings, trimmed the fat. She goes to Barry Manning at the first signs of anything, makes Geoff go too, for a yearly check-up. They have done all the walking, the crosswords. Geoff set up the computer so he could load things up from the Internet. Archaeology things, Words of the Day. He printed them out on the buzzing little printer and left the papers about the house. They have done it all: Rotary, gardening, tennis twice a week, art appreciation, *Life Writing* that one time. And she has been their vigilant guardian:

sunhats, sunscreen, hard green vegetables. Margaret feels tears of fury pricking at her eyes. She had been on at him, always: watch this, don't eat so much of that. And he had narrowed his eyes and looked more intently over the rims of his glasses into the fuse box, intoning, '*There is nothing to fear but fear itself,*' in a deep, mocking voice. And she would nod, sighing—she bored herself, even, with the ninnying nagging of her voice.

But she had been *right.*

She turns the corner into their street. She had been right to be fearful—only, it was of the wrong things. This is the insult, the outrage of it. It has got them by surprise, despite all the wretched, braying *watchfulness*. She sniffs her tears back, swallows. She noses the car into their driveway, automatically looking up to the windows to wonder if Geoff is home yet, before catching the thought and letting it pass.

She turns off the ignition, pulls on the handbrake, and sits very still, waiting, watching for movement from the corners of her eyes. But here in the car the creature too is still, and silent, and nowhere to be seen.

CHAPTER FOUR

THEY TRAVEL in the small blue hire car through the hot, dirty suburbs, then reach the motorway, climbing away from Sydney and out into the flat, dry country, towards Rundle.

Mandy stares through the passenger window at the sliding landscape while Chris drives. Cathy slouches in the back, drinking from a can of Coke through a straw, as if she is their teenage child.

At first Chris, and then Cathy, make effortful conversation, asking Mandy about her flight, about Baghdad, but when her answers only come in tight monosyllables they give up. Chris dips a hand into the console for a CD among the stack Cathy has brought. He fishes one out and passes it to Mandy. She presses the button for the disc to emerge, inserts the new one. She glances at Chris, deals him a brief, polite smile, then looks away again.

Once she reaches over and lets her hand rest stiffly for a moment on his thigh, but she doesn't look at him while she does it. Now and then, from her bag on the floor, her mobile beeps with messages. Each time, she pulls it out, peers at the phone's screen for a moment, and either texts quickly in reply, her thumb expert on the keypad, or simply presses one button and drops the phone back into her bag. She says nothing about any of the messages.

Chris reminds himself that the first awkward day is always the worst. Usually she sleeps through that day and into the next, when the strangeness can ease, when things between them can take on a slow and gradual restoration. But this time is different and, despite his protestations on the phone, he is now secretly relieved that Margaret convinced Cathy to wait so they could all travel together. He thinks of Margaret's high voice on the telephone, her suppressed panic. He feels the tears coming to his eyes again at the thought of her managing the last few days alone. He bites his lip and accelerates along a straight piece of highway, watching the speedometer needle rise.

'Why did they not fly him to Sydney?' Mandy asks once, staring out at the flat yellow paddocks stretching away on both sides.

Chris and Cathy both start to answer, then Cathy explains about Rundle's lauded new hospital wing, the new high dependency and intensive care units. 'The specialist reckons the care's better anyway. Because they're not so busy, and they consult with Westmead and Royal North Shore all the time anyway, blah blah blah.'

Mandy only mutters, under her breath, 'Huh.'

She is exhausted, trying to stay awake to fight off the jet lag to come. But for much of the trip she falls into a thick, syrupy traveller's sleep, her chin on her chest, or her head resting against the vibrating glass of the window. In the moments when she can haul herself awake, staring out at the dry flat land, she is visited by fragments of memory, old and recent, all slipping and merging in the wash of her tiredness and the landscape, so familiar but from so long ago. Faces and shreds from Baghdad in the days before she left—the militia commander's balaclava and dusty jeans; the bored young faces of the US soldiers at the checkpoint; packing her suitcase, stuffing some market trinkets alongside the flak jacket and helmet, some mini DV tapes and the sat phone—all this rushes into a pool of other images from years ago, to do with these paddocks, this sky, with childhood. A drive to Sydney with her first boyfriend when she was seventeen, drinking rum and coke. A mushroom-coloured, brushed cotton blouse she had seen, at thirteen, in the window of Rundle's one department store and wanted so desperately. The bloody spectacle of sheep mulesing at a school friend's farm when she was twelve, and afterwards dancing to Australian Crawl tapes in the girl's airless weatherboard bedroom. The dribble of boiling water from that farmhouse bathroom's chip-heater. All these stray memories, unthought of for decades.

She brings her gaze back from the paddocks to the whizzing bitumen before them. Occasionally the dark lump of a dead animal emerges up ahead—wallaby, or wombat—like fleabitten cushions squashed there on the roadside.

They drive north-west for hours, stopping now and then at a square dark brick public toilet in some abandoned small-town park, and once at Wollaroi for petrol and something to eat. Whenever they near a town with mobile reception Cathy dials Stephen's number once again. He still does not answer.

Now Mandy's phone beeps again, and once more she picks it out of her bag. Graham, the cameraman, has lost his mobile and wants all her phone numbers. And also the news desk want to know when she'll be back. Fuck.

'Have Mum and Dad got email?' she asks Cathy, twisting around in her seat.

'*Yeah*,' says Cathy, nonplussed. 'Don't you get their emails?'

'Oh yeah,' says Mandy. 'Sometimes.' She can't remember the last time she read one. They remain, subject lines in bold, piling up in her inbox beneath all the others. Mandy turns back to the phone, texts Graham—*on road. will email*—and tosses the phone back down into the cave of her bag.

She lets her head fall back into the soft plush of the headrest. And, lulled by the rhythmic hum of the car, sinks instantly back into sleep.

She is roused, eventually, by the slowing of the car. She lifts her heavy head, blinking, licking her lips. They are at the outskirts of Rundle. Chris slows the car again at the red and white speed sign.

The sisters straighten in their seats as their old home town draws them in. They are both wide awake now, but silent, sliding along the highway in the sinking afternoon, past the familiar clumps of industrial buildings, the caravan park, the disused skating rink. The first service station of the town, the Caltex, looms on the left.

'It's on empty, may as well fill up now,' says Chris, and steers into its driveway.

A dry wave of heat meets them as he opens the door and gets out, stretching. He walks around to fill the car, and as the pump noise begins, Mandy and Cathy watch the service station attendant who has appeared and begun cleaning the windscreen. She is a skinny, girlish-looking woman of about thirty-two with a tattoo—and, Mandy guesses, at least three teenage children. Her blonde ponytail is darkening with the years, her black jeans fading, and a sharp corner of the tattoo rises at her hip as she leans over the bonnet, reaching across the windscreen with the squeegee.

'That's Tracey Tessler's sister,' Cathy murmurs from the back.

Mandy recalls the Tesslers, from the schoolyard, from Mass, from that gaunt station wagon full of children and cricket stumps and netball bibs. Chris has finished with the petrol. He opens the door and begins searching down the side of his seat for his wallet.

'Pregnant in Year 9,' Cathy says in a monotone.

Chris looks up, sees them both watching the attendant. 'Wow,' he says.

They all watch the woman's body for a moment, moving back and forth across the windscreen. This is the shame of the country town, Mandy thinks; that people can watch your first mistake and predict the rest, and they can sit in their cars while you lean your body over their windscreens and they can see for themselves the line of your bra beneath the cheap fabric of the Caltex polo shirt, see the sweat at your armpits. The woman catches Mandy's eye through the windscreen as she yanks the squeegee back and forth. Something—recognition?—passes across her face and then drains instantly away, water into sand.

Mandy looks over at Chris, still rummaging for his wallet. She says, 'I'll get it,' and gets out of the car.

She arches her back in a stretch, and rolls her left, then right shoulder, following the young woman into the bright glass shop. Mandy pays with her credit card, watching the woman's expressionless face as she slides the card through the machine and waits, fingers poised, for the receipt to emerge. Mandy takes it, signs the docket, and the woman slides the credit card back across the counter. Mandy walks out to the car—but halfway there she turns, marches back in through the automatic sliding glass doors.

The young woman's head jerks up, and she looks suddenly alarmed, as if Mandy might have returned to say something to her, to challenge her.

'A packet of Benson & Hedges Extra Mild please,' says Mandy. And a relief, a till-now withheld energy, seems to flood the woman's limbs. She leaps off her stool and flips the cigarettes onto the counter with one hand, the other expertly blipping the green numbers on the till. 'Thanks,' Mandy says, and without meeting the woman's eyes, steps out again into the black concrete expanse and the smell of petrol. She is conscious, as she walks, of her clothes, of the sound her expensive shoes make as her heels strike the concrete. She sinks back into the cool, cushioned quiet of the car and seals herself in with the closing door.

'Oooh good,' says Cathy, seeing the cigarettes.

'I thought you gave those things up,' says Chris, turning the key in the ignition. Mandy shrugs. As the car moves off she sees the girl in the service station watching them leave.

I am not like her, Mandy tells herself as the car curves out onto the main street. But she feels the young woman watching from her little glass box.

THE OLD black dog, Leia, comes haring around the corner of the house as the car pulls into the driveway. She follows the car to the backyard and when the doors open, drops to the ground, scurrying low and sneaky, weaving in and out, waiting to be cursed.

The sun has disappeared below the trees at the end of the yard, the sky a pale, washed yellow.

'Princess *Leeeia*,' croons Cathy from the open back door, one bare foot planted on the ground and leaning out, low, to grab Leia by the collar as she passes. But the dog ducks and slinks around to the other side of the car, tail wagging.

'Stupid as ever,' Cathy sighs, and leans back along the seat to drag her bags out behind her.

Mandy looks up at the kitchen window, sees her mother waving with her whole arm, and then disappearing from view. Mandy stands on the driveway in the still, hot air, a confusion of childhood smells and sensations swelling up at her—the green acidity of broken geranium stalks, the metallic taste of concrete. The silty red dirt, the quiet of the streets, the rubber of bicycle tyres. All the long hours of all the flat, empty afternoons.

Leia pushes at her legs, and Mandy bends, stroking the old dog's shiny head, murmuring, 'You *still* here, old woman?'

Their mother appears at the top of the red concrete steps at the back door, calling out to them, hurrying down but holding all the time to the railing. She looks very small, in her neat khaki trousers, her blue cotton blouse tucked in at the elastic waist, bright white sneakers on her feet. They move quickly towards one another with their arms out, and Margaret says, 'Oh,' and at the same moment a rush of pressure seizes Mandy's chest, forcing tears into her eyes.

'Hi, Mum,' she murmurs, and they stand wrapped together for a moment, Mandy's chin over her mother's shoulder, smelling her familiar, sweetish smell. They release each other.

The pain of not crying has gone now, swallowed. Mandy glances into her mother's face and looks away again, but not before seeing that Margaret's eyes are glassy with emotion. Margaret only sighs out a word—'*Well!*'—before turning to Chris and Cathy.

Mandy drags her suitcase over the gravel with a grinding noise. Halfway up the steps she glances back across the roof of the car, where Chris is still holding her mother by the shoulders, though they are untangled from their hug now. They are murmuring together and looking into each other's faces. Her mother has a child's concentration as she listens to Chris, nodding and biting her lip and blinking slow, heavy blinks, as though his voice might now be the only thing keeping her from collapsing to the hot white gravel of the drive.

Cathy stands just beyond them, clutching a hat and a large black overnight bag, waiting for them to finish talking. As Mandy turns to step inside the back door it occurs to her that a stranger watching this scene might assume Cathy and Chris were the married ones, that Margaret was Chris's own mother. In her slurred tiredness she lets the thought rise and sink away, then pulls her suitcase over the ridge of the low step and pushes inside, the screen door banging behind her.

Soon Cathy is hauling her bags down the hallway to her old bedroom. 'Smells weird in here,' she calls out. In Mandy's own childhood room a new double bed sits squarely beneath the window.

'When did that get put in here?' Mandy says as Chris comes in.

Chris shrugs. 'Ages ago.'

At the far side of the bed Mandy sits down heavily. With a foot she levers off one shoe, then the other, and lies on her back on the quilted nylon bedspread. She wonders what her mother has done with the old crocheted bedspreads from the two single beds that used to be in here, one parallel to the window, the other nearer the door. From either of those beds you used to be able to see the big lilac bush outside. But from its new position the only view is of the louvred sliding doors of the built-in wardrobe, slightly apart, showing the shelves of stuffed shopping bags and boxes of unused things Margaret keeps in here now.

Mandy draws up her knees, making a swishing sound on the bed cover. The telephone rings. They hear Margaret's slow footsteps on the hallway carpet, and her nervous telephone-answering voice, same as it has always been, whispering into the gloom, 'Hello?'

Chris turns and leaves the room, closing the door quietly behind him.

Mandy sits up, feeling her body sinking further into the springs, listening to the voices of her mother, then Cathy and Chris, in the hallway. Then there is a silence, and then she hears them further away, down in the living room. She is staring at the bedside table when beneath a saucer holding hairpins and a tube of hand cream she sees a red, sticky pool. Her heart bolts—once, twice—until she makes out the glistening splotch as a wide, beaded red bracelet. It must be Cathy's, from an earlier visit. She reaches over and extracts it from beneath the saucer, winding it around her own wrist, concentrating on the tricky fastener. She holds up her arm to see it in the mirror across the room.

The deep bracelets of blood at the boy's thighs, the nonsensical arrangement of trouser legs and torn sandals in the dust, and her own heartbeat, *whoomp whoomp whoomp* as she ran with her arms hugging her head.

Cathy told her that on the first night when their mother got home from the hospital she had stood hosing their father's blood into the ground beneath the gravel.

The bedroom door clicks open and Chris comes in, stepping across the thick carpet. He sits down on the other side of the bed. He looks, puzzled, at her garlanded wrist for a second, but says nothing about it.

'Are you ready to go to the hospital?'

CHAPTER FIVE

TONY WARREN drives along the rutted track from the gate to his house in the sinking evening. It's a long time since a grader has been through, and he has to drive slowly, shouldering the ute up and over the road's ridges, lowering into and then easing up from the dips.

He stops in front of the shed and gets out, listening to the ticking of the car's engine and the dogs' barking. The fibro house is a grey hulk in the gloom. He feeds the dogs, tipping the yellowed pellets into the wide metal bowls as the kelpie lurches, gasping, on her chain. Her feet scrabble on the scraped earth, she makes a high grizzling whine. The collie stands stiff-legged, shoulders erect, as Tony shakes the food out. As soon as he moves off the dogs dive to their bowls, snouts turned sideways, long wet tongues flapping in and out.

Tony goes inside, switches on the kitchen light and waits for the fluorescent hum and the delayed flicker—on, off, on. In the living room he turns on the television. There is a game show, people grinning and blinking in the studio lights. He walks up the dark hallway, past his mother's dark, long-empty room, to get changed.

Later, in tracksuit pants and socks, his blue t-shirt hanging out, he sits with his legs stretched along the couch. The dinner plate with its sheen of butter, the three prongs of chop bones, lies on the floor. As he snaps open a can of beer and pours it into a glass he keeps his gaze on the television. Another car bomb has exploded.

'At least eight Iraqis have died in another series of attacks,' a woman's voice is saying. There is the usual cluster of men around a molten black car. *'It's ordinary Iraqis like these,'* the voice goes on. Tony stares at the screen, trying to picture the reporter. He knows it's not her, not Mandy Connolly—the voice is younger, sharper—but still he needs to be sure. On the screen some of the men squat, some stand, in the dusty air, wearing their high-waisted trousers, the pale shirts, their beards and the headscarves. *Kaffiyehs*, they are called. He looked it up on the net.

Now the screen shows the reporter, talking into her mike. Tony leans forward—and he is right, it's not her but some other younger, skinnier bird. *Woman*, he corrects himself in his head.

So he is right: she must be coming home. Tony takes another gulp of the beer. A weird feeling in his guts at the idea of seeing her face to face again. After all the years.

He thinks of the father, lying there with his wrecked balloon of face, all juiced up with wires and tubes and the life support. Tony talked to the mother this morning, seeing her gardening magazine. He talked to her about tomatoes, how it's almost too late now for plants but when his are finished he'll give her some of his seeds, and also about derris dust. He was careful not to ask her anything, but when he was hooking up another machine across the ward he heard her tell one of the nurses that 'the girls' were coming home.

Girls, not girl. Not the brother, not only the sister.

When he thinks she could be here, in town, even now—maybe driving out there on the highway past his gate—he has to take a big breath and then exhale again, to try to quell the nervy feeling in his guts.

He looks up at the dark bare pane of the window. It reflects only the room, the television's changing light, the furniture. The piles of *Time* magazine and the newspapers, all the World News sections he has not yet read, stacked on the floor beneath the window. His mother's hospital wheelchair and walking frame in the corner, that he's never gotten around to taking back.

He takes another gulp of beer, tries to focus again on the television. People are running—a woman's hooded black shape moving through the ruined street, a wail coming out of her like death. And now the camera pans back across the curved black fronds of the car's wreckage, and underneath the reporter's voice the men still squat or stand in the dust, their numb gazes moving from the ashen blob to stare into the camera, then back again to the car.

Tony knows their listlessness, their defeated eyes. He knows their empty, dangling hands.

# CHAPTER SIX

THEIR FATHER is unrecognisable. Obscenely swollen, his face patterned with terrible strange colours. A yellow-brown stain has dried across his cheek; a splash of something that has come, possibly days ago, from his mouth. The ripening plums of his eyes are bulbous, swelling out from beneath his brow. Around his neck is a plastic and foam brace. He wears a hospital gown but it has fallen away, and his shoulder and part of his chest, sparse with grey hairs, are exposed. Despite the hair, this private, bared part of him looks chubby, girlish.

They stand by the bed in the low-lit ward. The young nurses, a woman and a man, stop their talking at the desk and watch the family across the room.

Mandy wants to take a warm cloth and wash the yellow stain away, but there is sticking plaster and threadlike tubing all over her father's head. She holds her breath as she leans in to kiss him.

'Hello, Dad,' she whispers. But there's no room, between the tubes and the plasters, for a kiss. She puts her lips to his ear instead, just beneath the wound above his temple, the bruising of its edges leaching out from beneath the dressing.

On the other side of the bed Cathy stares in shock. Chris and their mother stand too, not saying anything.

He does not open his eyes. Mandy watches his face for any tiny movement, any sign he is aware of her, of any of them. Of touch, or sound. But there is nothing, except the quiet drone of the ventilator, forcing the breath in, then out. His chest rises and falls in a perfect, inhuman rhythm.

The tubes are everywhere. One—a thick, short concertina like the coil that used to hang from Margaret's old hairdryer with the shower-cap attachment—is plastered down over his forehead with tape. At this tube's end another sticking plaster joins it to a thinner, hard one thrust deep into his opened mouth. Into his throat. A tube snakes into his nostril too. Sacs and bottles of liquid hang from the drip stand.

Geoff's face, beneath his closed swollen eyes, is grizzled with uneven grey stubble. Mandy has almost never, except perhaps for meeting in an occasional night-time stumble to the bathroom as a child, seen her father unshaven.

Noises come from everywhere, nowhere. Not just beeps, but little trills, musical seesaws, as if the hospital is in fact full of birds: tiny, wheezing, beeping, mechanical birds.

On Geoff's right index finger is a grey rubber clamp; a thick, square thimble. His visible hand—the other is somewhere beneath the sheet—seems too large, and terribly white.

'What's that for?' says Chris, pointing to the end of the bed, where a flat computer screen is connected to a long, flexible metal coil curling down from the ceiling. Beneath it is a tall table with a keyboard, and a black leather stool on a wheeled stainless-steel stalk.

Margaret looks up. 'It's new. Everything's new.' She casts a glance around at the seven other beds, each with its suspended computer, then at the central desk and its small bank of phones and computers. 'We're very lucky,' she says glumly.

Mandy sits down in the mauve vinyl chair, and puts a hand through the bed's safety bars to rest on Geoff's blanketed leg. It seems the only part of him unmonitored, the only part perhaps undamaged. She does not want to lift the blankets to see if this is true.

She bites the inside of her cheek. 'He should be in Sydney,' she says. 'At a proper hospital.'

Nobody answers. Chris and Cathy and Margaret glance at one another, then back at Geoff.

On his chest are several small white adhesive plaster disks, each with a metal nipple in the middle, and coming from each nipple is a plastic-coated wire, flowing down over the bed to somewhere behind it, then to a bank of power points and computerised boxes.

A squat young man, the nurse, appears at the end of the bed and sits on the stool at the computer. His name is Nathan. He taps with two fingers at the keyboard, then peers up at the screen, troubled. Then he grins at them.

'We dunno how to work all this stuff yet,' he says cheerfully. 'Back in a tick.'

He saunters off to the desk to talk to the other nurse again, resting his elbows on the high bench with his chin in his hands as they chat quietly about their weekend plans. Nathan's going pig-shooting.

OUTSIDE THE hospital entrance, in the car park, the sky is dark, the air still warm.

Chris says, 'Are you okay?'

Mandy nods, her mouth closed. She juts her jaw, moving it slowly from side to side, standing with her arms folded across her body.

'Are you sure?' Chris's face is pale, stricken. 'He looks so *terrible*.'

'Mmm.'

It is all she can say. She swallows, looking down at the cement paving. She rubs the toe of her shoe, in a slow circular motion, over a spot on the paving. They stand apart from each other, in the fluorescent twilight of the entranceway. Chris steps to her, puts his arms around her shoulders. Mandy doesn't move, just stands stiffly in his embrace, her face turned so her cheek meets the dry fabric of his t-shirt and the warmth of his chest. She can hear a skateboard from a distance, growing louder and louder as it approaches, scraping the concrete path, gathering speed. The first time back from Bosnia when she'd heard this scouring of the air, her skin had gone instantly cold and she'd jerked wildly, looking for fighter planes. Now she only tells herself, *Breathe*, and waits for the crescendo of sound just beyond the hospital's hedge. Then it curves away down the hill.

ON THE way home they stop outside Liquorland, the only brightly lit shop in the main street apart from the supermarket. Mandy says, 'I'll get it,' and strides through the shop to the wall of fridges, yanks open a door and pulls down three bottles of white wine. She is the only customer.

The young woman behind the counter has a broad, open red face and light-brown hair pushed back behind her ears. She grins expectantly as Mandy moves to the counter. Mandy has two fifty-dollar notes ready in her hand, but the girl takes the bottles from Mandy slowly, still grinning widely, as if accepting a surprise gift.

'Looks like someone's having a party!' she cries cheerfully as she takes the bottles.

Mandy shakes her head with a grimace and says, 'Not really.'

The girl stands the bottles in a row on the counter and then picks one up in both hands, peering first at the price sticker, then twisting it around to read the label.

'CAPEL VALE,' she reads slowly in her flat, high voice, her brow furrowed. She looks up, beaming at Mandy who simply stares back, proffering the notes.

But the girl is still holding the bottle up, looking at the label. She cocks her head. 'Is this nice?'

Mandy shrugs. 'Think so.' She doesn't bother to return the girl's smile.

But the girl grins again, knowingly this time. 'It should be, at that price!' She puts the bottle down on the counter, but makes no move towards the till, or to take the money. Instead she shifts her weight, ready for a conversation. 'I'm new,' she says. She is oblivious to Mandy's expressionless face, to her fingernail now lightly tapping the counter.

'It's just good to know what's nice,' the girl chatters on, ''cos sometimes customers ask me.' She grins again. 'I don't drink wine. Don't like the taste.'

She looks back at the label. '*Sauvignon blanc*,' she reads aloud, sounding out the words phonetically. Then she smiles again. 'That's probly not how you say it!' She laughs, finally picking up the scanner and aiming it at the bottle's label. There's no embarrassment in her laughter; it's convivial, confident.

Mandy feels herself drawing back, but forces a tight smile as the girl finally takes the money and fusses at the till, then tips the change into Mandy's open hand. Then the girl drags each bottle towards her belly, bending awkwardly to slither one, then the second and third, into separate paper bags. Then she stretches out her arms to carefully gather the three bottles together into a neat triangle. Then she bends beneath the counter to begin searching for a plastic bag.

'Don't worry about that.' Mandy snatches up the bottles with a loud clunking sound. 'Thanks,' she grunts, and stalks off toward the glass doors and the headlights of the waiting car. She slumps in beside her mother on the back seat, heaves the bottles into the space between them and slams the door, muttering, *Jesus*, could she have been any slower.'

Nobody answers. As the car moves away, Margaret looks past Mandy through the window, sending a glance of sympathy to the girl at the counter, still staring after Mandy through the glass doors, bewildered.

BACK AT the house, Mandy fills wine glasses and, clutching her own, walks down the hallway to her room. While Margaret gets the dinner ready, the children drift between their rooms, unpacking, emerging now and then clutching something—a small tissue-wrapped present for Margaret from a Baghdad market, or a tube of toothpaste, a book—and then returning to rummage in suitcases and bags.

Chris leans in the doorway, watching Mandy pull the scarves and long-sleeved shirts, the loose, pastel-coloured cotton trousers and veils from her suitcase, then roll them into a ball and toss them to the floor of the open wardrobe.

He remembers her packing these strange clothes into her bag the first time she left for the Middle East, along with a pile of compact discs and DVDs. He had picked up the DVDs one by one. *My Big Fat Greek Wedding*, *Kath & Kim*, *Little Britain*, *Seinfeld*, *Shaun of the Dead*. But also *Full Metal Jacket*; the *Rambo* series; *Black Hawk Down*.

'Who's this crap for?' he'd said, flipping through them.

Mandy had been sorting through collections of other stuff on the bed. An old CD walkman, an MP3 player, boxes of tampons and a large mound of packets from the pharmacy: Panadol, amoxycillin, Xanax, Imodium, Sinutab, Berocca, multivitamins, Canesten, insect repellent, cold sore ointment.

'The reporters,' she'd said. 'They love all that shit.'

She would be joining the journalists and assorted stray people living in the Al Hamra hotel in Baghdad. Chris tried to picture her there.

'Do you have your own room?' he'd asked, trying to keep his voice light. Mandy had only laughed, not looking at him.

'Of course I do. Christ,' she'd said. And she had gone on shoving the boxes of medication into a plastic bag.

Now, here in the doorway, Chris shifts his weight and Mandy glances up. They smile briefly, politely.

Last night, as Chris lay alone in his—their—wide bed in Rose Bay, he'd stared up into the dark and tried to recall how long it had been since he and Mandy had had sex. Istanbul, maybe, when they had met there for her birthday. A long time ago. He imagined her there at home in the bed with him, imagined getting hard, climbing on top of her, pushing his way in. She would close her arms and legs around him and pull him inside, slick and satiny; he would feel the tough skin of her heels on his back. But the thought was only theoretical, and he did not get hard.

Sometimes, when she is far away from him, his wife takes tranquillisers in a Baghdad hotel, gets drunk and watches *Full Metal Jacket* with strangers. With men.

Chris turns toward the cupboard, sweeping the wire coat hangers to one end of the dark space, remembering the way that she had scowled at this double bed when they arrived today. He imagines sex again with her now, here on the bed. Their bodies, the slithering bedspread.

But once again, it is like thinking about being someone else.

THEY EAT in the dining room, and Margaret reports on the scans, the procedures, the doctors.

'They have to do something to him, all the time,' she says in a small voice, pinching some bread crumbs into a little pile on her side plate.

Chris says quietly, 'Oh Marg—' but she interrupts.

'They have to do a sort of draining thing. From his lungs. They push a tube down . . .' She trails off, blinking fast. 'I don't want any of you to watch it.'

Now that she has something authoritative to say, her voice loses its waver.

'If they do it, you must just stand outside the curtain— they prefer it, actually—until they're done,' she finishes firmly. The horror of that first time she watched Geoff in the dreadful soundless convulsion; one nurse cradling his head and shoulders, bracing him, while the other grasped the thin tube with both strong hands, pushing it down inside the thicker tube already in place in his throat. The nurse had had to work hard, leaning in, using her body weight and the strength of both shoulders to force the tube down, a little at a time. And with each push, Geoff's slumped body, jerking and jolting as if in a terrible gasping or coughing or vomiting fit—but not a sound. Not a sound, or a breath, escaping his colourless lips.

She looks down at the dog, who has been swaggling around the table, nosing for scraps. Margaret seems suddenly cheered.

'Leia bit Nola Gardiner's granddaughter at tennis.'

'Jesus, Mum!' says Cathy.

The little toddler had waddled over to the seats which Leia was lying beneath, and before anyone could stop her, had put out her pudgy fingers and clamped hold of Leia's snout.

'The screams were unbelievable. Bloodcurdling,' says Margaret, distractedly. There had been blood, she said, but only a little bit.

'Oh my God,' says Chris.

'It was only a tiny nip!' Margaret protests.

Mandy says, 'Mum, dogs get put down for that!'

'But Nola should have been watching her!' Margaret stares around at them, shaking her head. 'So anyway, I don't take her anymore. But they shouldn't be bringing little children to tennis anyway, it's not safe.'

Cathy sniggers softly. 'Not with Leia around.'

Margaret bristles. 'Not anyway. There's rusty wire and all kinds of things.'

It had been melodramatic of Nola, rushing off to hospital when a Bandaid would have done; but of course, once there, it had to be tetanus shots and dressings and God knew what else. And then Leia had slunk around the courts, in and out of the bench seats so Margaret couldn't catch her until after everyone had left.

Chris leans down to stroke Leia's glossy black back, fat as a slug. '*Naughty* Leia.' He whacks her a couple of times on the rump, making her jiggle with pleasure.

'Well, I'm not taking her anywhere, after last time,' he says.

Cathy and Margaret begin to smile, wine glasses raised to their lips.

'It wasn't very funny,' says Chris, but he too is smirking. Then he suddenly makes a wild scrabbling motion in the air before him with both hands, and Cathy bangs down her glass and clamps two hands over her mouth to stop her wine from spurting. They all turn to Mandy.

'Last time we came up,' Chris says, as Margaret and Cathy, who has swallowed now, struggle to hold back their laughter, 'there was a huge storm.'

Margaret butts in. 'She *hates* thunder,' and makes a sympathetic face at Leia.

The dog has always been terrified of thunder; for her whole life the family has had to shut her, shaking and cowering, in the bathroom whenever a storm approaches.

'I took her for a walk to the video shop,' says Chris. The others begin chortling, all telling Mandy the tale but watching each other as they speak, interrupting, talking over one another. How Leia had been waiting on the footpath outside the shop when a huge thunder clap struck, how she bolted in through the automatic doors and began streaking about the store, howling.

The three of them are squirming now.

'And Leia's charging round the shop, trying to *climb up* the video shelves!' Chris makes the scrabbling motion again, his face a mask of open-mouthed terror. 'And the girl in the shop,' he leaps up, hunching his shoulders and crying out in a high-pitched voice, 'she's screaming, I DON'T LIKE DOGS! And I'm chasing Leia all round the shop yelling at her, but she's *possessed*!'

Cathy pushes in, 'She destroyed *all* the shelves—DVDs and videos everywhere—and knocked a little boy over!'

Margaret cries, 'The general manager of Video Ezy in *Sydney* rang the Rundle *Council* to complain!'

Mandy has been smiling as she listens, but now she simply watches the three of them—Chris laughing with his head back, Margaret and Cathy tittering.

Eventually Margaret says, '*Anyway*, she's been very good since then. Haven't you, Leia. Yes.' And she tears a lump of bread and feeds it to the dog.

'Till the biting,' snorts Cathy into her glass, giggling again.

Margaret has noticed Mandy sitting silent across the table, tilting her wine glass on its base, turning it in small circles on the table.

'It was back before Christmas, love—in November, I think,' says Margaret, her voice steadying. She casts her gaze to the ceiling, trying to remember the date, as if a specific chronology will somehow ease the tension that has suddenly stretched over the moment.

'I think you were in—' she searches her mind again, flushing—'Oh. I'm not sure. Baghdad, I suppose.'

She shoots a testy glance at Cathy, who is still snickering with Chris and pawing the air. Chris catches Margaret's frown, and looks at Mandy, and stops laughing.

Mandy smiles tightly. She feels the muscles in her face.

For most of November she had been trying to get into Basra. A quick, rainy pattern of images and sensations ripples through her—the juddering of the car, the nights peppered with brightness. Adrenaline a taste in her saliva for days. The dead dogs rotting. She had not told Chris or her parents she went to Basra, and if they had seen any reports on television they didn't notice hers. Or had forgotten.

She leans across the table to collect their empty plates. 'I didn't know you were all here together then. I would have phoned,' she says, standing. She grips the plates and turns toward the kitchen. Her father lies lifeless in a hospital bed, and they are telling dog stories.

The other three glance at one another.

At the door Mandy stops, turns and says, 'I don't suppose anyone's heard from Stephen yet?'

CHAPTER SEVEN

Day two

MANDY WAKES at four into the stark blue space of her jet lag, eyes wide open. Chris breathes heavily beside her. She has had a dream, a bad one, but there is no clarity to her recall of it—only the familiar riverweed of dread, wrapping itself beneath the surface of the night.

She sits up, careful not to wake Chris, and eases out of the bed. She feels around in her suitcase on the floor for clothes, then carries them through the darkened house to the kitchen, where she dresses. She has never been more awake, alert. A streetlight and the moon fill the kitchen with a pallid light; enough for her to be able to put the kettle on.

She takes her hot cup and sits out on the back step with it, listening in the quiet, until the sky begins to lighten, revealing the simultaneous familiarity and strangeness of this house, this yard. Above her is a pergola of white painted wood that has been added in the last four years, and a sturdy jasmine has plaited itself around the nearest post. Next to the garage is the old neat square of tough lawn bordered by a hydrangea, some azaleas alongside the garage wall. The rusting basketball ring is gone from above the garage door. Some sparsely planted red-leafed cordylines now line the driveway, but the same old crazy pavers shine in the gloom, leading down to the fishpond at the bottom of the yard, fashioned from lumpen rocks by her father in the seventies.

In the middle of the square of lawn is a new-looking slatted teak table and heavy matching chairs, a closed shade umbrella held steady by a hole in the table's centre. She imagines the family gathered around the table, passing a bowl of curled pink prawns to one another in the white heat of Christmas Day.

She thinks back to where she was that day, to the story she filed. They went for the routine: the American soldiers' Christmas lunch (wild turkey cooked by locals) followed by some footage of the almost empty Catholic church service in Amariya (Iraqi Christians too afraid to go to Mass)—and then the day's list of atrocities. The assistant dean of Baghdad's medical college shot dead, latest figures showing around 300 academics murdered since the invasion. An interview—at the Hamra as usual now, since they no longer went to people's houses—with a middle-aged professor mourning his neighbours', and his own, lack of courage these days. That they must leave the bodies where they fall, go about their business, pretend not to see; it's become too dangerous to offer help to the dying. *'On my way home from work as I reached my street, I saw a man lying in a pool of blood. Someone had covered him with bits of cardboard. He wasn't dead. This was the best they could do. I drove on.'*

She and Graham had edited the package together, finished with a solemn piece to camera in the compound, sent it off. She'd reworked the details into an 800-word piece for the *Times*, then joined Graham in his room for a drink. He'd just got off the phone from his wife in Sydney—Shelley had had to wake their younger daughter at eight-thirty to find her Santa presents, while her sister had been up since dawn. Mandy and Graham had raised their beers to each other and muttered, Merry Christmas. Then they went downstairs to join the others for fatoush, beef jerky and more beer. Afterwards she watched DVDs in her room, and then left a message for Chris on the answering machine at Rose Bay. He was at his parents', she'd assumed.

But now, watching the light of dawn wash over the silent backyard of her childhood, she wonders if maybe Chris was here instead, sitting at that new table on the lawn alongside her father in a red paper hat. Cathy had texted her mobile, 'with love from us all', but maybe that included Chris too. Passing salads and slices of ham to one another, having Christmas without her.

But without Stephen either, apparently.

The last she heard of Stephen, from Cathy, he was working for the police service in some typing job. Mandy imagines him slouched in an office chair somewhere, typing at a computer. Charting, she supposes, the everyday failures of petty thieves and violent husbands, pathetic public servants with hard drives full of kiddy porn. Lost adolescents and their heroin drudgery. The routine miseries of the drowning unemployed.

Thinking of Stephen now, it seems to Mandy as though he himself has always been lost, even in the years before his physical drift from the family. He has always seemed, since adolescence and for no graspable reason, to carry within him a bedrock of resentment—towards her in particular—never articulated and never resolved, but which has formed the foundation for his every conversation, every glance from his guarded eyes.

Not that she has had what could be called a conversation with him in years.

She realises now she is relieved that he has not come home. And in this dusky backyard with the first chitterings of lorikeets sounding from somewhere across the roofs, it seems to her that this is a particularly Australian thing, that boys might go into the funk of adolescence and never come out. This destiny of innumerable young men to live their lives adrift.

When the sky has lightened some more she takes her cup inside, rinses it at the sink. She scrawls a note to the others, then shoves her feet into a pair of sneakers, finds her wallet on the kitchen bench and returns to the back door, steps through and closes it quietly behind her.

She walks across the spongy grass and down the driveway. At the front gate something small moves on the ground; an Indian mynah bird is stabbing at the grass. She nears the bird and it stops pecking but does not flee, simply stays where it is, motionless. As she passes, the bird seems to watch her over its shoulder, through its sly yellow-rimmed eye.

She thinks of the boy again, his watching: the dazed concentration of his gaze, the limp arms slick with blood. Perhaps this morning's dream was just another mutation of this too-familiar image. The mynah takes a few strides in its lazy gait, still watching her, waiting for her to leave before returning to its jabbing at the grass.

She lets herself out of the gate, and begins to walk through the streets of her childhood town. The sun is almost up, and the houses have begun to absorb this soft light, not yet hardened into day.

She walks down Aurora Street, past the familiar houses, all squat, post-war red brick, like her parents'. Some have long-past attempted gardens in front—a few leggy, squalid roses, a ragged pencil pine or two—others, neat but parched lawns and rangy cotoneaster hedges. The neighbours' cars are in garages or car ports, parked at the far ends of driveways, shining moulded shapes of white and silver.

At the corner she turns into Fitzroy Street, and the crepe myrtles are in shocking pink flower all down the road.

When she was little she loved their gaudy pinks and crimsons, but as she grew older she began to realise they were tawdry, that these were the colours of bargain shops and chemist-brand lipstick, and she became ashamed of them. Now, as she walks through the streets, the flaring crepe myrtles are the only bright shriek in all the dried-out anonymity of the town.

A few blocks on—past the Baillieus' house, past the play park—she reaches the fire station. On a square white perspex sign is the fire service badge and then, in red and black plastic, racks of removable capital letters: RUNDLE FIRE STATION. Another line beneath says EASTER MESSAGE: DON'T BE A BUNNY, BE FIRE SAFE. It's either almost a year old or two months early. The station is silent, the corrugated roll-a-door closed. She turns and stops here at the top of Monarch Street, the wide grey road sweeping downward. Rundle is spread out there below, a town of low red-brick and fibro buildings, with their whitened aluminium or painted tin roofs—but the town's scale is entirely dwarfed by the wide, wide plains beyond. The sky is enormous, and in the distance are the blue torn-tissue strips of the mountain range. It is a landscape of horizontals, and Rundle itself is only another one, smeared over the pale brown land. Across the road, in the gutter outside a beaten-up house with white roses blooming, is an abandoned stereo speaker on its side. Just near it on the grass, a blue sign on two short poles says HOSPITAL in white lettering, with an arrow. She steps across the road to follow it.

* * *

MARGARET FINDS herself awake in an odd position, on her side with her arms out in front of her chest, one leg kicked across the bed. Mid-hurdle. The bed has been a spacious shock each morning since the accident; but each morning too, the dislocation dissolves a little more quickly. She turns and lies on her back in the pale blue bedroom, her gaze tracing threads of cracks in the ceiling plaster. Then she remembers that the children are here. Her pulse enlivens, she is suddenly fully awake. Today Chris will help her to buy paint for the bathroom. She spoke to him about it yesterday, hurriedly, when the girls were out of the room. Now, here in her bed, she has a lovely feeling of extravagance, of order, as she imagines the smooth creamy expanse above her while she bathes.

But also she must go to the hospital, she thinks with a start. *First* she must go there. It is possible to feel guilty about the hospital not being her first thought. And also for secretly counting as if all the children were here when Chris is not really her son, and Stephen is not here but somewhere in Sydney.

She supposes he is somewhere in Sydney.

Margaret swallows down the small gasp that might come if she lets this unknowing about her son rise to the surface of her thoughts. She allows herself a quick vision again of the creamy bathroom—but then is filled instantly, and thoroughly this time, with shame. A catastrophe has befallen her family, her husband. Even to think of a painted bathroom is an obscenity.

She is probably tired, and she has been through a lot. This is something people have said to her often in these last few days, and although Margaret knows Geoff would scoff at such self-indulgence, she now tweaks the phrase into consciousness. *I have been through a lot.* The words have enough gravitas to allow her to squish into a small and manageable parcel her guilt at not thinking first of Geoff and the blank space of Stephen, and *later* of the children—and the bathroom—and Margaret sits up.

IN THE kitchen the ABC news blurs statically from the clock radio on top of the fridge. Chris wipes the bench with a pink dishcloth, his body jiggling with the vigour of his effort. Cathy, in striped cotton shortie pyjamas, is slouched in a chair at the table, a cup of coffee held in two hands. She has one brown foot resting on the seat of the chair opposite her. She flaps a sleepy wave at her mother as Margaret comes in, then rubs her itchy nose with the flat of her hand.

'Where's Mandy?' Margaret says.

'Hospital,' answer Cathy and Chris together.

Guilt flushes through Margaret again. 'Oh,' she says. She is moving towards the kettle when the radio newsreader's voice catches at the air. An American reporter held hostage in Iraq has appeared on a video, pleading for help.

'God,' breathes Cathy. All three have turned to look at each other, then quickly away, listening to the radio.

'*Jill Carroll was kidnapped on the seventh of January in Baghdad,*' says the newsreader.

They stare at the table, the kettle, the bench, hearing a hissing background and then the hollow, schoolgirl's voice echoing in some faraway room.

'*Please just do whatever they want . . . There is a very short time.*'

'God,' says Chris. They stay silent for a long second, until there's a pause and the newsreader says that supermodel Kate Moss will appear on the cover of *Vogue* despite being caught using cocaine.

Margaret exhales a long, slow breath.

Chris says, 'Sit down Marg, I'll make the tea.'

Margaret moves obediently to the table and pulls out a chair. The moment has passed. Cathy swigs from her cup.

'I'll try Stephen again,' she says, getting up from the table.

Chris switches the button on the kettle to red, and pushes two pieces of bread into the toaster. He watches the torn edges of the bread begin to smoke, listening to Cathy walking through the living room to the telephone in the hallway, and then pours the hot water into a cup for Margaret. Turning back to the table, the teabag label fluttering against the cup, he sees his mother-in-law's folded hands, her closed eyes and her silently moving lips.

He knows it is not the reporter, but the reporter's mother, for whom Margaret is saying her prayer.

# CHAPTER EIGHT

STEPHEN LISTENS to tapes of coppers asking people questions, of the people answering or not answering the questions, and types them into a computer. He works in an office in the city where there are other people typing with headphones on, typing out the flat voices, the evasions, the fright and the arguments, the bullshitting. The sniffing, the throat-clearing, the bewilderment. Since his first week, years ago now, every tape has sounded the same. A young bloke and his excuses; a weary or bored copper, repeating the same questions in that brainless way.

— Did you steal a Ford Falcon GX with the registration number SHY 768.

— Nup.

— Did you park the stolen vehicle at 55 Dalhousie Road, Matraville.

— Nup. I wanna see my girlfriend.

The coppers write their own statements to be read in court. *Then the defendant said the words, 'oink, oink, oink' in a loud and abusive tone.*

Stephen is not as fast as some, but he can decipher the words through accents or coughs or slurring, and he can make sense of what is said. They are not allowed to change the words of the defendants. They leave in the ums and ahs and fucks and shits. Sometimes they take the shits out of the coppers' words, but not always. They always take out the fucks when the coppers say them though. *You stupid fucking little cunt.* They take those out.

Stephen's mobile has rung several times each day since last week, with Cathy's number coming up. His phone has also beeped all week with texts from her, and she has emailed, the messages tagged with a red exclamation mark, every day.

But this time when he looks at the phone the number appearing is his parents', in Rundle. He lets it ring, watching it vibrate, a dying blowfly across his desk. He has long ago turned off the message bank.

Where were you at nine o'clock.

There have been no messages from Mandy.

When Stephen thinks of his older sister he recalls her as a tall, skinny teenager at the local swimming pool, a towel flicked over her shoulder. Or slouched along the living room couch, watching television in the heat of the school holidays, her flat eyes staring at him as he tried to explain the rules of cricket. She would just get up, stride across the room and change the channel while he was mid-sentence. His feelings toward Cathy are more benign—she's younger than him—but still, as they were growing up, whenever Mandy was around the girls seemed somehow perpetually organised against him.

Now Cathy is thirty-seven and Mandy forty-two, but it is their teenage years he lingers in.

The phone stops buzzing. He picks it up and clears the *1 missed call* message with a couple of thumbstrokes. As he turns back to his computer screen he wonders if Mandy is receiving the same phone calls, the emails. Wherever she is. Whichever Middle-East shithole she has chosen to live in for the month.

Sometimes he has watched her face on the television late at night, her accent changed, her voice charged with urgency, talking into a microphone but shabbily dressed in greens and browns, and always behind her some pale ruined building, and dust, or dug-up ground. Her voice never wavers or pauses. Sometimes he has watched her on the television in the pub, and has sat back on his stool, one hand on the bar and a schooner tilted in the other, looking up at his older sister talking about explosions or disease or looting or suicide bombings, and then her face has disappeared from the screen while the camera moves across more broken houses, wailing people, holes in the ground, burned cars, and underneath the television screen in the gloom there are always a few young people dancing around a pool table, a boy pinning a girl to a wall while she smiles drunkenly into his face and hooks her fingers through the belt loops of his jeans, and an old eighties song comes on the video hits machine, and the young people yell, *yeah!* And whoop and lean over the pool table, waggling their bums as they line up a shot and sing and get drunker. On these, like most, nights Stephen walks home alone up the dark footpath to the brightly lit door of his block of flats.

He lets the police tape resume, his fingers skittering across the keys, the headphones snug on his head.

CONSTABLE STEAD: [Indistinguishable] . . . February five, 2006, four oh five pm. Your name is Bradley Michael Stewart?

DEFENDANT: Yes.

CS: Did you break and enter . . .

Stephen types, the scene appearing before him—the boy mumbling and sniffing, the tired copper filling in pieces of paper, occasionally getting shitty when the kid won't speak loudly enough. Stephen imagines the kid, hands deep in his tracksuit pockets, his shuffling feet. The boy keeps sniffing as he talks, is by turns subdued and hostile. It is clear he has done all this before. Then Stephen has to rewind a bit of the tape.

. . . legal representation up to your parents.

DEFENDANT: Yeah. Excuse me?

The kid's voice is muffled but suddenly polite, hesitant.

CS: What?

DEFENDANT: Are the cells down under here? There is the sound of what Stephen thinks is his foot, scuffing a beat on the linoleum floor.

Stephen kicks the dictaphone's stop button on the floor beneath his desk, takes off the headphones and sits back in his chair. He gets up, stretching his arms above his head.

In the next booth a woman is typing fast, staring at her screen. Stephen can read, over the partition, that a man in the interview she is transcribing is screaming at the police to let him give his son his medication, and then he'll fucking answer the question. Stephen looks at the woman's, Angela's, face. She's oblivious to him standing there beside her. Her bottom lip pouts in concentration, and she stares at the screen as though past it, into it. Her expression doesn't change as her fingers flicker over the keys and the lines of type appear on the screen. She does a hundred and four words a minute, he has heard. He sneaks another look at the screen. No spelling mistakes either.

He walks past the supervisor, who is frowning, listening to someone on the telephone. Stephen slows as he nears her desk and dips his head, miming smoking a cigarette with two fingers. She nods, still frowning into the phone.

On the street it's raining, and Stephen has to squeeze himself into a jutting corner of the building so as not to get wet. He lights a cigarette and inhales. Across the road at the courthouse, small drifts of people stand beneath an awning, smoking and muttering. Two men stand in line, waiting for a small woman with long blonde hair to get off the public telephone. She holds the receiver with both hands, then hangs up and ducks sideways from the booth, avoiding the glances of the men.

An older woman and a young man sit together on a bench at the top of the stairs, staring straight ahead. The young man wears neat brown trousers, and a crew-necked green jumper conceals the lump of a tie at his throat. He's hunched forward, elbows on his knees, his hands dangling between them. The woman wears red lipstick and a camel-coloured raincoat. She could be his mother or his older sister. They don't speak.

A gust of wind sends a little shower of rain needles into Stephen's face. He draws back into his corner, pulling his collar up. On the brickwork at his shoulder he notices, in small, neat black texta handwriting: GOTH AS FUCK. He sucks on his cigarette again and rests his head back in the corner, closing his eyes against the smoke.

This morning there was another email from Cathy on his Hotmail address, as well as one—shockingly, with his father's name in the 'from' line—from his mother. She must have got his address from Cathy. His mother's began *Dear Stephen*, as though writing a letter. *I'm not very good at this machine as you can see, so I hope you get this message.* Then, *Dad would like to see you, if you can manage it.*

She doesn't tell him what Cathy already has, in her earlier messages—about their father's flailing limbs on the gravel driveway, their mother shouting into his ear to *hang on*, calling down the fluorescent hallways of his pain while the ambulance didn't arrive. She doesn't say, as

Cathy did, that Geoff is unconscious. She signs the email *All my love, Mum*.

Someone else's mobile rings, and a skinny man with a beard pulls a phone slowly from his pocket, then crouches down with his back against the building to talk. The tune of the ring-tone is familiar, yet Stephen can't quite place it. He pictures his mother trying to find the 'on' switch for the computer in the back bedroom of the house that his father has used for an office ever since they all left home. He imagines her peering at the screen as she obeys Cathy's telephone instructions on opening the email program. As he pictures his mother's hesitant, one-finger typing in the little airless bedroom he feels the lump of rising tears in his throat for the first time since he began getting the messages. He swallows it down with the last breath of smoke.

He tosses the cigarette down into the gutter and turns toward the stairs. His mind still echoes with the man's phone ring-tone, trying to place it. He pushes through the large glass doors and it comes to him; it's the theme from *The Greatest American Hero*, a television show from his adolescence. He hums the tune beneath his breath as he waits for the lift. *Believe it or not, I'm walking on air . . .*

Angela from the next booth upstairs is standing beside him at the lift, smiling, her shoulder bag clutched across her chest.

'I didn't know you smoked,' he says, hands in his pockets, but leaning slightly towards her.

She looks up at him, suddenly expressionless. 'What?'

He sees now that she has a mobile phone earplug in one

ear and the phone is lit up in her hand; that she is mid-conversation with someone else.

'Sorry,' he says, shaking his head.

Angela glares at him a second, then turns back to her phone, smiling exaggeratedly. '*Sorry*,' she says into her hand. 'I'm just going down to the car park now.' She takes a deliberate few steps from Stephen and looks at the floor, chattering away on her phone while the numbers of the floors bing in lights above the lift doors.

Stephen thinks of his half-transcribed interview, of the boy in the tracksuit, and then of the angry father and the medication in Angela's transcript, and all the while the familiar melody traces its way beneath the images in his head. The doors open and Angela steps in, still talking.

The doors close again, and he's alone in the lobby, thinking of a young boy wondering about bars on prison cell windows, and his own father convulsing, moaning in the gravel.

I never thought I could feel so free-hee-hee, hums the song in his head.

MANDY SITS alone by her father's hospital bed, watching the robotic rise and fall of his bare chest as the ventilator makes him breathe. On exhalation, his ribcage sinks and seems to reach an almost concave point, then jolts and swells again. It is a perfect, terrible rhythm each time; the exact same measured breath, forced in and out.

A wardsman is strolling about the ward, joking loudly with the nurses, offering to help them. He wears navy overalls, and a short metal chain of keys hangs from a loop at his hip pocket. He has brought the nurses a tray of polystyrene coffee cups with white lids, and deposited it at the sink around the corner. The nurses scurry behind there, one by one, to take sips of their coffee. No drinks are allowed at the new work station.

Mandy is sitting with her chin in her hands, a magazine in her lap, when she senses the wardsman approaching. She hopes he will pass, but his blue legs stop. Although she has not been reading, she places the tip of her index finger at a place in the magazine column, then looks up.

'G'day,' the man says, grinning, his hands on his hips.

She nods, gives a thin smile. 'Hi.'

He just stands, as if waiting for something. When she offers nothing else, he says, 'I been seein you on the telly.'

She nods again.

'I'm a wardsman these days. Wards*person*, political correctness.'

There are no pauses between the phrases; this line is something he has said many times before. His attention drifts as he speaks; he watches a nurse winding the handle of a patient's bed across the ward. Then he turns back to Mandy.

'War reporter,' he says gravely. He pronounces it *repordah*.

'Mmm, sort of,' she says. She hates the term, but can't be bothered arguing.

'Are you gunna do a report on me?' he says and then grins, looking around the room, ready to snigger, but no-one is watching. Without waiting for her to answer, he says, 'Nah, only jokin.'

He is used to people saying *no*, to their averted eyes, their fixed smiles.

'I seen you, anyway. On that.' Nodding up at the television screen.

Mandy raises her eyebrows in acknowledgement, nods again. Then she looks down at the magazine in her lap, at the line her finger is marking.

But the wardsman is undeterred. He pauses a moment, watching her.

'When you was on the ABC, then SBS.' He sniffs. 'And now Channel Four, over there,' he says. 'England.' He's nodding respectfully as he talks.

'Yeah,' Mandy says, surprised. Her own family doesn't appear to pay this much attention to her jobs. But it's a small town. And television attracts weirdos. She forces herself to keep her tight smile.

She looks over at her father, at the white hump in the bed, hinting at the wardsman to leave.

Then he says, 'You don't remember me, do ya.'

His grin has turned hopeful.

Shit. She searches her mind now, looking into his narrow, acne-bitten face. Her mind is blank. She half-smiles. 'Umm.' An apologetic shake of her head.

His brown eyes meet hers. 'We're the same,' he says quietly then, smiling shyly.

'What?'

A nurse's voice calls out then from across the ward.

'Tony, can you give me a hand?'

He looks toward the nurse's voice, then back to Mandy.

'Doesn't matter,' he says. He licks his lips quickly, then winks.

'Seeya,' he says, and strides off across the room.

'Seeya,' she says.

Relieved he's gone, she turns back to look at her father. He has not moved, save for the hissing shunting of his breath, forced in and out.

The bruises, yellow and black, a dreadful mosaic all down his body.

MANDY LEANS against the bars of the empty neighbouring bed, a red jumper tied around her waist. Margaret has earlier said, 'You're ruining that lovely jumper,' gazing at it sorrowfully.

'It's old, Mum,' Mandy said, taking the limp, hollow ends of the sleeves in her fingers, flipping them back and forth while watching the television and her father in alternating glances. Chris and Cathy—again the couple—delivered Margaret to the hospital and have gone to do some grocery shopping. As they left the ward together Mandy saw her mother's fond glance after them—and then noticed her take a deep, silent breath, as if to draw strength before turning back to her elder daughter, and the empty hours ahead of them.

'So is this what it's like all the time?' Mandy now asks her mother, who is reading a gardening magazine on the other side of the bed. Margaret takes a second to look up at her, then nods. 'Yes.' Then she juts her bottom lip and looks upward, thinking. 'Or sometimes people come and talk. The wardsman, or that nice nun who comes sometimes.' She pauses again, looking around the ward.

Mandy follows her gaze and sees the wardsman from earlier, leaning across the nurse manager's desk, offering her a biscuit, joking with her while she tries to work. Mandy turns back; she does not want to catch his eye.

Margaret is scanning the pelmet above the bed where a scattering of Get Well cards is taped. 'And visitors, sometimes.' She nods at the cards. 'Rotary people, mostly.' Then she looks back down at her magazine.

Mandy leans forward to inspect her father's face again, then the monitor screen with its series of green and red and yellow and pink lines. There has been no change in his condition, the doctor told them this morning, but he is *stable*. The thing now, it seems, is to wait for the swelling to subside, and for the results of the new lot of scans. When Mandy had asked about hospitals in Sydney she saw, from the corner of her eye, her mother suddenly turn her full attention to tucking in Geoff's blankets while the doctor said his piece firmly: the care here was *top-notch*; Sydney hospitals were overcrowded and anyway—his parting shot—both Westmead and Royal North Shore had made it clear they wouldn't take him. Mission accomplished, the doctor had smiled at Margaret and walked away.

Mandy sits back down in her plastic chair, and watches her mother across the bed. Margaret's skin is still pink over the cheeks—the healthful appearance she has always had, and which none of her children has inherited. They are more like their father, long-faced and sallow. Margaret's thick short hair sits over her head in orderly waves, its colour an almost perfectly uniform grey, like the colour in advertisements for 'platinum' hair dye. Mandy wonders if her mother has ever coloured her hair. She doubts it, from the way Margaret has exclaimed over whatever colour Mandy's own hair has been each time she has come home: 'Oh! *Red*, now!' The way she would stand back to stare at it a while, one hand across her chest, before lowering her eyes again to meet her daughter's.

Mandy sees it—this careful distance, always, between herself and her family.

Now she observes how her mother frowns as she reads, how concentration makes her bite one corner of her upper lip. Maybe she does dye her hair after all, Mandy thinks. For who knows what women do in country towns when their children are grown and gone; when their husbands fall and lie jerking, legs buckled the wrong way, on the blood-sodden gravel of their driveways.

ONE OF the nurses is a man Cathy recognises; a boy she slept with a few times years ago. Older now but still the same Jim Galvin, with his gaunt, sexy face and an earring. She sits by her father's bed with her chin cupped in her hand and watches Jim Galvin across the ward, on the phone. She remembers his flippy dark hair in front of his eyes, standing at the bar in The Royal, the guitar band loud behind them. Her own boyfriend was away in Perth—sleeping, she suspected from his letters, with his friend's sister—but still she jolted in shock when this boy Jim leaned down and kissed her long on the mouth. She saw her boyfriend's workmate Dave Shanahan watching interestedly from the end of the bar. But she was seized by the kiss, by its panache, the bald lustful declaration of it here in the open, and she saw then the eyebrows of girls from school, holding cigarettes and gin-and-squashes and leaning against their sturdy boyfriends. And there in the dank pub she had kissed Jim Galvin back even though she didn't know him, and she felt the lean length of his thigh against the inside of hers, and they left the pub and walked up Park Street to his flat above the pizza shop near the Commonwealth Bank, stopping here and there to press themselves against a wall, a windowpane, his hands gripping her bum through her jeans. In his flat he had gone down on her, pushing her thighs open and thrusting his face in, sliding his tongue all over and into her, and she'd lain there, dazzled and reeling at the pleasure, the astonishing luxury of all that pleasure.

Today Jim Galvin had recognised her slowly, reading her father's name on the card above the bed. He'd said, 'Cathy Connolly,' and she smiled, rocking on her heels with her hands jammed into her jeans pockets.

'Hi.' She wondered if he was plunged into the same memory, but he only glanced at her father's chart and then back at her, and said, 'Sorry about your dad.' Cathy murmured her thanks and then he walked off, with his clipboard and his clicking nurse's keys and tags.

She heard him a few moments later telling another nurse—a new girl, from Sydney—about his house extensions and his kids going to the Catholic school, about his wife who works at Western Electricity and her parents with the butchery in the plaza.

Everybody has a place here. Butchers and electricity company administration officers and nurses and builders and teachers; they are parents, and home-owners and renovators, and they can forget their hands around a girl's arse and kisses in pubs because that was years and years ago, and they aren't lonely anymore.

Cathy sits waiting for her sister and mother to come back from lunch. She looks at her father now and then. Nothing seems to have changed in his swollen, ripening face; the monitors bleep and the coloured lines trail in jagged, unhurried pace across the screen.

She wonders if she is heartless, for not yet crying. She had held her breath for it, feared it as they walked into the hospital but as soon as she saw him the need for tears evaporated. Perhaps it is shock. Perhaps she *is* heartless. Jim Galvin has gone on his lunch break, she supposes. Maybe to meet his wife, to sit in Sidewalks and eat a toasted ham and cheese sandwich together. Or maybe he's gone home to his half-renovated place on acres. She imagines him and his wife after the kids are in bed, sitting on a couch covered in a paint-spattered cloth, drinking wine from tumblers and eating pizza from a crate set on the unpolished floor, like the couples in home loan advertisements.

Cathy's studio bedsit in Surry Hills has a shower, a toilet, and an electric hotplate plugged into the wall. Years ago Chris gave her a couch and some dining chairs from a city hotel that his firm was redesigning, and she has a dining table made out of a bench top she found in a rubbish skip, now resting on the pedestal legs from two café tables dumped in the lane. In the corner is an old double bed of Mandy and Chris's, an ugly country-style one made of cheap wood with turned legs, but with a good mattress that is still comfortable.

When she first moved there, halfway through art school, she felt thrilled at the place, at the midday sun that slammed in through the tall, graceful window and washed light over the whole wide room. Back when the pharmacy was just a part-time job while she studied and painted, she would enjoy the dulled traffic sounds that came in waves like the sea, and she would light a cigarette and drink wine from a cardboard cask, and draw and draw.

At Chris and Mandy's, Chris had the little courtyard garden done by an expensive landscape designer from a television show. The sisters have joked to each other in whispers about the naff paving, the mondo grass and clipped little evergreens that are supposed to be natives.

'Holy shit, a *water* feature!' Cathy had yelled out the first time she saw it, clutching a champagne glass to her stomach and flicking cigarette ash towards the pool, into which a stone lion's pursed lips drooled water. The pool was filled with tiny green round leaves; it was cool, and the sound of it secretly pleased her. She put her hand into the water and then took it out, a stippled green glove of tiny leaves.

Cathy still loves going to their house, with its thick carpets and glossy floorboards, its acres of bench space, the white, white bathrooms and the water views. Whenever Chris travels to meet Mandy somewhere, Cathy stays at their place alone, catching the bus from the pharmacy across the city after work, not minding the trip because as soon as she arrives she can thump up the stairs to run a bath, then pour a big glass of gin and sink deep into the water.

Sometimes she stays on for a day or two when Chris comes home from the extravagant week-long trips to meet Mandy at some luxury hotel—in Sri Lanka, or Petra in Jordan, or Istanbul or Dubai—and the two of them watch DVDs, or sit on the balcony together watching the boats in the falling evening, not speaking much.

Chris is always quiet when he comes back from seeing Mandy.

Once Cathy said to him, 'Doesn't it ever piss you off, her being away all the time?' She had her feet up on the railing, rocking gently back and forth on her chair. The boats tinkled below.

Chris stared out at the water. 'Course it does.'

Cathy had been surprised. 'Oh. I thought you must be all right about it.' They had sat in silence. 'So,' Cathy said eventually, 'you should tell her that.' And then Chris had turned to face her in the dark and said in a tight, bitter voice: 'What makes you think I haven't?'

Later that evening Cathy flipped through the photos of him and Mandy smiling out from the lobbies of grand hotels, the tables at fancy restaurants, and then she patted Chris on the shoulder and left him to his lonely view, padding up the hallway to the wide, soft bed in the spare room.

A wardsman is walking from bed to bed, emptying the white garbage bags from their stainless-steel frames next to each bed. The bags are almost empty, Cathy can tell from the way they puff with air as he swings them.

Jim Galvin is back from lunch. He calls out, 'Tony, the cleaner is supposed to do that.'

Tony calls back, 'Doesn't matter, I don't mind.'

Then Jim Galvin drops his head, directing a mischievous look at the other nurse, a dark-haired young woman sitting at the long desk with a telephone receiver hunched in the crook of her neck, clicking the end of a pen over and over while she waits for someone to answer. Jim winks at her as he calls out to Tony, 'Well, if you want to do it—just don't let Gordon Bright see you.'

At the mention of this name Tony wheels around, and points a finger at Jim Galvin. The woman ducks her head beneath the ledge above the desk, laughing silently.

'I've told him, and I've told *you*,' Tony says, angrily, 'I don't believe in unions and Gordon can't bloody make me join.'

'*Okay*,' Jim Galvin says, nodding with mock sincerity, while the other nurse snickers, still out of sight, and Tony bends to the next bin.

The ward is filling up. This afternoon, two beds from Geoff, a man aged about sixty sits in his white gown and pyjama pants in the plastic chair next to his bed, a nebuliser mask strapped to his face. He looks exhausted. His chest rises and falls once—quickly, shallowly—and then he slumps motionless for a few long seconds before the next breath. Cathy can see his tired eyes following Tony's progression along the beds, and how he purposely drops his gaze to his lap as the wardsman approaches.

When Tony reaches the far side of the man's bed he takes his time, unrolling a new bin liner, leaning to try to catch the man's gaze. But the man has closed his eyes now. Tony stands waiting, slowly punching the billowing plastic bag into submission. Then he walks around the end of the bed and stands over the man.

'You're a better colour today, mate,' he calls to him through the hiss of the vapour and the nebuliser's low drone. The man opens his eyes and nods wearily. He breathes, the little rise and fall. Tony leans to see the man's name on the card above his bed. 'David Levak,' he reads loudly.

The man's gaze curves upwards, then he slowly blinks and moves his head in a tiny nod. The machine drones.

'*Dave* Levak. Hugo's brother!' Tony crows. 'Hugo the Yugo!' The man nods once again, exhausted.

The dark-haired nurse calls out from the desk, 'Better

just leave him, Tony; he's just got to be quiet there.'

Tony does not acknowledge the nurse's voice, but after a moment puts up a hand before him, as if to stop the man from speaking. 'You just relax, mate, okay? That thing'll fix you up.'

The man closes his eyes again. Tony moves on then, looking up and grinning as he approaches Geoff's bed. But when he sees Cathy sitting there his smile drops off, and he looks down at the floor and walks on, swishing his fat bouquet of white plastic along the ground.

LATE IN the afternoon Mandy and Cathy walk along the corridor of the new wing of the hospital, and out into the car park. Chris has come and then gone again, dropping Margaret at home on the way, then driving off to shop for a few dinner things he couldn't find in the supermarket.

While Cathy rummages in her bag for the keys to the hire car, Mandy looks back at the new intensive care unit. Its clean bright bricks, its aqua awnings and guttering are a shock beside the shadeless, faded yellow fibro panels and grubby brickwork of the old part of the hospital. But the new unit, too, is blocky, virtually windowless and unadorned. As with the rest of the Rundle Hospital building and the treeless car park and strips of concrete pathway, it is as if any more generous aesthetic, any concession towards human comfort or beauty, might be unhealthy.

Cathy follows Mandy's gaze. 'Bloody ugly, isn't it?' she says cheerfully, and then ducks, nimble as a child, into the car.

Mandy is buckling her seatbelt when she sees the wardsman emerge from the entrance and walk along the footpath. He moves slowly, as though without aim, his hands deep in the pockets of his overalls. Unaware he's being watched, all the needy eagerness of his expression from this morning has gone. He walks with his head down, frowning out from beneath the shelf of his brow. His thick, bluntly cut dark brown hair in a straight fringe across his forehead. Mandy can see that beneath the looseness of his overalls he has narrow, teenager's hips, no bum, a slight torso. His hands-in-pockets stance gives him a leaning profile as he walks, moving off to a red ute several car-lengths away from theirs, finally taking a hand from his pocket; silver keys flash, dangling, from his fist. Mandy watches him unlock the ute's door and drop into the driver's seat.

You don't remember me, do ya. As she watches him Mandy thinks hard, casting back through the years—to school, sport, then her time after leaving school, on the local paper. The hot afternoon sun on the venetian blinds in the newspaper office. Other images flit. A dead, rotting bird she saw wedged between some rocks at the creek, the day she left for university. The endless Lions Club giant-cheque presentations, a Hoof and Hook prizegiving where she stood with her camera, freezing among the waxy hanging carcasses in the abattoir. Maybe that was it. Perhaps he was one of the grinning men in white gumboots and puffy shower-caps, sloshing noisily through the bloody water on the cement floor.

'D'you know that guy?' she asks Cathy.

Cathy glances over her shoulder, then bends forward to the ignition. 'He's the wardsguy. I think his name's Tony.'

'Yeah, but do you remember him from when we were kids, or after you left school, or whatever?'

The motor of the red ute chiggers into life. On the rear window is a sticker, white letters on black. AUSTRALIA: LOVE IT OR LEAVE IT. But though the engine has started, Tony sits for a moment staring ahead, expressionless, his hands limp over the steering wheel. Something stirs in Mandy's mind, then is still. She doesn't know him.

Cathy backs the car out of the parking space, twisting to see over her shoulder, her left hand on the back of Mandy's seat. She changes gear and the car moves forward, slowing down as they drive closer to the ute. She squints to look at Tony's face.

'Dunno,' she says. 'School, maybe?'

At this moment he turns his head and sees them. His eyebrows shoot up and instantly the needy grin spreads across his face. His hand jerks in a wave as they pass.

'I don't know either,' Mandy says. 'He's sort of creepy, though.'

Cathy shoots her sister a sly look for a second, but says nothing, only flips down the sun visor and accelerates out of the car park onto the highway. Mandy folds her arms, saying nothing more, and stares out of the side window.

Cathy can still be amused by Mandy's dark instincts, her pride. She bites the inside of her cheek as she turns into the main street, considering this endlessly intriguing matter. Through the years Stephen has always been ready to explode into exasperation at the first glimmer of righteousness from Mandy, but Cathy has always simply found it curious.

Mandy has always had a gift for disagreeableness. It's as though without some constant irritation, some stone in her shoe, she is not properly herself. As though she enjoys—but how could she?—the hardening of other people's smiles in her presence; their gritting teeth as she begins her inevitable argument, when all they'd said was that they liked some movie or hated George Bush. Cathy can still feel a pang for Mandy in these situations, at the same time marvelling at this missing aspect of her sister's perception. Because the truth, Cathy knows, is that Mandy does not enjoy it; she simply cannot help herself. And although by now, in her forties, she seems resigned to being the killjoy, the puncturer of other people's blithe, ignorant pleasure, Cathy can still see in her eyes the bewilderment at their cooling expressions while she corrects their understanding of US foreign policy or begins to lecture on the political undertones in a crappy Chinese martial arts film. Her rigid inability to let things slide; her poignant, stubborn pride.

Once when they were girls sharing a bedroom, Mandy, in a fit of fury, threw a glass tankard at Cathy and hit her square on the cheekbone. And although the glass, solid as lead, did not break but only bounced softly into the bedclothes, at the instant it struck her both girls knew

Cathy had won. Her eye swelled beautifully, fungal and purple, and stayed that way for a week.

The monstrosity of Mandy's crime was repeated among Cathy's friends with awe (Glass! She could have been blinded!) and Cathy almost felt sorry for her sister, but pushed away the feeling whenever it threatened to pall her victory, instead imagining with a thrill the shattering glass, the brave rush to hospital, the life-threatening surgery.

But at school—with her blackened face in full public view—the telling of the tale flew from Cathy's control. Some kids she simply told to mind their own business, and others received a shortened, toned-down version. She maintained, within her circle of particular friends, the elaborate version of the incident, complete with the frisson of the various heightening factors (the fact of the nearby window, for example; or that the glass was hurled from the top bunk). But without the luxury of that judicious selection, Cathy's pleasure in her injury evaporated. The eye hurt if she bumped her head, and the whole area of her face throbbed with an insistent ache. And then she did feel sorry for Mandy, clumping glumly past her in the corridors, her eyes fixed on the floor while older boys stopped Cathy to examine her hideous face.

It was when Mandy's favourite teacher leaned down to Cathy during assembly on the second day and whispered, 'What *happened?*' that she did not pause, but replied coolly that she had slipped over at home and landed on one of her brother's metal Matchbox cars. The teacher looked doubtful, but flinched in sympathy anyway at the idea of the vicious lump of metal.

Cathy did not tell anyone, not even Mandy, that she had lied on her behalf. She was simply miserable, and prayed for the bruise to fade. The crunch came when the family was squeezed inside the station wagon after Mass, and a neighbour put her head in the window to talk to Dad. Catching sight of Cathy in the back, the neighbour was aghast.

'Oh my *God*, Cathy! What happened to you?'

The car went quiet, and each member of the family turned to look at Cathy. The moment stretched. A flush began at Mandy's throat as she sat on the other side of Stephen, awaiting the shame of exposure, her legs jammed together and her fists two clubs on her knees. Cathy cleared her throat and looked the neighbour in the eye.

'I fell,' she said. 'And hit my eye on one of Stephen's Matchbox cars which was on the floor. In the living room, next to the heater.'

Stephen's eyes were enormous. Mandy stared too, her face bright with shame and astonishment. Their parents sat twisted in their seats, stunned.

Then the moment cracked open. 'Oh Cathy,' their mother said kindly. And she could not be stopped from saying, 'You don't have to *lie*, honey,' and turning back to the neighbour and murmuring *sibling spat*. The neighbour saw Mandy's and Cathy's faces and said *Ah*, in a gratified way.

Nothing more was said in the car on the way home. Mandy—who could not be spared, and so was shamed even more by Cathy's attempted rescue—simply bit her lip, folded her arms and glared out of the window.

Exactly, Cathy thinks as she waits for an oncoming car to pass along the main road, as Mandy is doing now.

LATE IN the afternoon Tony sees the mother's white Corolla in the street—he knows the number plate, the cracked tail light. Only an hour ago he saw Mandy in a different car, with the sister, yet still his heartbeat skimmers as he follows the Corolla for a few blocks, up past the chemist in the main street, left into Slough Street. She could easily have had time to go home, then discover some reason to head out again.

The Corolla slows, then reverses into a parking spot opposite the library.

Tony slows the ute and then he parks too, easing backwards into the gutter half a block from the Corolla, watching all the time. Thinking what he will say to her about the thing that happened way back, binding them. *Witnessing*, maybe he will say. It is a good word. Full of power, full of what nobody else can understand.

But when the door opens it's the husband that gets out. Tony's pulse goes sludgy. He stays put, watching the husband fussing with keys, with pockets. Tall, scrawny, with a neat, clipped little poofter's beard. *Homosexual's* beard, he corrects. Women like her, he has realised, love blokes that look like homosexuals. He learned this a long time ago but the fact of it still mystifies him.

Tony had a beard himself once, but he shaved it off.

His was thick and bushy, not shaped or clipped like that. People called him Ned Kelly. They gave him the shits, so he shaved it off.

The husband has gone into the corner shop. Tony waits. Then he gets out of the ute and lets the door slam, walks to the shop's cool doorway. The husband is at the counter already. Tony passes within inches of him. He's smiling a lot at the checkout girl, calling her by the name he must've read off her tag. 'Hi, Jordan,' he's saying, all friendly and appreciative.

Tony waits in line behind a kid in a baseball cap, watching the husband gathering together his little bags of lettuce and lemons on the counter. The husband is asking the checkout girl if she's got any coriander, smiling at her.

Tony folds his arms, sees that the kid in front of him has his folded too. The checkout girl looks at the husband for a bit, and then says, firmly, 'No, we haven't.' But you can tell she doesn't know what coriander is. Tony clears his throat.

'Fruit Barn, mate. Wesley Street.'

The husband jerks around, surprised. Then he smiles at Tony in recognition, a big broad smile. 'Oh *hi*. Thanks. I'll try that.' Then he hesitates a second while he gathers up the bags, shifting sideways to let the kid move to the counter.

Tony says, gesturing toward the street, 'Straight down there, right, then left. Closes five-thirty.'

The husband is all grateful, clutching his plastic bags in his skinny fingers, nodding at Tony. 'Much appreciated, thanks. See you soon,' he says in his girly way, crinkling up his face in another smile. He goes out through the open door into the street.

'Longbeach twennyfives,' the kid mumbles at the checkout girl. As she reaches up to the smokes rack she and the kid and Tony all watch through the door the husband flapping at the car with his plastic bags, putting them on the roof, fiddling in his pockets for keys again. The girl tosses the packet of cigarettes on the counter, and she and the kid smirk at each other then, about the useless knob out there in the street.

Tony says, 'He's all right.'

The girl and the boy glance at Tony in silence. She takes the boy's money, and then as she gives him his change they flick a knowing look at each other. The kid grunts his thanks, stepping aside as he puts his cigarettes in his pocket and folds up his wallet.

The girl is staring at Tony in a bored way.

'Packet of Dunhill Blue thanks,' says Tony. She reaches above her head again, fingers trailing along the rack, and tilts out a packet.

'He's Mandy Connolly's husband,' Tony says, looking out again at the husband, who is finally folding himself inside the Corolla's open door.

The boy and girl just stare at him again, blank-faced.

'On television? *War* reporter?' Tony says, gruffly now.

They keep staring.

Anger surges through him. 'Ever watched the bloody news? Heard of *Iraq*?' He smacks down a note and some coins on the black rubber belt of the counter.

The boy shrugs, says 'Huh.' His and the girl's eyes meet again in their private joke. Tony rips the clear, staticky wrapper off the cigarette packet and tears out the piece of foil. He glares at the two of them, flicking his fingers to free himself from the clear plastic, letting it flutter to the counter-top.

'This place is so fucken *ignorant*,' he growls, and pushes past the boy into the street.

The Corolla is gone, and the street is now almost empty of cars. Tony gets into his ute and sits for a moment staring out at the street, still hot with anger. Fucking morons. He sniffs. It occurs to him that he might be the only one in the whole frigging town who knows anything about her.

He juts his jaw at the thought.

A green and yellow chip packet flips, in a listless leapfrogging, across the bitumen.

STEPHEN'S ARRIVAL at the back door is as though he has simply stepped in from the rain. He walks in, scratching the back of his neck, and slings an overnight bag to the laundry floor. Margaret turns from the sink, where she's holding a spiky posy of knives and forks—and then she sees him, and something drains out of her, a tautness escaping her body with a gasp, and she drops the cutlery into the sink, calling '*Oh!*' and then she begins to cry, squeaking out in gratitude as Stephen steps across the old linoleum squares, red and green as Christmas, to dip his head and bend to put his arms around his mother.

In the grateful, muffled space of this long-awaited

embrace, Margaret hears the girls coming in the back door, their yelps of surprise and recognition. And with one look over Stephen's shoulder at their faces Margaret lays down the law: Stephen's years of mottled absence will remain undiscussed, unchallenged. For all three women know it could take only a single wrong word for Stephen to step outside the back door as if to hang a bath towel on the line, and then to slip noiselessly into the driver's seat of his old Subaru ute, close the door with a small thud, reverse down the driveway and out onto the road in a slick pirouette, and be gone from them again.

So Cathy and Mandy stop, wait for their mother to disentangle herself, and then call out to him. Cathy murmurs, '*Thank you,*' into the rough warmth of their hard, dry embrace, and then turns again to their mother, who is talking already of where Stephen will sleep—in his old room, Dad's office. As Margaret exclaims, Cathy watches Mandy step around the kitchen table to Stephen. They smile warily, briefly, murmur 'Hello,' and bump cheeks in a kiss, their uncertain hands touching each other's shoulders for a second before retreating instantly to the space of their own bodies.

'When did you get here?' Stephen asks her.

'Yesterday, with Cath. And Chris. He's—' she motions toward the street, 'shopping, or something.'

Margaret is calling now from the hallway, pulling sheets from the linen cupboard.

Stephen says, 'Have you seen Dad?'

Mandy nods, chews her lip. 'Not good.'

He looks at Cathy where she stands by the table with her hands on her hips, but she is just nodding too, and biting down on her bottom lip to stop herself from crying. She sniffs then, and wipes her nose with her fingers.

Margaret is still calling to Stephen. He looks from one sister to the other—from Mandy's shadowed expression to Cathy's face, smooth and open like an actress's—and then goes to the laundry, picks up his bag and turns to follow his mother's voice down the hall to his childhood room.

Chris walks in a few minutes later. 'Whose car is that?' he says, dumping the shopping bags on the table. When they tell him his eyes widen.

'Blimey,' he says.

WHEN MARGARET has gone from the room—after making up the bed, refusing Stephen's help as she bent to tuck in the faded yellow floral sheets—he flops down on the single bed, lying on his back and staring around the room. In recent years Geoff has set up a computer and a little inkjet printer on Stephen's little school desk near the window, and a stout grey two-drawer filing cabinet has replaced the old fake-teak laminate bedside table. Stephen used to stare at its pale, ice-creamy streaks as he fell into sleep at night. The computer on the desk is old: one of those grey, bulbous-screened jobs, the monitor and keyboard grubby with age. The printer is also grey, but newer.

Stephen wonders what the old man actually does at the computer. He can picture him there, peering over his half-moon glasses into the screen, his concerned old face reflected in the glass as the monitor warms up. *University of the Third Age* is printed on a sheet of paper lying on the desk; notes on some course, something archaeological. He imagines Geoff taking trips out to Lake Mungo with a whole busload of other old coots, clutching clipboards and clamping canvas sunhats to their bald old heads. The desert sun boring down to grow a few more opalescent scales of skin cancer at the open necks of their shirts.

The room smells the same. Or maybe it's just the sheets, musty with linen-cupboard camphor or lavender or the waxy little lumps of whatever his mother has always hidden in there in the dark among the towels and sheets and other mysterious slabs of folded fabric.

Next to the open door is the same paintworn wooden wardrobe that has always been in here. With a deep and sudden pleasure Stephen notices his old stickers still plastered over its side. He sits up, leaning forward for a closer look: a turquoise diamond with *Hey Charger!* and the Chrysler logo in black; a three-inch square sticker of an AC/DC album cover. A 'signed' poster of Dennis Lillee that he remembers tearing out of the Sunday paper, then rolling thick with glue and sticking to the door, smoothing it over and over, admiringly, with the side of his hand. Near to it, in studied disarray, other smaller stickers of band logos in red and black; all the schoolboy's pub-rock role models he'd loved—Cold Chisel, The Angels, The Saints.

He flops onto the bed again. Down the hallway he can

hear his mother calling to Cathy; the back screen door bangs. He should get up.

On top of the wardrobe is a small stack of board games, the box lids scuffed and worn at the corners. Monopoly; draughts; Ludo; Trivial Pursuit with one blue panel of its lid torn, flapping open. A quoits stick lies on its side, two hairy green rings hooked over it. Tipped crookedly among the quoits and the games is his father's old straw beach hat, frayed, with a sizable hole in the crown.

When Stephen was a kid Geoff would occasionally dump that hat on his head at the beach. He remembers its humid smell, the taste of its leather chin-strap, the wooden bead rolling in his mouth.

Once, far away when they went visiting cousins at Culburra one Christmas, he and his father took Stephen's new fishing rod to the wharf, leaving the others at the beach. When a baby whiting flipped at the end of his line Stephen almost dropped the rod in excitement, but his father leaned and steadied his grip, helping him begin to reel in the fish. But then suddenly a seagull dropped from the sky, and swooped the fish, still on his hook, high up into the air above them! They both let out a cry of astonishment and laughter, and for a few long seconds Stephen and his father held a flying bird on the end of a line, the reel whirling and tumbling. Then the gull tore the whiting away, snapping the line, and flew off. The cobweb of fishing thread fell down through the air.

It was *marvellous*, the word Geoff kept using. Whenever Stephen heard someone say 'marvellous' over the years, he thought of that day by the sea far from home, when he and his father held a bird flying in the air on the end of a fishing line.

He lies on the bed, listening. He can hear the television in the living room now. Stephen can't remember the last time they were all here together. But they are not all here. His father lies hooked to a machine, half-dead, in the hospital.

Suddenly Stephen wishes he had not come. The feeling that had grown as he drove the long hours of highway—that something might crack open the closed feeling he has had for so long about his family—has dissolved in an instant. He should have known it was a mistake to come. He doesn't want to see the old man. In the morning he will leave.

But—his mother's face when he arrived. Her pathetic gratefulness.

He hauls himself upright, pulls off the sweaty t-shirt, bunches it into a ball and tosses it to the floor, then reaches into his bag for a clean one.

'Wanna beer, Stephen?' Cathy shouts from the living room.

'Yeah,' he yells back, shrugging the t-shirt on.

On his way out of the room he stops by the noticeboard Geoff had made from six cork tiles when Stephen was doing his school certificate, pinning a 'study schedule' there in the vain hope his son would take any notice of it. Now the board is pinned with bits of paper, lists of stuff from the old man's so-called university courses, it looks like, and a large black-and-white aerial photograph of Rundle that hangs off the lower edge. Stephen bends to peer at it, orienting himself using the dark ribbon of highway. The main road's thin offshoot from the highway, then the grid of the town: the white dots of roof-smudges in rows, some obscured by trees. The tree-dotted wiggle of river, the white-scored outline of the cricket oval. Stephen finds Aurora Street, tracing it with his finger, counting the houses to theirs. An inch away, the stubble of the bush reserve starts. The town really is small, he thinks, taking in the irregular patchwork of grazing land beyond the reserve. Stretching away from the town on all sides, thousands and thousands of acres.

The reserve had seemed so vast when they were kids. Stephen would often labour up the hill to the bush, stomping up the hot street after a fight with Mandy or his father, in tears of rage and self-pity. He would scuff along the wide dirt track, smelling the bush, imagining getting himself lost; his family's shame and remorse when he didn't return that night. They would know it was their fault.

The reserve held all kinds of dusty secrets. Once he found a hole filled with dirty clothes. He had hoped it was a grave, or something illicit and sexual, but after a while it looked only like someone's stolen washing. Jumpers and handkerchiefs. He'd spat on the pile anyway.

Another time he climbed the highest rock up near the ridge, and imagined jumping off, crashing to the boulders and jagged shrubs below. But then he felt a bit sick, so he sat down, and then crawled on his belly over to the very edge of the rock. When he looked down into the valley, a sudden thrill swept over him, making his guts squirl. There, far below, was an enormous, silent compound. He recognised it immediately, fizzing with exhilaration, as some secret industrial lair. Spies, or some other sort of elaborate criminal enterprise. There were several vast, circular pits, each with a clothesline-style apparatus turning slowly through the containers' coal-black, lumpy liquid. And beyond those, a series of rectangular pools of water, or something worse. The whole compound was fenced and a tiny red-brick building stood at one corner. Stephen strained to focus, and made out a tiny guard patrolling near the compound gate. He had sat up on the warm rock, pulse racing, breathless with the responsibility of his discovery.

He would tell no-one about it. A satisfying wave of superiority had coursed through him. Even Mandy wouldn't know about this.

Months later, one Sunday after Mass they had driven down a strange street at the far end of town, for Dad to drop off some tools he was lending to a man from Rotary. They passed a large, fenced-off area and Stephen began to feel a confused, panicky recognition in his chest. Then he realised—it was the secret compound! The brick building—and beyond, the walls of the huge cement pits! He looked wildly around for his family's astonishment, opening his mouth to tell them what he knew—but they were unconcerned: Mandy only gave him her usual scowl, Cathy ogled from her baby's seat, Mum chattered on, Dad kept driving as if nothing at all was happening.

Then Stephen saw the sign: RUNDLE SEWAGE TREATMENT—WASTE WATER MANAGEMENT PLANT.

Standing here in the bedroom Stephen can't help but feel again the hot humiliation of that moment. *They all knew.* Except him. Cathy didn't count; she was a baby. But Dad and Mandy—even Mum—had known all along, that his secret was nothing special after all, only another bit of Rundle's ordinary ugliness, like the rubbish tip or the water tower. He looks for the sewage works now on the photograph—and there it is, a series of dark blobs just near the racetrack. He stares at it, recalling the drab shock, the hollow lesson of that day: that specialness had passed him by.

He walks out into the hallway's gloom.

TO CATHY, the house seems simply to shrug, and realign itself to Stephen's presence. He is asked no questions. When he comes out of his room Chris strides over to him—'*Mate*'—proffering a bottle of beer, and they settle into the safety of handshakes, talk of roads and travelling times, the safety of brothers-in-law twisting lids off beers.

And then, after Stephen's stroll around the yard, his lavish greeting of Leia—his face close to hers, hands cupping her slavering chin—it is, impossibly, as if he has always been here, as if he has not held himself apart from them for so long, making his parents and Cathy push through the twitchy, twice-yearly monosyllabic phone conversations to confirm he's still alive.

It is as though their father's falling has torn in their family an opening through which Stephen might come sidling back.

CHRIS AND Mandy sit watching the SBS news while Cathy and Margaret make dinner in the kitchen. Across the living room Stephen leans into the bookshelves, head tilted to read the spines, a glass of beer in his hand.

Mandy watches the blurred image of the missing journalist Jill Carroll, the tape leached of almost all colour, without speaking. Chris flicks her a look now and then but she seems completely unmoved. The bulletin moves on: the Australian Wheat Board managing director has resigned over the kickbacks; Parliament debates the abortion pill. The health minister's carved angular face, the stones of his eyes, fill the screen.

Stephen walks along the shelves, head bent, taking in the titles of the books still familiar from his adolescence. He looks up when the kidnapped journo comes on, watching Mandy for a reaction. But she says nothing. He turns back to the books: the Time Life World Library series on different countries, with their thin white spines. The thick hardback novels from the seventies and tightly packed non-fiction paperbacks, spanning the years—*Government, Power and Politics in Australia*; *Who's Who of Jazz*; *The Fatal Shore*. Then Margaret's novels—*The Plague Dogs*, *Three Cheers for the Paraclete*, a Doris Lessing autobiography, *Cloudstreet*. There's a two-volume encyclopaedic-looking set called, simply, *Catholicism*; some cookbooks; the long shelf of Geoff's old Isaac Asimovs.

Then there are the books attached to Geoff's various fads—camping, soldering, bicycle maintenance. Stephen tilts one, pulling it off the shelf.

'Hey!' he calls in delight. He pulls out two more: *The Magnificent Book of Kites*, and *Kites Across the World*.

'Remember these?' he says to the air, not looking up.

Mandy glances over her shoulder, then back, attentive only to the television. A visiting American anti-terrorism expert is saying the insurgency in Iraq has demoralised many coalition partners. Onto the screen flick images of car bombs and US tanks.

Stephen plonks himself onto the couch beside Mandy with the books, holding his glass aloft to stop it spilling as he sits. He ignores the television, turning pages.

Cathy comes in and leans over the back of the couch, peering past Stephen's shoulder at the books in his lap. They are both making little sounds of recognition, of discovery, at this kite picture or that one.

Chris gets up. 'Anyone want another drink?' Nobody replies. After a second he blinks, and wanders off into the kitchen to find Margaret.

'I loved going kite-flying,' Stephen says, his voice lost and wistful.

Mandy glances sideways at her brother and sister, then back at the television screen. The news has moved on to sport. But there is something tensing in her.

'You weren't even there,' she says then, still watching the screen. The annoyance in her voice makes both Cathy and Stephen look up.

Mandy turns. 'Well, you weren't,' she says matter-of-factly. 'You were a baby.' She forces a smile; she is being reasonable.

Stephen stares at her for a second. 'I was there. I've seen photos.'

Mandy sighs. 'Okay. You might have *been* there, but you can't re*member* it. You were just in the pram.'

Cathy rolls her eyes, eases herself up from her elbow-dent in the couch, and leaves the room. Mandy turns back to the television, saying, 'You didn't *do* it, you just always sat in a pram or on a blanket off in the corner. It was just me and Dad.'

She doesn't know why she cares, why this insistence has risen up in her, but the wearying tide of logic pulls her on. She turns back to Stephen again, who hasn't answered. He's staring straight at her, biting his lip. Under her brother's vengeful stare she feels her face grow hot.

'You didn't fly them,' she finishes flatly.

He's still looking at her, saying nothing. He takes a slow swig from his glass and swallows. Then he says, 'Well, so fucking what?'

She licks her lips. 'So nothing. It's no big deal. All I'm saying is, you can't remember doing it, because you didn't do it. You weren't a part of it.'

She gets up and takes her empty glass to the kitchen, leaving Stephen sitting on the couch staring at the open book in his lap.

The ruined mystery of the sewage works returns to him and with it the stale, left-behind feeling of his childhood.

And now he realises he has always associated this feeling with Mandy, and also with his father—this refusal of the world to offer its grander gifts to him.

Fuck the both of them, he thinks. I'm leaving.

But, but. This silver kite against a blue sky on the page. His mother's face today, full of stupid love and terror. And his father fallen. And why or how that might turn things inside out he doesn't begin to know, but as he stares back down at the book he can't get it out of his head: the day a seagull snatched a fish in the clear blue sky, the moment when he held astonishment in his hands. That marvellous moment only he and his father knew.

GEOFF'S KITE-FLYING obsession had lasted only a brief year or so, when Mandy was five and Stephen a toddler, just before Cathy was born. For several months their father would drive Mandy and baby Stephen to the highest of the bare hills near the town, where the grey transmission tower reached into the sky above them. He would lift his kites—delicate creations of dowel and bright tissue paper—from the boot of the car. Mandy would huddle, sullen, in her nylon parka, hair whipping her face in the freezing wind.

'I told you to wear something warmer,' Geoff would growl while he untangled a cord. But Mandy had insisted on her pink tartan skirt and bare legs, and the wind was icy. Geoff plonked Stephen on a blanket on the hard ground with a bucket of plastic toys, rugged so tightly and bulkily in his little hooded jacket he was rendered almost immobile.

When he turned to try to watch them the hood stayed where it was, and his face would half disappear inside it.

Mandy had to stand in the buffeting wind, holding the skein of nylon line in both hands, while her father strode up the hill ahead of her. Then he would throw the kite up, and shout at her, 'Hold it tight! Up!' and she would lean, her feet planted on the tussocky ground, holding the line up above her head. The kite would mostly swirl once or twice and arrow straight into the stony ground. But sometimes, sometimes, it would lift, the spool whirling and tumbling in her hands, the green box kite lifting higher and higher, and Mandy would begin to smile and then to shriek, standing with her head thrown back as the kite rose so high it was difficult to see, her feet gripping the spinning earth, laughing with her mouth wide open.

And Geoff would stand watching his daughter falling in love with the gamble, the chance of it. Falling in love with the high space beyond this town, and the possibility of flight.

Once, many years later, Mandy had called her father from Sarajevo for his birthday. Sitting on the floor in her room she had watched the window and listened. There had been no shots for an hour. She had twisted the satellite phone's rubber aerial, pressed the numbers.

'Hello,' said Geoff's voice then, in the way he always answered, with the downward, unexpectant inflexion.

'Happy birthday, Dad,' she'd said, smiling at the dingy carpet. She heard him breathing; there was a pause, like fright. But then he said loudly, gratefully, 'Mandy.'

'How's the weather there?' she asked, but didn't wait for an answer. 'How's Mum? What's the news?'

Her father cleared his throat across the oceans. 'Sunny here today; you can probably hear the lawnmowers.'

'What did you get for your birthday? I've tried to send you something, but the post . . . it might not get there.'

She had bought a battered old kite from a woman in the street who was selling her children's possessions, clumped deep inside the doorway of an apartment block. The absurdity of the kite, red and orange against the gritty misery of the dusty, blasted city. The bright precariousness of it. She had wrapped it in the ruins of a plastic bag and some paper, and persuaded another journalist to take it out with him through the tunnel, made him promise to post it when he got home to Athens. Crouched there with the sat phone on the hotel room floor, she had already given it up as long-gone, tossed perhaps into the mud of that foul underground passage.

'Mum's well, we're all well,' said her father.

Their voices fell across the world, passing each other, halting and starting, father and daughter seeking each other out in the delays, in the small scurrying sentences. Then in the middle of her saying something, Geoff cut in. 'We've been worried.'

She allowed the pause, felt the pain of tears building behind her eyes. 'But it's okay, Dad, I'm being very careful.'

She lay down on her back on the floor with the phone, blinking away her tears, watching the stained ceiling. Tell the truth, he had said to them all, all through the petty lies of their childhoods and adolescence. And now they were nearing the truth of her own life she could feel her throat constricting, her voice wavering.

'What?' her father said. He sounded older than he should, deafer.

'I'm being *careful*,' she repeated, louder, more definite. 'I'm safe.'

'Are you near that hotel? The one on TV?'

Tell the truth.

'No, Dad, I'm a long way from there.'

His answer was lost under a loud noise from outside, something huge and metallic falling. They both paused. And then he began telling her about the garden, about Rotary. Snatches of images came to her: the backyard with its apricot tree; the crepe myrtles all down the street; the blue and gold Rotary Club name badge he kept with the spare change in a little Indonesian bowl by the telephone, and which he pinned to his sports jacket lapel every Thursday evening.

Then there was the staccato of gunfire, and she crawled to the window, the phone in her hand. Two soldiers were dragging the sobbing driver from the cabin of a car.

Geoff stopped. 'What was that?'

'Nothing, go on, Dad,' Mandy urged, and he began to speak again. But he knew she was lying, she heard the knowing in his voice as he tried to cocoon her with the Anzac Day barbecue, the mown grass, the last of the peaches.

She closed her eyes to imagine these things, and her father's voice came gentle and rhythmic across the world, trying to help her stop the images dissolving, as she opened her eyes and watched the three young soldiers, each with a cigarette in one hand and an AK47 in the other, begin to kick the man to death in the cold street.

Three months later Geoff unwrapped a battered parcel, stickered with stamps and glossy with tape. Inside was a bent birthday card, and a folded paper kite. He held it up against the window and it glowed, red and orange as embers.

MANDY WATCHES late-night current affairs once everyone else has drifted to bed. Chris had told her he was ready for bed, and waited beside her on the couch for her to say something. When she just nodded at him he looked back, meaningfully, but said nothing for a moment. Then he let his hand rest lightly on her thigh and said, 'Are you okay?'

Mandy looked down at his hand, then put hers over it. She held his warm hand and looked up, meeting his gaze steadily for the first time since she got off the plane. She nodded. 'Thank you. I'm sorry,' she murmured. 'I'll be there in a minute.'

Chris let his hand rest in hers for a long moment, and then got up from the couch and left the room.

Her neck aches. On the television screen a Palestinian boy is crawling, dragging himself across the flat concrete roof of his apartment block. He is demonstrating for the reporter how he dragged his dead sister, who was shot while hanging laundry, across the roof. He shows the reporter how, as he dragged her, he tore a bath towel from the line as the shots kept coming, and he kept crawling and hauling, bunching the towel—*like this*—around her bloody, opened head. When the report is finished Mandy switches off the television.

She lowers herself into the bed next to Chris and lies there, gazing up into the dark. She breathes as silently as possible. She thinks of her father in the hospital, and she slows her breathing more, matching it to the slow, motorised rhythm of his.

When she wakes again, at three, the vision before her opened eyes is an old woman she saw once in Rafah, on the Gaza border. The woman's back was horribly deformed, the great hump of it forcing her to bend so her face was almost level with her hands, clutching the handlebars of a battered aluminium walking frame. A young man, her son, walked beside the old lady, hands in his pockets. The woman's legs were sturdy, but she could only take little scuffing steps like a baby, gripping the bars of her frame. Her son carried a large pack, and nervously scanned the street around them as they walked. He licked his lips, but he spoke all the time to his mother in a calm, low voice, the withheld, whizzing energy of his body only allowed expression in the jittering fingers, the fast blinking, against his mother's slow, excruciating steps.

The son was hit in the legs, and he screamed at her to *move, go!* as he fell. But she was stuck, motionless, in the middle of the road. Why did they let her stand there for so long, sobbing into the dirt, holding to the ridged rubber handles of her frame? She could not bend to her son, could not straighten. Eventually, howling into her own chest, she began to push the frame forward again, one dragged step at a time. She wailed his name again and again, perhaps apologising for leaving him. He was no longer moving; blood was everywhere. No-one else came for her. The wind blew rubbish along the road.

Only when she had reached the other side did the sniper hit her. She fell without a sound, except the light clatter of her walking frame falling to the ground beside her.

Mandy forces her breath to come slowly again, lets her mind's lapping waves enclose the woman and her son, waits for them to sink back away beneath the surface of the night. When she finally returns to sleep she dreams of coming home, of driving the Rundle streets, but the crepe myrtles and jacarandas are festooned with shreds of her father's skin and flesh.

CHAPTER NINE

TONY STANDS motionless in the doorway to his living room, staring at the TV.

A kidnapped journalist has appeared on a video, begging for her life; the newsreader's voice is tight with importance. Tony's gut lurches before his brain even kicks up *it's not her*, before the millionth-second's reasoning that he's seen Mandy here in Rundle with his own eyes just hours ago.

The American girl's photograph appears behind the newsreader's head. She is nothing like Mandy at all. There is no reason for him to keep watching, for this panic in his body. But still his guts knot. He swigs from his beer glass, the kitchen lit up behind him. The living room is gloomy but for the bright square of television; he's not yet bothered to switch on the light. He has fed the dogs, but not himself. A bowl of microwaved pasta sits congealing on the kitchen table behind him. He tilts his glass steeply, watching the television's blur through its base. And now there she is, the Yank girl. She's wearing a headscarf. *Hijab*. Or is it *abayah*? Behind her is a giant flower, on some rug or curtain. The video is all blurry black-and-white. But in the middle of the flower and the hijab is her young girl's face, while she says, '*Please, just do whatever they want, give them whatever they want as quickly as possible.*'

Her voice is American, calm, as if she is acting. There is no emotion.

'There is a very short time; please do it fast. That's all.'

She makes a weird half-smile.

The shot changes to file footage of the street where the girl and her translator were grabbed. On the street people walk about in their robes, there are cars beetling. All the dusty colourless decay.

'*Carroll is the thirty-first foreign journalist to be kidnapped in Iraq since the Iraq War began,*' the newsreader says.

Tony swallows, and exhales a long, slow breath. *It's a Yank*, he tells himself, over and over like a mantra as he goes to the kitchen drawer for a fork.

But if it happened to her. His gut squirl begins again. Tony has seen the crappy video footage each time on the TV, on the net; each person unrecognisable from their smiling staff photos. He remembers the French woman, appearing against the dark, featureless background with her knees up, her big bony hands clutched together around them. She wore a grey, too-big sweater and her hair was stringy, her face haggard and filthy. Her choppy accent. *My halss iz vary bud*, she had said. *I'm very bad sichologically also*.

He has watched them all, their hair bushy and dirty, all the muscles of their face gone slack and their skin grey, crouched with their ankles bound on the concrete floor of some grey shithole. Once, that poor Yank boy with the orange overalls on. Everything grey but the overalls, a blob of terrible colour. But each one, talking always like they're already dead, talking to the camera with their eyes rolled back like a corpse's, giving their name, maybe holding their passport open on their chest. Maybe saying, *I don't want to die.* Maybe asking the government to do something. But mostly sitting there, with the guns pointed, or the masked faces behind them, just waiting for it to be over, staring out of their dead, scooped-out eyes.

If it was her, could he watch it?

He watched it once, on the net. The orange overalls kid, pushed to the floor and then the awful screaming. The connection kept dropping out and Tony was glad of it, sitting there at the corner table in his living room, sweat on his forehead, his hand over his mouth. He saw the first dreadful movement of the knife, the sawing wrench of it, and then he ran to the bathroom and retched into the toilet. When he came back the silence told him the footage had frozen with the dropped-out line and he turned the computer off without looking back at the screen and then he sat in the dark, wishing away what he had seen.

If it was Mandy he couldn't watch it. Crouched there, her ponytail showing the slender, naked back of her neck. Sobbing probably. Or maybe not, maybe so half-dead and sick with terror she would only just be breathing.

Tony realises he is crying himself now, standing here over the opened kitchen drawer. He sniffs, wipes his face on his arm. *It isn't her.* You fuckwit. But still he can't stop the tears coming as he shoves the drawer back in, goes to the table, pulls out a chair and sits, dragging the bowl towards him. He peels back the plastic wrap from the bowl and leaves it in a sodden gob on the tabletop, jabs the fork into the pale lumps of the pasta, sniffing back the tears.

Then it comes to him. If it happened to her, he would offer himself. The simplicity of it stops his guts quivering, stops his bawling. He would go to Baghdad, they would let her go, shoving her through a doorway into some stinking laneway. She would cry, thank him, and then they would shake hands and he would open the door and go inside. He would pull on those stiff orange overalls, and he would kneel down in the concrete room and wait.

After the first blow, perhaps it would not be so terrible. Perhaps even just one blow, and that would be it—living, done with. Hasn't he wished it, sometimes? One sharp shock, the rabbit's wrung neck?

He almost tried it once, that early release. A rope, a tree in one of the back paddocks. He climbed the tree, winding the rope around and around the branch. He found he liked the feeling of it, the rope running through his fingers, raspy like the bark. The little flick of its end, each time he pulled it up. It was a warm afternoon. It was a useless thing, doing that, but it felt useful, pulling up the rope like he was winding something in, then letting it fall: *flick*, *flip*. After a while up there the thick hard force churning in his chest had gone slow, and he was knackered again. So he just sat, feeling the bone of the tree branch under his arse, looking down and across the paddocks, and way off he heard the dogs whining for their dinner. He sort of lost the need for it then, in that moment. He felt too buggered even to get down. But eventually he did—half-climbed, half-slithered down, felt the bark rasping against his belly as he slid.

He left the rope there, for the next time, and he got back in the ute and drove back across the knobbled paddocks, the grasses lain over in tufts like the hair on a Scotty dog. In his rear-vision mirror he saw that small loop just hanging there, waiting for him, and then he put his foot down and drove back to feed the dogs.

He thought about her then too, while he drove across the paddocks. That maybe she sometimes felt like this.

Sometimes he thinks about joining up in the army. He watches the news, like tonight, and he thinks sometimes about the places, about all the people that've got nothing. He could go to one of those dusty, hot places and give stuff to the kids that haven't got anyone. Lollies and things. He could have an M16 and drive an APC and all that, but mainly he would be nice to the people with nothing. He wouldn't let the kids hold his gun or anything. But then on the news he heard some kids got blown up when some soldiers were giving them lollies, and after that he couldn't sleep for a while, not in bed anyway. He could go to sleep on the couch with the television on, orange and blue in the dark.

He wouldn't let those kids touch a gun. He could get one of those iPods, let the people listen through the little earphones.

The last time he looked the rope was rotting away, with a lumpy sort of knot at its end. It probably wouldn't even hold his weight anymore.

Before he goes to bed, he has a piss and then stands for a moment in front of the bathroom mirror beneath the dangling globe, staring at the stubble of his own face.

It is not possible that she doesn't remember. Tomorrow he will talk to her properly. About their being the same. About how in all the years since the fire he has followed her, paid attention to her life, its importance. Tomorrow it will be possible to say the words of it: the car, the burned corpse. How they saved one another.

CHAPTER TEN

Day three

CATHY ROUNDS the corner and there's something different about Dad's face there in the distance, a different light spread over his bed. As she walks closer she realises what it is—he's been shaven, somehow, beneath the drips and tubes and plasters. And then she sees Stephen, sitting in the chair, a hand resting on the white blanket through the bars of the bed. He sees her and stands up.

Cathy says, 'I thought your car was at home.'

'Walked,' says Stephen. They both turn to look at their father.

'Looks pretty terrible, doesn't he.'

They stare at his ballooned, blotchy face.

Cathy moves to fetch the other chair from the side of the bed, pulls it across the waxy lino. 'Yep.'

'Did you shave him?' she says then.

Stephen nods, reddening for a moment. 'Couldn't stand him looking like that.' He looks at her, then seems guilty. 'They said I could,' he says, jerking his head towards the nurses' station. 'I asked them first.'

He stretches, scratching his back over his shoulder with a large hand. He wears a faded red polo shirt, the collar bent and whitened with age. His sneakers squeak on the floor as he moves. He and Cathy both sit back down in the chairs.

Stephen had arrived early, creeping into the ward and whispering to the duty nurse. He'd sat in the low light, holding his old man's white hand, tilting his weight forward, setting the plastic chair rocking in a slow, deliberate tremor.

After a while he had stepped silently back across the floor to the nurse at her desk and asked, 'Can I shave him?'

She'd raised her tired eyes. 'Sure, I suppose. If I can find some stuff . . .' and she trailed off across the ward, fiddling with a bunch of keys.

Shortly she presented Stephen with a bowl of hot water, a towel and soap and a razor on a tray. 'We just have to be really careful with the tubes and stuff,' she said, easing the grubby plastering off Geoff's sweaty forehead, peeling it away and then taping the large ventilator tube to the pillow beside his face.

She stood beside the bed while Stephen took the washer and lathered his father's face with soap, lifting the nostril tubing carefully, watching Geoff for any sign of discomfort, any reaction. The machines buzzed and beeped their arrhythmic melodies.

After a minute or two the nurse said, 'You'll be right,' and left him.

Stephen bent over his father, smoothing the old skin and turning his face, drawing the razor across the skin—gently, gently—and dipping the razor in and out of the water. Eventually he took the bowl into the bathroom and tipped the soapy water out, rinsed the washer under the tap, then came back with a bowl of clean hot water. With the clean washer he wiped his father's face again, lifting and setting the tubes back, sponging his cheeks, nostrils, the corners of his closed eyes, smoothing up into his hairline, into and behind each ear. The nurse came back, picking at a roll of tape, and repositioned the big white tube with a square of clean, unrumpled tape.

'Much better,' she said, and smiled at him.

He took the bowl once again to the bathroom, once again rinsed the washer under the hot tap. Then he drew it over his own face, pressing the steaming cloth into his eyes.

Now, as he sits beside Cathy and their father's motionless body, the hospital is coming to life, there is the sound of people arriving and equipment moving. They hear talking rising from the corner near the desk. It's a man's voice, insistent about a tent he lent someone.

'Worth two hundred and sixty-four bucks, and brand new. The prick.'

Another man murmurs in answer, but the first man cuts in.

'Just for a week, he reckoned, the prick.' He looks around, sniffs once. 'Anyway, that solicitor, East Ward? He reckons he can write me a letter,' he says.

Stephen sits, elbow on his knees, chin cupped in his hands.

'Two hundred and sixty-four bucks,' Tony is saying again, leaning against the wall while the other wardsman inspects a piece of paper in his hand. 'But I reckon I could get more, because the arsehole said one week and now it's been five months. When he gets out anyhow, that solicitor bloke reckons he can write me a letter.'

The other man folds his paper into a wedge and sticks it in his pocket.

'We gotta get down to Recovery.'

Tony nods, trailing his gaze bed by bed around the ward. His colleague goes to the door but Tony, hands in his pockets, lifts an elbow at him and says, 'Hang on a sec,' as he moves toward Stephen and Cathy.

'G'day,' he says, standing at the end of the bed, feet apart, hands still in his pockets.

Stephen and Cathy murmur hello, smile. Tony looks down at the pile of books and magazines on the tray. 'What's that?' he says, nodding at the book on top.

Stephen picks it up. 'Kites. He used to make them.'

Tony nods as if listening, but then immediately says, a grin faint at his mouth, 'Your sister still 'ere?'

They nod. 'Yeah.' Tony is about to speak again when the other wardsman yells out.

'Tony! Come on!' He motions from the door.

Tony hesitates—then seems to change his mind about something. He winks at Stephen and Cathy, then rolls his eyes, saying, 'In trouble again. Checkya.' He saunters off across the ward.

As they watch him leave, Stephen says, 'Who's that wally?'

Cathy says, 'Tony someone. He's a wardsman.' Then she smirks. 'Mandy thinks he's creepy.'

Stephen snorts. 'Of course she does,' he says, widening his eyes, mocking the grim Mandy expression they know so well. He is about to add something else, but Cathy, instantly regretting what she's said, butts in.

'Well, *you* called him a wally,' she says, looking towards the empty doorway. Then, brightening, she says: 'I reckon we should have a drink at the pub this afternoon. Don't you think? And tomorrow night Mum wants to take us to the new restaurant at the club. It's called *Ciphers*.'

They grin, then Cathy turns to the magazine in her lap, Stephen to the book in his. The earliest kites consisted of a huge leaf attached to a long string, he reads. He turns the pages, looking at all those kites, stamped bright into all the skies around the world, each one suspended there like a held breath.

JUST BEFORE Stephen turned seventeen—as he has told a girlfriend once or twice over the years—his father threw him out of home. Just for coming home drunk—once, Stephen says—in the early darkened hours.

Stephen has never known that his father lay awake, listening to his motorbike roaring too fast into the driveway, hearing the lurching brakes and Stephen's long, noisy dismount while he struggled to keep the bike upright. Geoff had heard Stephen's unsteady footsteps, and then a pause, and then heard him vomiting on the front stairs, before stumbling through the house to bed.

In the morning Geoff raged into Stephen's room, shouting, '*Get UP, you filthy pig. UP!*'

Margaret had already cleaned up the vomit, standing on the verandah and hosing it off the stairs into the garden with a hard jet of water, sprinkling the concrete with disinfectant and boiling water, and then tipping leaves from the compost over the patch in the garden. The vomit was invisible now, there was none of its sour smell. But earlier Geoff had had to step over the pale smatter of it, its horrifying little lumps, when he went to collect the newspapers from the driveway.

In Stephen's doorway he shouted, '*You're disGUSTING!*' and lunged at Stephen in the bed, ripping the blankets away. Margaret was in the hallway, calling after Geoff to stop. From behind her husband she saw Stephen lying there on his brown polycotton sheets, naked except for blue underpants, still a small boy despite his long pale legs and his motorbike boots on the floor. He yelped, squinting at his father's looming form, wiping his grey, sleepy face with his hand and drawing his legs up.

'Geoff!' Margaret called. But he was still shouting, and Stephen was yelling back, shocked and awake, his hair matted on one side of his head, scuttling across the room and pulling on his jeans, shouting, 'Fuck you, Dad.'

Geoff had lunged again then, grabbing up Stephen's motorbike boots and his helmet and jacket that had cost too much, and marching through the house to the front door, white with rage. He stood on the verandah and hurled the things from his arms. The helmet bounced twice, cracking, down the stairs. The boots and the jacket fell in loose, dark humps over the lawn. Geoff turned, rigid with fury, and let his son stride barefoot past him, pulling on a t-shirt and muttering, 'You're fucking insane, old man.'

Geoff stood inside the door, paralysed, breathing heavily through his nose, while Margaret pushed past him, tears spilling, calling to Stephen to wait. Halfway down the stairs he had stopped, looking wildly back for his mother. He looked up, his face full of hurt and headache, hands tucked beneath his armpits, taking small side-to-side steps with his bare feet on the freezing concrete.

'What did I even *do*?' he shouted, his voice breaking into tears. Then immediately he crouched to pick up his helmet, checking the damage, then lurched around the lawn for his boots and the jacket.

Margaret turned back to Geoff. 'Go and talk to him!'

But Geoff couldn't. He looked at his wife, his eyes all fear and tears and fury. 'I *hate* that bloody bike,' he whispered.

Margaret ran down the stairs to Stephen. He was on his motorbike, about to jump on the starter pedal.

'Don't, love,' she said, peering into his helmet. 'He was worried.'

Stephen's red eyes looked out at her. She couldn't hear what he said.

'Where are you going?' she asked, holding on to the waxy canvas of his sleeve. He took his helmet off. She wanted to smooth down his sticking-out hair. But he said, 'I don't want to see that bastard ever again.'

'Don't be *ridiculous*, Stephen,' Margaret called as he jammed his helmet back on and jumped heavily on the pedal. He backed the bike slowly out of the drive and then roared off again down the Saturday morning street.

Geoff stood silent with shock in the hallway as Margaret went back in. She took his hand. 'He'll come back,' she said. But Geoff shook her hand away, walked down the hallway to the bathroom, and closed the door behind him.

Stephen did not come back that day, or the next.

On the third evening, as Geoff sat watching *Four Corners*, the front door opened and Stephen walked through it. He did not look at his father but marched past him into the kitchen, and only when Geoff heard Margaret's voice from the next room did he allow his body to slump with relief into the soft upholstery of his armchair.

Margaret had wheeled around from the sink where she was drying the last of the dinner dishes, her face thin with anxiety and exhaustion. But before she could speak

Stephen held out a finger before him and said, 'I'm only here because of you.' And he whipped around, walking from the kitchen in his lean stride.

Margaret went into the living room and sat down in the chair beside Geoff, putting out a hand. He let her hand rest in his cool one for a tender moment, and they glanced at one another without needing to speak, and then Margaret withdrew her hand in the soft new calm of the room's air, and on the television screen they watched some colourfully dressed Africans scooping muddy water from a puddle.

After this Stephen came and went between home, the technical college and his mechanic apprentice's job at the Toyota dealership with an aloof woodenness. He stopped eating with his parents and Cathy, and no longer wrestled with her or Mandy, on her visits home from university, over a packet of chips or the remote control.

And over slow time, the story of Stephen's three runaway days became instead the story he carried inside himself, against which no-one in the family had the strength or sense to argue: that when Stephen turned seventeen his father had cast him out. If his determination to have only the coolest, most formal relations with his father sometimes faltered, he needed only to remember this fact and hold it fast, and soon enough it grew over any softer, more complicated feelings for his family like the smooth new skin of a scar.

Now and then, during these years, Mandy or Cathy would tease him about his clothes, or a girl, and there would be a flicker of his old ease as he stuck two fingers up at them or suddenly flicked a tea towel at one to make her screech. But mostly, with habit, his expression remained guarded and he would yield information only when absolutely necessary, in grudging little pieces.

Once, when Mandy was home from uni, she drove her lime-green Gemini to his work to ask him to look at the clutch. As she pulled into the concrete yard she saw him squatting on his haunches, leaning back against the white corrugated-tin wall, smoking and sulking. It was exactly the look he had so often had during childhood when she beat him at a game. Mandy sat in her car for a moment and watched. An older mechanic stood in front of Stephen, hands on his hips. Mandy could tell from the way Stephen held his own body that he was tearful with fury as he talked, spitting out the words. She was astonished at the power of her urge to run and stand between him and the other man, to put her hands on her own hips and square up to the older man. Instead, she nosed her car forward into a parking spot, not looking at Stephen but knowing he would see her. And then, watching in the rear-vision mirror, she let him stand and throw his cigarette butt down in a gentle arc, and turn away into the cool dark of the workshop before she got out of the car.

That evening as they were spread over the couch watching television Mandy said, 'How's work?'

Stephen moved his jaw sideways a little, working his tongue into a tooth. He didn't take his gaze from the television. 'Fine,' he said.

Mandy offered him her half-eaten bowl of ice cream, and said mildly, 'I reckon that's bullshit.'

He took the bowl, still not looking at her.

'Whatever you say, Mand,' he said, and licked the spoon, holding it over his tongue for a long cool moment. 'You're the investigative reporter.' And then he threw her a menacing look and whispered the *60 Minutes* clock's *chk chk chk chk chk*, as he scooped the last of the ice cream from the bowl.

Nobody could remember the year that he eventually stopped talking to them altogether.

THE YOUNG woman in the bed at the far end of the ward wears a green and blue cotton scarf in awkward, baggy folds around her head. A friend arrives, and the young woman's tall shaggy boyfriend hauls himself up from his chair, offers it to the visitor, says he'll get a coffee. As he walks past her Mandy sees his smile drop away; he is exhausted. Back at the bed the woman's friend clutches plastic bags of offerings; a shrink-wrapped jigsaw puzzle is clamped under one arm. She glances around the ward, lowers her voice to murmur, 'Why are you in *here*?' She doesn't want her friend in this ward, infected by the old and the lifeless.

Mandy had said the same thing this morning, to a nurse named Jenny. 'She shouldn't be in intensive care, surely?'

The nurse was blasé. 'Not enough beds in the other wards,' she said, flicking at one of Geoff's tubes with her clean pink fingernails. 'She's the healthiest person in the place,' she said then, smiling firmly. A hint of *get over it.* Then she strode away.

The healthy are so obvious here, Mandy thinks. Their quickness, their life.

She shifts on the plastic chair, turns the novel she's been reading face down, pages open, in her lap. She bends sideways to stretch her neck one way, then the other. Two hours have gone by since she arrived and the others left; Chris has gone off with her mother to help choose some bathroom paint. Mandy had frowned as her mother discussed this with Chris, and said, 'We're not on *holidays*, Mum.' Her mother looked guilty, but Chris put his hand on her arm and said, 'It's fine, Marg,' and glared back at Mandy.

She picks up her book again, but this grey ward, this moment, the girl with leukaemia and her faded boyfriend won't fuse with the book's tone. It's a new Australian novel her mother bought her, all landscape and imagery and symbols and no plot, the kind Mandy herself half-heartedly sends sometimes to friends in Europe.

She hears a voice, the sound of small wheels, and flicks her gaze quickly into concentration on the page. But she knows the wardsman is coming over to her again: she can smell him, the overscented men's deodorant and cigarettes.

In her ears she hears the click of her own swallowed saliva, and the wet clicking of maggots comes to her, the millions of maggots in a vast clay grave. A rubbish-tip of clothes, that one boot with the slender bone sticking cleanly out. The sudden pearly wash of nausea, the hurtling vomit.

'Remember yet?' his voice says.

She must look up. Tony stands there, his fingers curled around the upright rod of a quivering drip stand. On the fourth finger he wears a slim silver ring in the shape of a snake. It curls twice around his finger, the small head separating itself at the end. Around his wrist is a thick silver bracelet, its links flat and smooth. Like a reptile's scales, thinks Mandy. In a repelled way, she would like to touch it, to stroke its links one way, and then the reverse, to feel the scales' abrasive edges.

She meets his eyes. He is waiting for an answer. That expectant grin. *Does* she remember something? But the only image that comes to her from years ago is a rotting bird, its matted feathers, wedged between rocks at the river.

She is aware that she has stood up and moved to place herself between the wardsman and her father in the bed. She glances behind her at Geoff, and then smiles in Tony's direction. She can't bring herself to meet his eyes again.

'I'm sorry,' she says, shaking her head, staring at the chair. 'I've been away such a long time—'

'Yeah, doesn't matter,' he cuts in, nodding. 'I knew you wouldn't.' But when she looks at him again his face is mournful.

Mandy sees that in his other hand he carries a plastic shopping bag. She keeps her smile stiff. Through the hours of sitting here yesterday, she made a methodical search of her memory, sifting through categories for one that could contain this man—the school years, or more probably her year on the local paper, some netball- or soccer- or golf-club function photograph she'd taken once, twenty years ago; or some sheepdog trial or Rundle Show or cattle sale. When he tells her she will raise her eyebrows, pretend recognition, say *Ahhh, of course.*

But Tony is staring at Geoff now, at the deep dark wound on his head. He steps nearer the bed, dumps the plastic bag and its contents on the tray table, still peering at the wound.

Mandy wants him to stop. There is something in the way he is entranced by her father's injury that makes her want to splay out her hands, hide the damage from his gaze.

She stretches her arms along the rail of the bed each side of her, trying to take up space. 'So what is it,' she says in a rush, 'that I should remember?'

Tony turns to face her again with a rueful smile. He exhales a brief, single sigh—as if they both know she's being untruthful; as if, in a disappointed way, he understands why. As if something is a matter of time.

He points to the plastic bag.

'That's for your mum. Said I'd bring it.' He's still gazing at her in that sorrowful way. 'Derris dust. For her tomatoes.'

Mandy is aware she is licking her own lips now. She is careful to keep her fingers curled around the bars of Geoff's bed; she cannot be certain there would be no tremor if she lifted her hands.

Tony is waiting for her to ask him again. But she will not. She nods at the plastic bag, says, 'Great. I'll tell her.'

He is still intrigued by Geoff's head. He takes a step to look past her, to inspect it.

'He's not gunna last, is he,' he says then, slowly. He draws out the vowel: *laast*.

And now Mandy is free to hate him. She looks him in the eye for one long second and then away, staring at the floor, breathing deeply. She feels the tips of her fingers pressing into the cool metal of the bars. Then Tony suddenly steps back, grabbing the drip stand in one hand, expertly spinning it on its wheels.

'You'll remember,' he says in a firm, sullen voice. Without waiting for her reply he stalks off, rattling the drip stand before him.

Mandy stands there, gripping the bars of the bed, waiting until the blue of his overalls has gone completely from her peripheral vision before she can exhale and let her grip relax.

Inhale, exhale. The maggots and their glistening sound.

A SMELL—floral, or appleish, but with a surgical chemical undertone—emanated from the floor as Chris and Margaret walked along the new corridor with its bright lights and its shining, speckled grey linoleum. Margaret had felt her shoes pressing her weight into the new lino. Soon it would look like the rest of the hospital's floors, she supposed, dreary with age and the foot-trafficked burden of sickness.

'I'll drive,' Chris said, and Margaret gratefully handed him the keys.

Now they've had coffee and are standing in the gloom of Macquarie Hardware before a slanting wall of coloured cards. As Margaret peers around, it seems they are almost alone in the enormous cave of the building. Off in the timber section she can hear heavy things being moved but can't see anyone. Nearer by, at the paint counter, a young man in a dark green apron stands peering down at a paint tin, glancing over at Margaret and Chris now and then but making no move toward them. Margaret is thankful. Talking to strangers seems to take such an enormous effort. Although this young fellow, she thinks, might be one of Alan Gutteridge's sons—he has the same narrow forehead and sagging pouches beneath the eyes—and therefore is not quite a stranger.

'What about Promised Land?' Chris proffers her a little piece of cream-painted cardboard, his head cocked in concentration as he frowns down at it.

Margaret holds a fan of the little pieces in her hand already. They have narrowed it down to Clouded Pearl 2, Frayed Hessian, Cracked Clay and Twisted Bamboo 9. Chris has patiently explained the difference between Fresh Neutrals and Warm Neutrals, and now without irony he holds out the Promised Land with a hopeful expression.

On the way here, stopped in the car at the traffic lights, Margaret had looked out at the caged magazine and newspaper headlines in their frames on the footpath, propped in a row against the dingy blue-tiled wall of the newsagent. *Summer Super Food Ideas. Four Marines Dead in Roadside Bomb Attack. Find out what Inspires Simone Warne and Bill Granger.* At the door of the newsagent one of the Barron girls struggled to push a stroller over the step. Then the lights turned green, and Chris turned the car left. Margaret had said then, 'Mandy is right, isn't she, about not being on holidays.'

Chris had kept looking at the road, annoyance crossing his face.

'It's got nothing to do with holidays.'

He brought the car to a stop at the next corner, hunching forward, looking past Margaret for oncoming cars. He glanced at her, then past her again, and said in a firm, meaningful voice, 'I think it's a lovely idea. It can be a surprise for Geoff.'

Margaret felt the tears of gratitude spring to her eyes as they coasted out onto Monarch Street and were carried across town towards the hardware store, towards this pearly new possibility, of Geoff's homecoming.

But now, standing here in the muggy warehouse with the paint strips in her hand, the whirring fans high above making no difference to the prickling of sweat at her brow, Margaret is drenched with a sudden and complete exhaustion.

'I don't know . . .' she says in a small voice.

Chris looks up from the paint swatches.

'It's okay,' he says, taking the fan of cardboard strips from her hand and putting them in his pocket. 'We can do it later.'

And he puts his arm about his mother-in-law's bony, narrow shoulders and guides her past the rows of tins, past the dump bins of brooms and cheap drill bits, back out into the shock of sunlight in the car park. Once inside the car he watches Margaret allow herself to fall back into the comfort of the passenger seat and close her eyes.

He starts the ignition, easing the Corolla out of the parking spot. He too is exhausted. By watching Margaret for signs of collapse, by the monstrous mess of his father-in-law's body. By trying to keep at bay a cold, looming acceptance—of the thing he sees he has for years been turning away from—that Mandy is finally almost completely transformed from the person she once was.

Margaret's frightened face in the hardware shop had caused him to hurtle back into a memory of Mandy, on one of her first trips home from Bosnia.

They were buying the papers in a Rose Bay newsagent and she said, 'I need a pen.' He'd waited at the door for long minutes before going to look for her. He had found her hunched in front of a rack of pens—crying, noiseless but unstoppable, into the wet privacy of her hands. He had taken a minute to realise that what had triggered this was the shock—of a homecoming to a rich, peaceful country, all injustice suddenly crystallising in the obscenity of too many pens, too easily gotten. But today, as Chris drives along the hot dry streets of her childhood town and recalls her hardened face in the hospital ward, the cold monotone in which she speaks to her mother, he cannot imagine Mandy ever softening to the point of tears again.

MANDY LIFTS her father's hand, lays it down again on the white cotton blanket. She has been here an hour, perhaps two. Someone raised the head of the bed when she went to the toilet. The ventilator pushes the air in, out. The monitors beep and sing but nobody takes any notice; in here these are only the sounds of existence, not of alarm. There is some sort of staff meeting going on at the end of the ward; the nurses stand at a whiteboard marked with the few patients' names, talking in a group.

All this waiting is unbearable. She sits down again.

Three beds along, the television comes to life. The young man with the amputation lies holding the remote control against his bare chest, watching the screen sleepily. A young woman—girlfriend, or sister, scrawny with the same neglected look as his—spent most of yesterday and today sitting there with him, but she has gone. A plastic shopping bag and a motorbike helmet are on the tray table. Then Mandy hears the television voice say *'Luke Russell, familiar to many of you—'* Startled, she leans to see the picture. The presenter is saying *'BBC reports from political hotspots like Africa and Iraq,'* and then the picture changes to a satellite feed, a man sitting in a chair with a nightscape of blocky buildings behind him. He holds a book in his hands. Then the screen flicks to another scene, Cate Blanchett talking with cameras flashing about her, and then the station's promotional logo appears before an ad for carpet cleaning comes on.

Luke Russell.

A nurse has broken away from the group and is walking past the young man's bed. He appears to have fallen asleep. She takes the remote control from his chest, snaps the television off. He doesn't wake.

All the correspondents Luke Russell's age had eventually merged, for Mandy, into one sort of Luke: the carefully tousled hair, the British public school voice, the cheekbones, hints of a drug-troubled past, the expensive shoes battered into war chic. In her early days she had slept with too many of them. Out of fear, out of loneliness, from boredom or exhaustion. Or to protect herself from the crashing noise of mortar fire, from nightmares.

All through her high school and university years Mandy had been sexually cautious—the idea then of a one-night stand was unbearable. Having a boyfriend, even, was horrifying if she let herself think of it. To sleep naked with someone else, someone who knew how she looked, smelt, *tasted*. Occasionally she has wondered if she married Chris so early simply to get it over with, to reduce the number of people through her life who could possibly know these things about her.

But once you had seen a woman's opened head. Once you had heard the fifteen-year-old Kosovar girls' toneless horror stories (the bloodstained mattresses, *they rubbed me with body lotion first*) and smelt the graves, crouched watching with your hands over your nose and mouth, not moving lest you lose your footing and begin a madwoman's screaming as you fell. Once you'd knelt in your jeans on a dry road with your hands clasped like prayer over the back of your head and felt the gun tip at your neck, tasted the dust of stones in your mouth and heard your own hoarse voice calling *Ani Sahafiya, Ani Sahafiya, I am a journalist* over and over into the dirt, smelt your own shit squirting out.

After these things, then 'reputation', 'marriage'—these words were only some distant, formless haze. Every part of you was risk, every taste adrenaline. So for a time she lived as they all did; she unshackled herself from fear. It no longer existed. At the end of assignment in some destroyed city, the reporters' parties took on a raucous, savage abandon. Once she had returned to a room to see one of the correspondents mimicking fucking her against a wall, imitating the sound she made. It was as though all their lost adolescence was being called up, and they hurled themselves into it—the drinking, the drugs, the desperate sex, to obliterate the months of what they had smelt, what they had seen.

On the trip home from Bosnia the first time, this adolescence subsided, and she stepped out of the plane's captured air to resume her old life. But something had changed. She found she could no longer move easily through familiar rooms or streets; she felt a layer of something impenetrable—some thick, elastic membrane—between herself and her ordinary life. The scenes, sensations she had cried for, imagined so desperately while she was away—a walk in the botanic gardens by the harbour, while she watched a dog in Sarajevo devouring a human hand; a glass of cold wine on the jasmine-scented balcony in Rose Bay, as she had shuddered freezing and boneshaken in a Bosnian army truck—these homecoming experiences had somehow shrivelled, become joyless. And she was shocked to hear, repeated in her head, something one of the journalists had said to her before she left, grinning drunkenly out of the dark in a bar in Split. *Admit it*, he had said. *War is fun.* It sickened her, but the notion lay in her mind, half-submerged like the latticed bones of a dead baby whale she had seen once dredged up on a beach. And as soon as she came home she found that she wanted to go back.

War is fun.

Mandy hears a noise behind her here in the ward, feels herself jump.

It's Stephen. He falls into the chair beside her, tossing his car keys from hand to hand.

'D'you think he hears anything?' he says after a minute, watching their father's body.

Mandy shrugs, shakes her head. They look at Geoff, say nothing. After a minute Stephen leans down to fossick in his backpack on the floor.

Mandy drags her chair forward again to the bed, reaches to pick up her father's hand, holds it in hers. Its corpse's weight.

She sits cradling his hand once more and goes back to thinking of Luke, with his long limbs and his rich-boy's wide, marble-carved lips. The way he hung himself off chairs, slouching so low that he always seemed louche and decadent, no matter what fleapit hotel or hole in the ground they inhabited. Luke, who spoke to her directly, asked her opinion in tricky moments, looked her in the eye. Who loved his sister, whose parents were normal. Who said the thing he hated most about this job was the vanity, the memoirs with their sarcastic one-liners and the insiders' nicknames for every fucking thing—*Baggers, Dixie*—the boring, insistent *I was there, I was there, I was there.* She bites her lip. A moment ago on the television Luke had been holding a book with his own face on the cover.

In Sarajevo once they'd stayed in the small fifth-floor apartment of an old woman named Hana. She spoke no English, but as she ushered them in she spoke in a constant stream of Bosnian, occasionally pausing to repeat a word, emphasising some point they did not understand.

'Take your shoes off,' Mandy had murmured to Luke in the dark entranceway. She eased her own off as she spoke, pushing them with her foot to join the little collection of worn shoes next to the wall, but then Hana saw Luke bending to untie his laces.

'*No, no* . . .' The old woman waved a hand, smiling, to show she didn't mind. He stopped.

'Go on,' said Mandy, but Luke straightened. 'She doesn't care,' he said, and trudged into the next room in his filthy boots, dipping his head low under the ceilings.

Hana's apartment had a window looking out onto a vacant block. There used to be trees, she indicated with some gestures. The city was framed in the window, bare and gritty. This, her living room, was where they would sleep. It was large by Sarajevo standards, carpeted with thick shag pile in swirling caramel. How, without electricity, did Hana manage to keep her house so clean? Mandy looked again at Luke's encrusted boots.

The beds were two couches, on opposite sides of the room. They had told her they were married. The back cushions of the couches had been removed and the makeshift beds were already made up with clean flannelette sheets. The pillows were pillowcases stuffed with clothes.

As they put down their bags Hana babbled in a questioning voice, repeating a word again and again. Mandy smiled helplessly, shaking her head and raising her hands. Hana disappeared and then appeared again in the doorway, holding a *dzezva*, a small Turkish coffee pot. 'Ah!' Mandy said.

'We haven't got time,' Luke muttered to her, fiddling with the sat phone.

She murmured in reply, 'Yes we have,' and nodded, smiling at Hana. 'Yes! Thank you!'

In a minute Hana returned, gesturing with her bony hands for them to follow her into the kitchen. In the middle of this tiny room, jammed between the window and the fridge, was a red plush velvet sofa, firmly upholstered, with delicately turned wooden legs. It was spotless.

Mandy hesitated, but Hana pointed, and Luke sat heavily down. Mandy watched the sofa take his weight and then lowered herself to perch on the edge. She gestured to Hana, patting its cushioned arm: 'Beautiful.'

Hana smiled wide, showing her yellowed teeth. As she passed them each a tiny, bird's-egg-blue coffee cup she put out her own fingers to the sofa's velvet, stroking it with a single fingertip, as gently as she would a newborn baby's head. The skin on her wrists and forearms was fretted with fine, dry lines, like fibreglass. But so frail and fine, her skin seemed, a simple jolt against a table corner might tear it open.

Hana began talking, gesturing again. Her voice was high and childish, and now and then she whimpered and crooned as she indicated how the mortars came, how she and the rest of the apartment block dwellers had to sleep in the basement; how three people—she held up her bony fingers—in the block had been killed. She showed them how she had cried—rocking, mewling rhythmically, *hroo, hroo*, tracing tears down her face with her index fingers as she acted—and then she got up from her chair, and cowered near the stove—*boom, boom*—and drew her own arms around her shoulders, crying again. They nodded and listened, and Mandy thought of this old woman struggling in her nightclothes down the concrete stairs to a dirty basement to sleep on the hard floor with men and children and other women in the cold and dark.

After the coffee, as they left for the day, through the kitchen doorway Mandy saw Hana bent lovingly over her couch, smoothing the nap of the velvet with the flat of her hand.

That night Mandy had listened to the mortars across the city, lying in the dark, watching the window glow now and then. Then there was a louder one, near the apartment. 'Christ,' she had whispered to the ceiling.

'Are you okay?' Luke whispered back. She had got out of her bed and went to his, and lay with her back against him, watching the space of the window, listening. As the noises grew louder, the sky brighter, Luke pulled her closer, nuzzling her neck, his hand reaching her breast. She could feel his erection, and she closed her eyes, allowed herself to be drawn in, and the more the air cracked and the louder the threat, the more urgent came Luke's breath, and behind her closed eyes the city exploded, again and again.

When she woke in the morning Luke was already up; she dressed and grabbed her toothbrush. Hana had shown Mandy a pair of faded slippers for indoor wear, and she put them on, repelled by the greasy intimacy of the concaves worn by Hana's feet. Mandy shuffled in the slippers to the bathroom, passing the kitchen, and through the crack in the door she heard Hana's high voice and saw Luke slouched across the sofa, one of the little blue coffee cups in its saucer on his knee.

Soon afterward they left the apartment, squeezing past Hana in the tiny vestibule, Luke shouting their thanks and shoving a handful of US dollars at her. She seemed distressed, repeating something in her crooning, whiny voice, but they were in a rush. It was only as they turned out of the front door that Mandy caught sight of Hana through the doorway again, scrubbing and scrubbing with a soapy cloth at a coffee stain on the sofa.

AT ONE o'clock Stephen is still sitting in the plastic chair, one ankle resting across his other knee, and picking at a frayed piece of rubber on his sneaker. 'I'll drop you home,' he says.

Their mother is waiting at the house to serve lunch.

'Why, where are you going?' asks Mandy as she gathers up her book and bag.

'Hardware. For kite stuff,' he says, still picking at his

shoe. Then he looks at her. 'I'm going to make a kite.' He stands up and leans over the railings of their father's bed. Mandy can't see his face.

'What for?' she says. 'You don't think he's going to see it, do you?'

Stephen is holding Geoff's thick, meaty hand now. Mandy thinks, if he presses too hard on the swollen pad of the palm it might burst, pale and wet as a plum.

'He won't, you know,' she says.

Stephen turns to face her, and he looks as though he would like to hit her with a brick. He turns back to Geoff's hand, examining it. But his foot begins to jiggle, there at the bedside, and he says in a low voice: 'I'm not *doing* it for him.'

They drive back to the house in silence, along the wide, bright main street, past the optometrist and White's Jeweller, past RLK Enterprises and Sloane's Footwear with its racks of work boots and dark court shoes, past shady Jubilee Park with its struggling Bicentennial Heritage Rose Garden, past the Retravision and Eagle Boys Pizza and the Aboriginal Housing office, the Bi-Lo supermarket and Target, past Tooheys Newsagent and Abbott's Amcal chemist. The streets lined with pale Falcons and Commodores and white tray-top utes, all neatly angled with their rears to the kerb.

At the top of Monarch Street they turn right into Fitzroy, pass the fire station. DON'T BE A BUNNY. They turn into Aurora Street, pass the low brick houses with their brick fences, their little squares of dusty grass, their cement-strip driveways.

They arrive at their childhood home, still not speaking, and Leia lollops up to the car from behind the house.

AFTER LUNCH Chris shifts about in the kitchen, opening cupboards, the fridge, and calls things out to Mandy to write on a list.

'Coffee,' he says. He picks up a bottle of oil and tips it from side to side, the inch of gold glazing the glass. He puts it back on the shelf. 'Olive oil.'

Mandy looks down at the list. They have argued mildly about the need for more shopping; Chris is obsessed with groceries. There must be fifteen new things on the notepad now.

The ABC news mutters from the clock radio on top of the fridge. A young woman in a Bali jail will today find out if she's to spend another twenty years behind bars. Mandy thinks of the television shots she's seen since coming back to Australia: the girl's expressionless, sweaty face; her slightly bulbous eyes, always staring out, blank, from behind the bars of that dirty tiled cell.

Nobody has asked Mandy how long she is staying. But here, alone in the kitchen with Chris, the weight of this unasked question presses the air from the room, and she knows his every addition to the shopping list is an attempt to anchor her here. She has not yet rung the news desk back, though they have left three messages on her mobile, and her phone beeps constantly with text messages from other reporters, from Graham, from her translator Jassim.

'*The Prime Minister has labelled a Greens senator's t-shirt offensive,*' says the modulated ABC voice. '*Get your rosaries off my ovaries, the t-shirt slogan read.*'

Mandy looks out of the window and suddenly wants, more than anything, to leave. To walk out of the back door, down the stairs, to get into the hire car and drive away from this house, this street, this town. She feels a wash of loathing for Rundle, for the whole country, with its caged refugees, its despair-bludgeoned Aborigines. Its cunning, passionless prime minister.

'*Mr Howard said the t-shirt was deeply offensive to Catholics and called it an undergraduate stunt.*'

'Fuckwit,' Mandy hisses at the radio.

But even as she says this she knows it isn't the prime minister causing this sourness, this loathing sweeping through her. It is closer, more basic—Chris's hurt, her mother's need, the ugly windowless hospital and its strange, horrible wardsman. This creeping dread. Chris has his head deep in the pantry now and does not appear to notice when she puts down the notepad and creeps out of the kitchen and up the carpeted hallway to the bedroom.

She closes the door and lies down on the soft bed. She thinks of Tony staring at her father's head wound, but as soon as this image comes she slides it shut. In its place the boy comes to her again, his smooth glossy black hair cut close over his head. She imagines the feel of it under her fingers. If she had touched him.

When she wakes a while later she can tell from the hollow silence that the house is empty. Chris has gone to the shops, she supposes. The others are out, at the hospital, the supermarket, somewhere in the bright town.

On the white net curtain and the closed venetian blind are sharp shadows of the moving leaves of the lilac bush. She has been asleep long enough for the sun to move to this side of the house. A breeze carries occasional noises from the street, and she lies on the bedclothes and listens to the world outside. A car accelerates in a distant street. Boys, she thinks. An air-conditioner rattles somewhere. After a while two women—their heels clopping on the cement footpath—stop and admire the lavender down by the fence. 'Simple planting,' one of them says. 'But striking.' The other woman murmurs in boredom or assent. There are birds, their rhythmic *chueek* like the creak of a turning Hills Hoist. There is the trudge of a fast walker and then a slamming, heavy car door nearby. A few loose piano notes, unconnected, come from somewhere far off.

In lying here she feels some familiar, hollow staleness she does not understand. And then she realises that what comes to her through the open window is the crippling boredom of every weekend afternoon of her adolescence. The aimless trudging she would do through the empty town, sometimes with a school friend but more often alone. She would walk along Aurora Street, then slowly across town to the disused railway tracks, or the dusty dry grass of the oval when the netball and cricket and football games were finished; or she would wander up along the track through the bush reserve, smelling all the hot emptiness of her existence.

She supposes it could not have been like that, so lonely through all her growing up. She knows she had friends—she remembers their names, their houses, the smell of their bedrooms—but beneath each image is the feeling she always had through those years, of having to keep silent, to bite down upon her instinct for saying what she thought, lest she hurt someone's feelings, or, more usually, be met simply with a blank stare of incomprehension.

She spent most of her teenage years staring out of windows, it seems to her now. Sitting jammed beside Cathy and Stephen in the back seat of the car on the way to Mass, or the rubbish tip, or the river, she would bring her focus to the spinning pink gravel of the roadside, making her eyes blur with its speed, and imagine flinging open the door and hurling herself out. She would count it out—one, two—with her hand on the door latch, enjoying the skimming pace of her pulse, feeling at last as if something might happen.

On her first trip to Sarajevo, as a field producer, she recognised that feeling. As she hurried with the reporter and the sound recordist across the stone bridge and someone told her where they were, she felt that same whizzing in her pulse again. At the end of the bridge she stopped for a second—it was dangerous to do but she couldn't help herself—and put out her hand to touch the stone of the place where Franz Ferdinand was shot, and she thought, I am standing at the centre of history. And then she ran on, feeling her feet strike the hard street, the air cold on her skin. That night, as she lay in the dark listening to the crack of gunfire coming from the hills, the same words thrilled in her head, her blood. She was *standing at the centre of history*, and for the first time in her life to say out loud what she was seeing was not only allowed, but was her duty. Important things—lives even, perhaps—depended on her very willingness not just to observe, but to *say what she had seen*. In the years since, every time her courage has begun to fail, every time she loses her way, she says inside her head those words that have been large enough through history to bring down governments, to save lives, to give voice to those who no longer have their own. *I am a witness*. I am telling you what I have seen.

From outside in the street there is the throaty rumble of a car engine starting, then falling silent. It starts again, then stops. When it begins again it's the constipated *yerr-yerr-yerr* of a motor that won't start. Silence, then the straining, impotent motor again. Mandy sits up on the bed and turns to kneel at the window, making an aperture in the venetian blind with two fingers. Just beyond the fence a large orange Torana is parked, rear to the kerb. A girl's forearm and hand extend from the driver's window, and in the hand is a cigarette, trailing wisps of smoke. The hand moves back inside, arm hinged at the elbow, and then out again. Eventually, on the downward arc the girl lets her cigarette fall to the ground. She tries the motor again. Nothing has changed: the motor's *yerr-yerring* begins again, but through the rear window Mandy can see the girl clinging with both hands to the steering wheel, jolting in her seat, as if to force the car into motion with the thrust of her own hips. The motor is quiet again, and Mandy hears a muffled 'fuck'.

She knows she should get off the bed, go out and offer to help the girl. But the idea fills her with exhaustion. The car door opens and the girl unfolds herself into the street. She leans her long body against the car and pulls a hot-pink mobile telephone from her pocket. Mandy lets the blind slats snap back into place, and slides to lie down again.

She thinks of Stephen and the kites. Her stomach tightens. She does not know why she has been so disturbed by it, but the leaden feeling in her gut remains. The kites were *her* thing, and Geoff's. Even as she thinks this she knows how ridiculous it is, how childish. But she feels like a child here in her parents' house, bickering with her siblings, thirteen again. Flat-chested, big-nosed and sallow-skinned. In this wallpapered room she had lain on the bed and howled at the injustice of her looks: her limp, badly cut hair; the nose, long and bulbous like a man's, obscene in her narrow face. Once Geoff had come into the room and sat on the bed, listening to her hacking sobs. She had told him to go away, she didn't want to talk to him. But he stayed, and this intrusion enraged her more, and she screamed into her pillow that she was *ugly*, that was the matter. Her *nose*. Her father had sat in silence, absorbing her rage and self-pity.

Then he'd said, did she know that Caesar would only choose large-nosed men to keep about him?

He sounded pleased.

Mandy's sobs stopped, from shock, and from the drawing up of energy required to explode. Her father mistook the stunned instant for comfort, and he added with the relish of certainty, 'Caesar thought big-nosed men were noble, and honest.'

He had not known what to do then, when Mandy lurched upright, convulsing with fury. She was a *thirteen-year-old* GIRL, she had shrieked into his face, *in Rundle! Nobody bloody cares about fucking* CAESAR!

He had sat in his own shock then, watching his howling daughter, and then he nodded sadly, sighed, and left the room.

Here in the same room now Mandy lies face down on the bed. She sniffs in amusement at the memory. And then her breath catches and she cannot stop herself from starting to cry, for her father, her beautiful father, too noble, too honest to call her 'princess' and tell her she was pretty.

CHRIS DOES hear Mandy walk up the hallway to the bedroom and shut the door. He goes and sits at the kitchen table with the notepad, looks at the list written in Mandy's hand; the upright capitals, the emphatic lines of her pen. On the flipped-up previous page, Margaret has written a name and a telephone number in her soft, looping cursive. There is nothing similar about their handwriting, at all.

When Chris first met Mandy, her directness had unnerved him. He was used to girls who sulked, or who cried softly in bed with their backs to him rather than say what was wrong. Mandy was not like these other university girls whose every move, every expression was designed for effect. Those girls wore op-shop clothes studiously collected and paraded, but Mandy wore oversized t-shirts and one outdated style of jeans, oblivious of fashion. The obliviousness made her sexy. And her unchecked opinions were rare at university, where to Chris it seemed everyone—including him—made a furtive calibration towards irony before they spoke. To laugh too loudly, or to stomp across the library lawn with your head down; to argue using your own reasoning without defaulting to the student's worn grid of left-wing opinions, was to expose yourself utterly. To Chris, the fact that Mandy didn't know any of this made her more exciting still.

When she said she didn't know who The Smiths were he was incredulous. This was at a party early in second year, when Chris had never travelled west of the Blue Mountains. He reddens now, when he thinks he'd boasted to her of that.

'*Morrissey*,' he'd said, taking the cigarette from his mouth and blowing a long stream of smoke. 'The *Smiths*.' But Mandy had just looked blank and unconcerned. 'Sorry,' she'd said, and exhaled her own smoke to the ceiling.

Chris liked to call her a country girl after that, and he liked to drive with her out to Rundle in the holidays. He'd found the town romantic in a way Mandy just scoffed at. He'd even talked about moving out here when they finished uni. Once he'd said it in the car with her parents, as they drove along Monarch Street and the trees were yellowing.

'It's quite beautiful here really,' he'd said. 'I could live here.' And he didn't look at Mandy but watched the back of her father's head. Marg had made excited, approving noises but Geoff had stared only at the road.

Still at university, Chris and Mandy made a good couple. He softened her, nudging her at parties when she was in danger of offending someone. She would turn back to the person in shock, her face completely erased of its previous scorn, and apologise with genuine warmth. And Mandy made Chris tougher, braver. He learned to trust his own opinions, to voice them without embarrassment. He learned to shout when they argued, without quaking for hours afterwards. She taught him to stand up for himself. Once, during a fight of glittering ferocity, when Mandy's yelling had suddenly swerved into tearfulness, Chris had begun to *clap*.

When he occasionally remembers that moment—his slow, bitter applause, the thrill at his own callousness—he loses his breath. He cannot imagine them ever having such majestic fights again. Now their disagreements are stiff, low-toned, polite.

Their decision to marry was a shout of defiance in their circle of arts student friends. Their parents—especially Geoff and Chris's own mother—agreed that they were too young, but stood smiling tightly in the wedding photographs all the same.

Chris tears the page from the notepad and folds it. He goes to the window and looks out to see Cathy unpegging clothes from the line, Margaret folding them into a basket.

Their voices murmur but he can't hear what they are saying.

He leans on the sink, watching his mother- and sister-in-law, and it hits him, as it has sometimes over the years, that the kind of love he has for them is not normal. Other people complain about their spouses' families; they roll their eyes and talk about Christmas as an ordeal to be survived. But Chris knows he feels more for the Connollys than for his own family, who seem held together more by his mother's nervy energy than any real emotion. His mother Jeanette has a quick, anxious line of questioning, and her children's achievements are too quickly reported to her friends. She is often to be heard on the telephone, exaggerating any mild success—Chris's firm winning a routine contract, or a kindergarten award for his sister Fiona's daughter—into a sort of triumph of her family over someone else's. And with repeated calls to other friends on the same subject, the stories grow longer, more smug. Her body is wiry from her morning power walks, and whenever Chris sees her she hugs him too hard and too often. She's forever organising some public family event—it used to be elaborate twenty-firsts, then weddings, and now it is Fiona's kids' christenings or birthday parties—designed to prove, it seems to Chris, how overwhelmingly *loving* the whole family is. And both she and his father speak of any ordinary human failing that might occur among their friends' children—divorce, treatment for depression—with a terrible, reverent sympathy. Despite their watchfulness, it seems never to occur to them that their own children might at any time be struck by such disasters.

Compared to his own parents then, Margaret and Geoff have always seemed to Chris to be marvellously negligent, too busy with their own pottering lives to notice what their children are doing. He knows this isn't true. But there are no weekly, hurt-sounding phone calls to any of their offspring, and they have none of his own parents' habit of interrogation for snippets with which to impress their friends. In fact, the more successful Mandy has become as a reporter, the more baffled her parents have seemed. Chris has thought sometimes that perhaps he should be offended on Mandy's behalf—that Margaret accepts news of her awards or promotions or other glories with a surprised, 'Oh!' and does not rush to the phone breathlessly to tell her friends. Geoff is harder to read, but he too has seemed to suspect that taking pride in his children would be a sort of personal conceit.

Marg and Geoff have always seemed to accept Chris's comings and goings at their home without surprise, without fanfare. One weekend years ago, after a slow and lonely week at Rose Bay, he even went to visit them alone, without even Cathy. They tootled about Rundle together, going to the orchard for apples, building a new compost bin, and somehow they seemed unembarrassed at the strangeness of this visit. Cathy—even Stephen, in the rare times they've shared a weekend or a Christmas—operates in this same benign way, seeming to accept him as part of the scenery, warmly enough but without remark. It feels to him miraculous and lucky.

And as he stares at Marg and Cathy now through the kitchen window, bent over their sheets and pillow-slips in a plastic basket, Chris knows, as plain as the faded floral laundry, that he loves them.

He turns back to the table, reaching for his keys, and he wonders if he has any love left for his wife.

Mostly he manages not to wonder this. When he senses the question looming in his mind he simply turns away from it. It has been easy enough, with the years of her absence. And whatever it is that has happened in their marriage happened so long ago, and in a manner so slow and undefined, that he has never been forced to articulate it to himself, let alone bring it into the light with Mandy.

It is a politeness concealing something harder and colder. *Encased*, is the word that comes to him now, staring at the folded shopping list in his hand. He used to think that something other than himself would make Mandy come home, would revive things—he used to think that they would have a baby—but now it is as though deep inside this marriage is a coffin, the lid forever nailed.

It would be simplest to blame her job, of course. Enough people have intimated this—the unspeakable things she must have seen, the gut-wrenching fear she must have felt, these things must affect a person, mustn't they? Obliterate some capacity for tenderness? One or two of their friends have even said, out loud, *post-traumatic stress*—but not to Mandy. Nobody is strong enough to contemplate the withering stare this would provoke, but it is tempting, so tempting, for Chris to agree.

He has sometimes looked at women—in the office, or at someone's dinner party—and thought, I'm going to have an affair. Sometimes the imagining has gone on for weeks, in mostly garden-variety sexual fantasies: one of the women greedily sucking his penis in the Barretts' bathroom during a dinner party, for example, the soft sheet of her hair hiding her face. And then taking her home and doing it again in his and Mandy's bed, her sheeny breasts jolting above him as he rammed upwards into her. But in the fantasies the women always long for him across the dinner table or the office desk with open, easily readable lust. In reality they either smile in a pitying way when they hear about Mandy's job, or just switch off altogether and turn to speak to someone else.

He would like to blame Mandy's job for his own decay. But he suspects—he knows—it is worse, and more banal. For why would she have gone in the first place, if things were all right? He remembers his face turning hot, then cold, the day she'd told him of the offer to go to the Balkans as a field producer. A one-off. He had turned away to hide his humiliation, gone to sit on the toilet, staring at the floor tiles in shock. That his wife would go to a war rather than stay at home with him. And an hour later he had congratulated her, they had spoken of the opportunity. What sort of a man does that, if he has any balls?

They had already, he supposes now, begun to *grow apart*. It is the kind of phrase his parents would use. The flat desolation of it makes him sick.

This morning he noticed with a cold, nauseated shock—and has no idea how long it has been the case—that Mandy's wedding ring is missing from her finger. This, he knows, should be the last straw.

He trails out of the side door and calls out to Marg and Cathy that he's off to the shops. Cathy yells back for him to wait, asking for a lift to the hospital. He stands leaning against the car in the driveway, facing out at the street. Some neighbours' kids are playing tennis on the road; their shouts and muffled footsteps echo in the quiet air. And as Chris waits here in the soft sunshine, imagining that this could be the last time he comes here to Rundle, to this house, he must close his eyes against his tears.

But in a moment he opens his eyes again, blinks the tears down. He knows there is such a thing as self-respect. Mandy taught it to him herself.

ACROSS THE road from the hospital's side entrance is a little milk bar and takeaway café, The Tuck Inn. Cathy slams the door of the car and Chris drives off. She crosses the footpath and steps in through the grubby clear plastic straps that hang across the doorway to keep out the flies. It is almost the same as when they were children. Same dank smell, the same wall of greasy deep-fryers and hotplates, a deep freezer against the wall in the same place it used to be. The counter is new though, and a sharp-lined modern glass food cabinet stands in place of the old rounded one. At the drinks fridge Cathy takes down a bottle of water, and then stands to wait behind the few customers before her.

She hears the small *whump* of the freezer lid dropping and looks around; a man stands with a Cornetto in each fist. It always makes her think of Mandy now, that sound. The time she had jumped out of her skin when Cathy flung the freezer door shut once, in Chris and Mandy's kitchen. Apparently it sounds like a fired mortar. Cathy still doesn't get this—how could it? Such a benign, soft little thud—but she won't forget that frozen second of Mandy's jolt, her terrified expression. It is the only time Cathy has ever been able to glimpse a fraction of what goes on in Mandy's life when she's away.

In front of Cathy, a loud male voice is braying at the young woman behind the counter.

'Can't believe you're not married yet, with cookin' like that,' says the voice. It's Tony from the hospital. A couple of waiting customers look at each other.

'What?' the girl says, leaning down onto the lid of a bulging plastic container on the counter. All the customers have turned now towards Tony's booming voice.

'I said, bein' such a good cook you'd reckon you'd be married by now,' Tony says again, leering. 'Or at least have a boyfriend.'

The lid snaps on. 'It's fruit salad,' says the girl, looking at him in disgust.

She bats the container into a brown paper bag, snatches up a plastic fork and napkin and dumps the lot up on the glass top of the cabinet beside another brown-wrapped bundle. 'Seven-fifty,' she says, resting her open palm on the counter alongside Tony's lunch.

Cathy moves aside for Tony to shoulder his way out through the shop. As he passes she notices his heavy silver bracelet, the bright contrasting patterns on his sneakers.

A little later she is alone at her father's bedside when the wardsman comes in. She sees him watching her while he talks to the nurse, and the sly way he looks around as he strides over to her.

'Hi there,' she says, smiling at him.

'G'day,' says Tony, then steps past her to stare with open distaste at her father. 'Jeez, he's still not lookin' good is he?' he says, wincing.

'No,' Cathy says. He's like a child, she thinks. She remembers boys like him at school—no capacity for artifice, their compliments to girls always falling flat and them never understanding why. She feels sorry for him.

'Your sister still 'ere?' he says then.

'Yeah,' Cathy says. 'At home with Mum.'

Tony lifts his chin and gives her an open, appraising stare, as though he's working out whether to trust her with some confidence. Then he suddenly dips his hand in his pocket and pulls something out.

'Want one?'

He holds two biscuits in his open palm.

'No, thanks,' Cathy says, grinning.

Tony looks surprised. 'Huh.' He takes a bite from one of the biscuits and begins munching away, shoving the other one back in his pocket. 'It's a Kingston,' he says warningly through the mouthful, as if this might make her change her mind. A fleck of biscuit spittle lands on her arm.

'I'm right, thanks.'

Tony only raises his eyebrows, swallowing the last of the biscuit and running his tongue around his teeth. Then he gives a workman-like sigh and turns to go. 'Seeya.'

'Seeya,' Cathy says, watching him saunter over toward the door. He even walks like a kid, she thinks: hands in his pockets, staring at the ground with an open mouth, swaying as he goes. Near the door he falls into step with Nathan, the nurse who is back from his pig-shooting weekend in Mudgee.

'So what are Mudgee girls like?' she hears Tony asking, too loudly, as he whacks the button beside the automatic door. It opens and they turn out into the wide bright corridor.

# CHAPTER ELEVEN

TONY PERCHES on a bar stool at one of the tall tables near the front door and hunches, both elbows on the table, talking to another man while he smokes. The second man is shorn-headed, wears an open-necked white business shirt, sleeves rolled to the elbows, and grey trousers. They are laughing together, but not in the way of friends. Tony could be the man's mechanic, or they might meet weekly on the soccer field. Tony looks thinner here, without the bulk of his blue overalls. He wears loose grey jeans and a navy-blue collared giveaway t-shirt, with

CPG Western embossed across the chest in small yellow lettering. The town is full of these mysterious acronyms, of failing local businesses with obscure, joined-together names—Ad-Nu 65 or KGK Alliance or RundlePak System 300.

The other man taps a packet of cigarettes once on the table with gusto and says '*Anyway—*' in a clipped voice, snatching up his wallet. Tony has already turned to scan the room as he says, 'Yeah seeya,' and exhales a plume of smoke through his nostrils.

THIS IS the pub where Cathy kissed Jim Galvin; where Mandy used to sit with her newspaper workmates among the first of the Friday afternoon drinkers (and where once, a few gin and squashes into the evening, one of the printers whinged to her about his marriage and had challenged her to tell him how often she had sex. She refused, but he kept going: twice a week? Once a fortnight? She'd said nothing, but her face must have given it away because he sat back, satisfied. 'Yeah. Try twice a year.' Her boyfriend then was a soft-faced footballer who left her tiny notes hidden in her sock drawer, that said in his tiny writing, *I love you*). It is the pub where Stephen had snuck in to see bands when he was under-age—Chisel had played here once—and where he played pool with the other apprentices.

On this late afternoon the three siblings sit at one of the dark polished tables in the gloom, chins in their hands, watching Chris order drinks at the bar. He leans towards the barmaid, smiling, eyebrows raised in friendliness as he speaks.

'City boy,' says Stephen. The sisters smile. The girl behind the bar only draws in her chin at Chris, and moves without a word to the beer taps. When she shoves the glasses across the bar, Chris is too friendly again as he pays, asks for a tray, says *sorry*, and *thanks so much*. The girl flat-eyes him in return.

'He should tell her to get fucked,' says Mandy idly. 'Rude little bitch.'

Cathy and Stephen smirk.

'Look,' says Cathy then, as Chris lowers the tray of drinks to the table. 'There's that ward guy.' Then she calls, 'Hiya, Tony,' raising her glass at him across the room.

Stephen says, 'Oh yeah,' and then calls too—'How're you going'—and nods across the tables.

Mandy looks up and sees Tony staring at her. Chris is still preoccupied with the glasses and the tray.

'Jesus, he's not going to come over, is he?' she mutters, looking down at the table quickly and taking a gulp from her beer. The others don't reply, and Chris plonks down, looking around him. Then he too lifts his head in Tony's direction, makes an oversized smile and raises his glass.

Stephen turns to Mandy. 'You could just say hello,' he says.

She blows out a sharp puff of breath.

'Why not?'

'Because I don't like him.'

'Why not?' says Cathy.

They're all looking at her now, and she knows that when she glances away her siblings will roll their eyes at each other. She knows that she could answer the question, or just shut up and let it go. She takes another sip of beer. It has always been like this, the weighing up, the calibration, the reining in.

But why should she always have to be the silenced one?

'Because he's intrusive, and he's threatening. He gives me the creeps.'

She hears her own snotty voice, its melodrama. But something flares through her. This town is no more their place than hers, she wants to shout. No matter their (occasional!) visits to Mum and Dad; their once-a-decade trips with a carful of city friends, the ironic tours to childhood schoolyards and cricket grounds. And her snitchy voice, her opinions, Cathy's and Stephen's eye-rolling at what they think is the great yawning distance between her present life and their childhoods—*none* of it is different from when they all lived here together, from every day at primary school or high school or her year on the newspaper. Her conceit, her refusal to accept what is acceptable to everyone else—this grotesque, shameful need for something *beyond*—has always been what separated her from here. And from them. She raises her head and stares back at them both.

Chris looks from his wife to her siblings, and feels a sudden, surprising stab of love and pity for her, knowing Cathy and Stephen see all the defiance and none of the hurt, but he can do nothing to stop them all being swept apart on the unpredictable tides of their complicated, silent sea.

TONY'S HEART moves. He feels the actual shove of it in his chest when he sees her across the tables. But he waits, watches the husband buy the drinks. Two Tooheys New and two Heineken. He swallows deep from his own drink.

If they stay, if he can talk to her. Away from the old man—it's too hard in there. After this morning Tony walked the hospital corridors, ashamed of his own selfishness, of putting his own need first. Dickhead. He wanted to go back and apologise, to tell her he could wait, till the old man, till she was ready. But he knew he'd made her nervous. He'd walked the corridors, saying *fuckwit*, *fuckwit* in his head, making himself breathe in deep to stop from bawling at the idea of upsetting her.

But now. Relaxed. Have a few beers, go over.

And now the sister's seen him, the brother. His heart hammering again.

'G'day,' he calls back. His voice loud.

She looks up. They lock eyes and he again feels it, the thick slide of his heart muscle, its slippery drop.

The husband looks over now, the skinny poofter.

'G'day,' Tony calls again, lifts his glass. He licks his lips. Please, he thinks, waits for her to look up again. She doesn't look up.

He turns to face the video screen. A one-day match, the players coloured all over the field. He can wait. He breathes deep, in, out. *Just wait.* When she's ready, they will talk, about that smoky morning, his heartbeat while he walked alone to the blackened car. How he and she became two halves of the same thing that day. And nobody else can ever understand. *We are the same.*

He looks quickly over his shoulder at the table again, the four of them talking away. One more beer—not too fast—and then he'll go over.

The camera moves slowly around the cricket field, the players. The camera lands on Katich where he stands scratching his balls and then lifts his arms up like he's going to hug something and twists his torso, yanking, side to side. Then it's Hussey, arms folded, white nose pointed in the air, waiting.

We are all waiting, Tony thinks.

He hears a voice mutter his name then, and Nathan from the hospital has brushed past him towards the bar. Tony glances back at the table where Mandy still is with the others. He's got time. He shifts on his bar stool, swiping his smokes away to allow room at the table for Nathan's beer, checks with a kick of his foot that the other stool is still there. But when he looks up again Nathan is walking away, carrying his beer down to the far end of the bar. Tony sniffs. Doesn't matter. Probably wants to watch the cricket. They yarned this arvo anyway. Nathan said he didn't know about the Mudgee girls, but Tony thinks he probably lied. Doesn't matter.

He looks back towards her table, and his heart starts yammering again. What matters is, she's still here.

Now. He tips back his head and finishes his beer in one long double gulp. Have a piss, then two Tooheys New, two Heineken. He breathes out. He clears his throat because it's like the heartbeat is filling up his windpipe, his mouth.

He feels his legs move, he dumps the empty glass on the bar, and pushes himself to walk past their table. He doesn't look down at them but he walks close, fast, by her chair. He thinks one of them looks up at him but he doesn't look at her, though he can smell something nice, some shampoo or perfume smell, as he passes. It might be her, that powdery female smell. And then he's swinging open the toilet door and it's all gone in the piss-stink.

He closes his eyes. Thinks, if he was ever to touch that hair. Just a single smooth stroke, the hair falling between her shoulderblades. He wouldn't touch her, but if he did.

He takes his time, washes his hands slowly, pushes open the door and then walks back into the gloom, walks back to the front bar the long way round, through the back bar with its circus of pokies, past the little hallway counter with its narrow rack of racing forms and the pencils. Two Tooheys New, two Heineken. Past the stairs to the cocktail bar, and past the bistro door, wishing to fuck his heart would slow down.

They're gone.

The chairs pushed out and the four glasses on the table. Tony's guts churn and he wants to shit and cry suddenly, at the same time. The beer glasses empty and the chairs opened out from the table like a crashed abandoned car.

But she looked up for him once. She looked.

***

CATHY AND Stephen have gone in his car. On the way to the hire car a short blonde woman steps toward Mandy and Chris, smiling. She has a stocky, muscular build, and Mandy suddenly recognises her as Leanne, a girl she had been to high school with. She remembers Leanne darting around a basketball court, leaping into the air and scoring lots of goals. Leanne had had a footballer boyfriend who had already left school. Mandy remembers wondering why Leanne—athletic, bouncy and popular—would be friends with her. Whenever Mandy and the other girls from school saw Leanne's boyfriend he would be standing apart, waiting—at the school gate, or next to his big car. He wore sunglasses, all the time. He gave Leanne Valentine's Day presents, large teddy bears and heart-shaped balloons.

'Leanne!' Mandy calls now, bending to kiss her cheek. She says, 'Chris, this is Leanne. We went to school together.'

Leanne smiles at Chris. 'Nice to meet you,' she says, then glances aside to a nearby car, where Mandy can see a couple of blonde kids scowling from the back seat. Mandy forces surprise into her voice: 'Are they yours?'

Leanne laughs. 'Yeah, the little fiends.' She calls out to the children, 'I'll be one second.' She flips keys in her hand. 'Amanda, I'm so sorry to hear about your dad.'

Mandy nods. 'Thanks. You don't have to call me Amanda. Nobody but the TV calls me that.'

'Oh,' says Leanne, looking confused. 'Why do they, then?'

Mandy feels a blush, murmurs that she's not sure.

The children begin fighting over something between them in the car, but Leanne, unfazed, ignores them. She asks about Geoff, about Margaret and Cathy and Stephen. Then she smiles at Chris. 'So do you two have any kids?'

Chris doesn't return the smile. Instead he shakes his head. 'Bit hard with Mandy's job.'

Leanne's face turns instantly red. 'Oh, of course! I'm an idiot!' She is shaking her head in embarrassment.

Chris, expressionless, watches Leanne's fluster without comment, and then he turns and looks down the length of the street, and for this long second Mandy hates him. She should change the subject, but instead she says, smiling, 'Well, nearly all the blokes who do this job have kids, so it's an entirely reasonable question.' She looks at Chris, then back to Leanne. 'It's just that they have wives who stay home and do all the work.'

Leanne sees a lifeline, leaps at it. 'Ha!' she says, relieved. 'Then it's just the same as normal people, isn't it!' The sound of her children's fighting grows louder. 'Anyway,' she says with a big grin, jerking her head towards the car, 'Why would you want that?'

Chris turns to watch the children for a moment. When he turns back his face is softer, and he smiles at Leanne. 'Doesn't look so bad to me, actually.'

It's Mandy's turn for silence, and Leanne's smile stiffens.

'Oh,' she says, glancing from one to the other. 'It's not all it's cracked up to be, let me tell you.' It's clear she wishes she was somewhere else. She flips her keys in her hand again, and leans forward to kiss Mandy goodbye, offers to help Margaret.

As Leanne steps away to her car Mandy sees that in the passenger seat is the same old boyfriend, still waiting.

Chris and Mandy start walking again. Mandy says, 'You didn't have to be so rude to her.'

Chris does not look at her. He's walking fast, so she has to trot to keep up. When she reaches his side she sees that his eyes are glistening with fury.

'Where's your wedding ring?' His voice is strained.

Mandy gasps. 'Oh, *shit*. Chris. I meant to tell you before.' She puts a hand out to touch his arm, says, 'I'm sorry.' She wants him to slow down, but he keeps striding along, not looking at her.

She struggles to keep pace. 'I'm really sorry, Chris. I gave it away—it was in a hospital, a nurse. I know it's terrible, but I knew you would understand. I thought about it, and I knew you would have done exactly—'

He lets out a sound to stop her talking; a cough, or a snort. Or, Mandy thinks with horror, the start of a sob. He has stopped now. Beside them is a milk bar, with a large ice-cream advertisement on the window. When Chris finally turns to her his eyes shine and he says in a hard, bitter voice: 'I would *never* give away my wedding ring.'

Mandy swallows. She stares at the poster. A tanned girl's profiled face is puckering her lips around the rounded tip of a long yellow ice-block. The background is a bright, bare blue. Mandy hauls herself up, squares her shoulders as she opens her mouth again to plead, explain.

But the truth is that in that noisy, crowded moment in the Yarmouk hospital with the exhausted young nurse, she did not think of Chris at all.

She remembers the screaming and the shouts, and running feet as they brought in the bodies—'*another roadside bomb in Baghdad*' is all she says later in her reports—and she remembers pressing herself back against the cold tiles of the wall to keep out of the way as she watched the young woman running between beds with bags of saline and syringes, shouting instructions, and she remembers the lumpen white dressings clamped over so much blood. The dazed, stilled faces of the injured, and she did not know if they were alive or dead, and the noise from outside. The high, endless screaming.

None of this is explicable here in the subsiding evening heat of an Australian country town, beside an enormous picture of a thin, rich, white woman fellating an ice cream. It is not explicable that in the alien fluorescent light of the dingy hospital later that night, she had listened to the nurse say in her dead voice that she was supposed to be getting married, was supposed to be going to university, was going to study medicine. Her boyfriend had gone missing though, she said. Mandy had stood there with her and held her hand while they both stared, unseeing, at a blood-smear on the floor tiles. And then the nurse had moved her index finger to touch Mandy's wedding ring, and said, 'You married.'

Mandy nodded, and then out from the dark street there came another siren, and the girl's whole body began to shake, and Mandy pulled her own hand away and removed her ring, and pushed it onto the nurse's finger. 'You'll find him,' she had said into the girl's ear while the doors banged open again and the sirens whined, and she had held tight to the girl's hand and called through the noise and both their tears, 'You will get married, you will go to university, you will have beautiful children,' and the girl had held Mandy's hand to her chest and nodded, unable to stop crying.

Mandy had looked for her the next morning. She saw her asleep on a chair in a corner, her smooth face tilted upward, the dark thumbprints under her closed eyes, her shoulders slumped. On the fourth finger of the girl's left hand she wore Mandy's ring.

Through the doorway of the milk bar a young woman in a red uniform is visible, laughing with a boy, standing on the single kitchen step at the back of the shop. She's holding on to the door frame with both her hands, raising and lowering herself, on and off the step, in small flirty movements toward him and then away and back again, her cap stuck sexily into the back pocket of her trousers.

Mandy says, 'I'm sorry, Chris.' Her voice flat. 'I thought we could buy another one together.'

She does not expect an answer, and does not get one, as they begin walking again towards the car. Chris takes the key tag from his pocket and points it at the car; its lights flash once as Mandy walks around to the other side.

Chris says something, muttering across the roof of the car. Mandy looks at him.

'What? I can't *hear* you.'

He leans toward her, his eyes moist. 'I can't *stand this anymore*,' he hisses. 'When this is over—' he gestures to the street, towards the hospital—'we have to do something. I can't fucking *stand it.*'

He falls miserably into his seat and slams his door.

Mandy stands there, not moving, with her hand on the warm roof of the car, and she looks along the roofs of the other cars in a pale silvery row all the way up Monarch Street, and she remembers all the Saturdays of her childhood, sitting on the hot bonnet of the car in the main street, waiting for something to happen, for their father to come back from wherever he was and drive them home.

She's still standing there staring when she hears the friendly *peep-peep* of a car horn and turns automatically to raise her hand. Leanne is talking animatedly to her husband as she waves. The husband is smiling, and the children's little blonde heads bob up and down as the silver car carries the family away.

ONCE, IN Sydney, Mandy had looked after her friend Susie's daughter for an afternoon. Susie had crept out through the house while Essie, who was three, was crouching at the water feature's pond, her hands clenched into little fists on her knees. When Essie realised her mother had gone she stepped back, staring at Mandy in terror. Then she'd stood with her small solid feet planted on the bleached paving and opened her mouth to howl.

It was astonishing how instantly the tears came pouring down her face, and her cry became a rising, convulsive shriek. She backed away from Mandy as she screamed, casting wildly about her with her arms out from her sides. She stumbled against a potted shrub, eyes wide with horror. Soon she could not breathe properly; she began to drag in the air in arrhythmic gasps, awful croaks and shudders as she screamed.

Mandy tried to speak calmly, then began begging Essie to calm down, but her voice was only a murmur beneath the noise of the girl's screaming filling the air, the street. Mandy put her arms around Essie then, and wondered for a moment if she should take her to hospital—her whole body was jolting and spinning in Mandy's arms, she spluttered liquidly for breath, and the screaming would not stop. And soon, held fast but still struggling, it was as if she had lost consciousness of Mandy, of where she was, even of her own mother's absence. It seemed she had burrowed a deep tunnel inside herself, breath by gasping breath, and was now a prisoner there, inside this catastrophic, hypnotic trance of screaming from which she would never, ever emerge.

Mandy remembered the pram then, and carried Essie's tough little body, still twisting and jerking and screaming, to the hallway and lowered her into the pram. It was like trying to capture a vulture—the flapping, the clawing—but eventually by keeping her forearm and her flat hand steady across the girl's body, she managed to bend her in the middle and snap the fastener shut. She grabbed her keys, heard her own pathetic voice, *Shhh, shhhh, it's all right, baby*, over and over.

After she had pushed the pram for a block, Essie's shrieks became rhythmic, and an exhausted pattern emerged; the jolting had stopped. Block after block they walked, and Mandy's slamming heart slowed, and she could listen then with a kind of fascination to the waves of Essie's rage slowing, retreating into a mournful, self-pitying howl. And then—Mandy held her breath, praying for it to last—the remnant spasms stopped altogether and she fell into a deep, exhausted sleep.

Later, after she had come home and moved the sleeping child, Mandy too fell heavily asleep on the bed beside Essie. She woke in the gloomy afternoon, her mouth sticky. She opened her eyes, and right there—closer than her own skin, it seemed—were Essie's huge brown eyes. Mandy froze for an instant and closed her eyes again, feeling Essie's little soft breaths on her cheek. Then she opened her eyes and stared back. They lay there in the silence of the afternoon, perfectly still, observing each other's pupils, the flecks in each other's irises, the soft, soft rings delineating brown from white.

After Essie's mother came to collect her in the evening, Mandy wandered through the house collecting strewn cushions, a plastic dinosaur, some hairclips. When she recalled the hour of screaming, it was as though from an afternoon many years ago. Instead, when she thought of the day, the only image was those round, dark eyes staring into hers in the cool bedroom. *This is why people have children*, she had thought, there in the gloom. Because they could watch you like this forever, staring right inside you, without flinching.

AFTER DINNER Mandy wanders through the backyard in the soft evening, hosing the garden beds for her mother.

She and Chris have moved cautiously about each other, as if bruised, since they got home, hiding themselves in the blurred noise and movement of the family, careful not to touch. If they have met one another's glance they have held it for only a half-second before looking away.

She directs the spray of water into the hard dry soil beneath the oleander, watches the water shifting the grains of earth. The quiet work of the men in Hatra comes to her, their scraping and brushing and dusting at the dry sand. She had squatted on her haunches, watching the ground deliver them up. A man dusted and brushed the dirt and with one movement of his hand an eyelid opened there in the ground. With the next sweep, a lip curled. A little further away the flap of an ear unfolded; a man's jawline appeared. Then the ground became all faces, all the sand-coloured faces of the dead, and Mandy squatted, listening to the camera shutters and the silence, and the *sweep sweep sweep* of the uncovering. The sun shone down and she stood, surveying the ghastly emerging eyes and lips and teeth of the ground beneath her feet.

When she finally goes to the bedroom Chris is already asleep, hunched into a ball. She wants to take a sheet to the couch, or the floor, but instead she gets into the bed in the dark.

A smell wakes her in the night. Something rotting and dangerous. She sits up full of dread, and then hurries barefoot through the dark house. But by the kitchen she is awake, and she knows the only smell is the lingering dinner, the greasy bolognese Margaret had made, still clinging to the air. It's raining a little, and there is no sound but the dripping of water in downpipes.

She goes back to bed and lies there, listening to Chris's steady sleeping breath. He's on his stomach, his arms bent beneath the pillow, face hidden. In the dark his body has the strong elegance of a landscape. The planes of his shoulders are beautiful. His bent legs mirror his arms; in sleep, even, he is measured.

She tries to think whether she loves him, what kind of love is available to them now, whether it is possible that he loves her.

A gunshot cracks the air outside.

Mandy jolts at the sound—the single, unmistakable reverberation. Chris's body has contracted. 'Whatsamatter,' he murmurs through sleep, pushing a hand across the mattress to her.

'A gun. Outside.' Her voice is loud in the dark.

He's awake now, on his back. 'What?'

Mandy lies rigid, listening, waiting for another shot, for sirens, for breaking glass or screeching tyres. Chris puts out his hand to touch her stiff body. She allows herself to be pulled into the shelter of his chest. She can feel the ricochet of her own pulse against his skin.

'Must be a car,' he murmurs, but she can hear tension in his voice.

'No,' she whispers back. 'It was a gun shot.'

They listen, their hearts beating, watching the ceiling. The gunman walks the wet streets beyond the house, in running shoes, breathing silently. Watching the windows, deciding, choosing theirs beyond the branches of the lilac bush. Would he aim low, gauging the height of the bed? She thinks of Martin Bryant, his slow, cool walk.

There is no sound. Chris shifts and she moves so that one of his arms can stay beneath the crook of her neck, the other soft across her chest. They listen to the silence, the dripping water, for a long time.

'Okay?' Chris whispers eventually, his lips at her temple.

She nods. 'Thank you,' she says. And then she tilts her head to kiss his soft, shaven cheek, and whispers, 'I'm sorry.' She kisses him again, and he moves and makes a sound that might be relief or pain or fright, and she turns to press herself hard against him, pushing herself into him, into their lonely, sorrowful desire.

When she comes it is with an enormous force, a vast, expelled breath.

CHAPTER TWELVE

Day four

STEPHEN IS at the dining table, a piece of toast with peanut butter held in one hand. His father's kite books are spread over the table and he's writing in pencil on an envelope beside him as his mother comes into the room. She wears a yellow floral nightie with a white nylon lace trim. The nightie is gathered across the bust and a white ribbon loops into a little bow at her freckled chest.

'Hello, love,' Margaret says, her voice croaky with sleep. She walks stiffly past him, her feet a little swollen in pale green towelling scuffs.

'Hi, Mum,' Stephen mumbles. He's looking at a picture of a birdman kite, made from bark and cloth and leaves by a Maori tribesman.

Mandy comes in from the kitchen, stands behind Stephen with a coffee cup in her hand. 'What are you doing with them?' she says, nodding at the books.

Stephen keeps making his notes on his envelope. 'Nothing,' he says. He looks around. 'I told you. I'm going to make one.'

Mandy sniffs, then takes a swig from her cup, looking at the books over Stephen's shoulder.

Cathy comes in wearing a red satin kimono too big for her. She bangs her cereal bowl onto the table and slumps down opposite Stephen, the gown gaping open to show the flat bony centre of her chest.

'*Please*,' says Stephen. Cathy grins through her mouthful of cereal and milk, shifts to close the gown. She waves her spoon at Mandy in greeting.

'Did you guys hear the gun shot in the night?' Mandy says.

Stephen and Cathy look at one another.

'Nup,' they both say at once.

'Well, there was a gun shot.' She sees them not looking at each other now. 'Chris heard it too.'

Stephen tilts his head back, giving her a bare, amused look. 'Sorry. Didn't hear a thing.'

Mandy sighs. 'Well, there was one.' She looks at Cathy, who only raises her eyebrows and shrugs, her mouth full of cereal.

When Mandy leaves the room Stephen and Cathy widen their eyes at each other, but then Cathy stops herself and Stephen bends back to his book. He can hear the crunching of Cathy's cereal. Margaret and Chris and Mandy are talking in the kitchen, there is the clank of dishes in the sink.

'What're you doing with them?' Cathy slurs, tilting her chin at the books in exactly the same mannerism as Mandy's.

'Reading 'em,' he says.

Cathy reaches out and swipes away his envelope before he can pin it down with the pencil, and reads silently. 'Huh.' She puts the list down, flips it back across the table to him. 'Dad's having another scan today.'

'I know.'

'So why are you making kites?'

He shrugs. Cathy hunches over her bowl, and then shifts to read a newspaper lying on the table.

They are silent, companionable.

Stephen had been one of those lean, wiry teenagers whom, were he not her brother, Cathy would have found attractive. He would occasionally give her a cigarette in the schoolyard if he was in a good mood. Most of the time, though, he just looked at her with a pained expression if she came near him. Mandy had already left school by then.

When Stephen was in Year 11, Cathy was in Year 9. His presence at the school brought her a kind of muted respect among the girls in her class; while he was not one of the desirable boys, nor was he among the dorks. He was gruffly nice to Cathy's friends on the bus, or if they came to the house. Once when Jane Bourke walked into the kitchen behind Cathy, Stephen made her a cup of coffee without asking if she wanted it, and remembered how many sugars she liked. He slid it along the bench to Jane and said, 'There y'go, coffee girl.' Cathy was secretly proud of him in that moment, of the way Jane's neck briefly mottled red. But at school he mainly hung around in the slope-shouldered group of boys who muttered among themselves and kicked things along the cement in front of them, swinging heavily into bus seats without seeming to notice if anyone was noticing them.

Here at the dining table, the siblings have slipped back into the time of their adolescence where the two of them could be together without speaking, each appreciating the other's desire not for solitude but for silence, anticipating one another's small needs, passing things or moving their feet out of the way without looking up. These moments where each privately loved the other, and knew they were loved in return.

There is a loud knock at the front door.

As Stephen reaches the hallway he can see the shape of someone unfamiliar behind the frosted glass. When he opens the door a short, balding man is standing on the verandah. He's about forty, wearing a grubby white sports shirt and faintly shining turquoise tracksuit pants.

'Hullo,' Stephen says. The man seems about to ask directions, or some neighbourly favour. He nods with a businesslike smile and glances past Stephen into the house. Then he leans forward and says in a low, conspiratorial voice: 'You heard of that number *six-six-six* round here?'

Stephen rears back, stops himself barking out a laugh.

'Yeah, mate.' He puts a hand out to the screen door, beginning to draw it towards him, smiling. 'Not interested though, sorry.'

The man looks glum. 'Huh,' he says. But he appears to change his mind about something, and he puts his hand out too, to grip the edge of the screen door before it closes. 'Well,' he says, in a challenging tone, staring at Stephen. 'It's the Mark of the Beast.'

Stephen nods, waiting for the man to continue.

The man smiles now, satisfied. 'So.'

But with that he seems to have played his trump card. And when Stephen gives no response the man's expression turns gloomy again, and he looks down to the doormat, nudging it with the toe of his large white sandshoe. He looks back up at Stephen and exhales a long, dejected breath through his nose. He turns away, saying no more, and trudges off down the front stairs.

Stephen watches him leave and then clicks the door shut, hooting with laughter.

The others are washing up in the kitchen while he leans in the doorway and tells them about the Mark of the Beast. Even Mandy smiles.

And for a second then, standing next to her, Stephen recalls some distant teenage fondness, some possibility of playfulness between them. 'Give us a look under your fringe, Mand,' he says, and lunges at her. She ducks away—lurching in surprise, and then chortling 'Fuck off,' in a low voice, glancing through the laundry door to make sure their mother can't hear from the washing machine. Stephen says again, '*It's the Mark of the Beast, y'know*' and they all snicker, Mandy as she wipes a baking dish with a tea towel, and Chris snorting into the washing-up water. Cathy laughs a high, relieved hoot as she reaches down to put a saucepan away.

Margaret, bent peering into the washing machine, hears her almost middle-aged children, shiacking and jostling in the kitchen behind her, bickering like cheerful teenagers. Perhaps they *are* still teenagers, she thinks suddenly, staring at the tangle of coloured clothes wound around the machine's pedestal, her hand gripping the opened lid. Perhaps there *is* something not properly grown-up about them. Perhaps this is why none of them has children.

This is a question that has sometimes kept her awake at night. Geoff will not hear about it, saying only *don't be stupid*; but sometimes lying there in the dark Margaret has been troubled by the suspicion that they—she—has done something terribly wrong. With Mandy, especially.

She lets the lid of the washing machine drop with its little hollow boom, and pulls out the dial to start the water pouring in. She turns to the kitchen and notices, perhaps for the first time in a year, some old postcards from Mandy, greased and filmed with dust, pinned to the noticeboard by the door. Three or four postcards sent over the same number of years, from places in the world Margaret had never heard of. All scrawled with single witty sentences, Mandy's large signature and small, solitary *x*.

The Mark of the Beast. Margaret recalls, from decades ago, a woman they had seen once when Mandy was a girl. The woman was crossing the road in town; a perfectly ordinary middle-aged woman like herself. She wore a pale green skirt and a neat white cardigan, and carried a string shopping bag. And one entire side of her ordinary middle-aged face was a shocking dark blotchy purple. The birthmark, if that is what you could call it, covered her neck and head, visible on her scalp through her mousy hair. And in the middle of this dreadful, violent colour, a two-inch patch of her face—part of her cheek, and lip, and chin—was covered in a thick tuft of long, white *hair*. The shock of it had made Margaret gulp. The hair, and the neat square shape of the woman's face, reminded Margaret of nothing so much as the face of a terrier dog.

Margaret had gripped Mandy's hand and looked at the ground as they passed her. She had no time to say *don't stare* without the woman hearing, and so Mandy, five years old, stared right into the woman's terrible face, twisting her head to keep watching her, as she passed. Once across the road Margaret hissed, too late, 'Don't stare, Mandy,' and dropped her hand.

When Mandy had asked why, too loudly, Margaret could not answer. But she saw a seriousness overcome Mandy, watching the gravel path moving beneath her feet in silence as they walked. And Margaret knew then that something in the world had changed for her daughter that day; that Mandy had learnt both the existence of misery and the obligation not to speak of it.

But that evening in the muggy kitchen at home, listening to the children's routine quarrelling and Geoff's volley of scolding, a storm of gratitude swept through Margaret. For she could believe that Mandy had forgotten the woman's dreadful face, and so she could grant herself permission too, to fold away that fearful, lonely knowledge and forget it.

You bring your children up to escape sorrow. You spend your best years trying to stop them from witnessing it—on television, in you, in your neighbours' faces. Then you realise, slowly, that there is no escape, that they must steer their own way through life's cruelties.

But when your first, your brightest, seeks it out, steeps herself in violence. When she fuses herself to this brutal intimacy with suffering, what then?

IN THE bathroom Mandy switches on Geoff's old clock radio for the local news as she brushes her teeth. The newsreader speaks about the drought, a light plane crash near Gunnedah, a high school principal retiring. There is nothing about a gun shot, nor any arrests, nor reports of the noise. A single shot in the dark streets of a country town goes unnoticed, and has disappeared.

She rinses her toothbrush, drops it into the slot at the end of the rack with the others, next to Chris's. She picks up his toothbrush and looks at it, running her thumbnail down its handle's plastic ridges. They have not spoken since last night, but their movements around each other in the bedroom, in the kitchen, have been respectful, accommodating. He poured her a cup of coffee; she buttered his toast; there is in these small gestures the air of a truce. *When this is over*, he had said in the street. Which means, Mandy realises now for the first time, when Geoff is dead.

She stares at the toothbrush in her hand, and puts it back into the rack beside the others. She thinks of her father's teeth, of his stale breath now, of the ulcers that might be forming in his dry, unswallowing mouth. He is alive and not alive, a corpse and not a corpse. Yet the notion of his death, being dead—that her father might *end*—is a catastrophic disorder of logic. She slams the idea shut.

THE HOSPITAL ward is unchanged. Geoff is unchanged. Mandy and Stephen sit on either side of the bed, chins in their hands. The ward shrugs now and then with movement: a nurse comes to Geoff's bed to perform some ritual—check the monitor, pat the tape over his face, write something down and then sling the clipboard with its notes back on the hooks at the end of the bed as she walks away.

Mandy has asked about his mouth this morning, whether he might have a painful mouth. Could the tube cut into his gums? Might he feel pain? But the nurse said, 'Oh, I don't think so,' and then the doctor shook his head before her questions were even complete, and changed the subject to morphine dosages and today's scan, which is to take place at eleven.

Mandy watches Stephen bent over his kite book, across the bed. He is looking at a diagram of a diamond kite.

'Dad's were a lot more complicated than that,' she says.

Stephen looks up. 'I know.' He bends back to the diagram.

She says, 'Do you want any help?'

Stephen looks at her for a long second, the ventilator droning.

'No thanks,' he says evenly, and returns to the book.

Mandy sighs. She thinks she might scream if she has to stay here, like this, for much longer. She says, 'Remember Mum wants to take us out for dinner tonight, at the RSL restaurant.'

Stephen nods, not looking up.

'It's called Ciphers,' she says. Stephen smiles into his book, but still does not look up.

Mandy counts to fifty, then backwards. She gets up, walks down the corridors to the volunteers' kiosk, where the woman from the Red Cross is trapped inside her little cave of magazines and lollies. She buys a magazine, carries it rolled in her hands back to the ward, where she sits again, for another silent hour. Eventually someone comes and they roll Geoff away for the new scan, leaving Stephen and Mandy sitting across from one another, their arms folded, the white space where the bed has been between them. Geoff is eventually brought back, the ventilator switched over from its battery and plugged into the wall once again. Stephen and Mandy stand on either side of his bed, leaning in, trying to remember if his face looks any different. He breathes the same mechanical breath. He has new tape over the tube near his left ear. They lift the blanket and lower it, straighten the sheet.

There is nothing they can do but lift the blanket, straighten the sheet, lift their father's heavy hands and put them down again.

'I'm going,' says Stephen then. He lifts a bag up from the floor. 'Pick you up after.'

He walks past the nurses' station, along the alley between the beds, presses the button at the hydraulic door. Mandy watches the door opening, *pssshh*.

Then she hears the voice, and Tony appears out in the corridor, talking to a nurse. As the nurse walks off he looks straight through the open doorway to Mandy, and grins. Fear lurches in her: she stiffens, wants to call Stephen back. But then as Stephen passes him Tony stops. 'Whaddya got there?' she hears him asking, jerking his chin at Stephen's book and leaning back with his hands in his blue pockets. Stephen replies, saying something she can't hear, and then the door closes with its slow hiss, leaving them both in the corridor. And she hears Tony's loud, stupid voice sinking away.

Mandy exhales with relief, returns to the magazine on her lap. Something in Tony's blank, dumb face has spun her mind back to an axolotl in a glass tank that she'd had to baby-sit once, in a house she'd stayed in in London. The tank was empty but for the murky water, a thick layer of pebbles, and the fat, pale, fishy thing with legs and six horrible ears. A greasy, spotted, hairless dog with a cuttlefish tail and fronds for toes. It had a face with a wide, stupid grin, and the whole creature was furred with slime. She wondered its body did not rot away. She had sat staring at it in horror. Sometimes it stood up on its front legs and slid about, but mostly it either lay motionless on the filthy floor of the tank, as if dead, or paddled slowly back and forth on its skinny legs, bumping into the glass walls when it reached the end: *paddle, paddle, paddle, bump.* Its pointy ear things—three on each side—flicked up now and then, wafting in the grimy water. The backs of its ears were furred like anemones.

A note from the owners of the house said the axolotl was blind and deaf, and quite aggressive, and she had to *hand-feed* it with pellets—*of beef heart*—from the freezer. She was almost physically sick at the idea; there was no way she was putting her hand in that water.

The first time she lifted the lid of the tank the thing nearly had a heart attack, plunging and sloshing about, so the filthy water splashed up at her. *Don't fucking jump out*, she had prayed. But it was just frightened. She found a wooden skewer in the kitchen and used it to lower the tile of jellied meat slowly into the tank. The thing was motionless there in the water, even as she moved the skewer closer and closer. Then she nudged it, and the creature suddenly leapt and seized at the meat, snapping at the skewer. Mandy splashed water over herself with the fright of it. She dropped the glass lid down with a crack.

The tank water was littered with little dark morsels of slimy, slowly rotting meat, or was it shit? She had wanted to vomit. She hated the axolotl, was surprised at how she could hate a thing so much.

She watched its slow-motion crawl, paddle paddle *bump*. Then it nestled back on its legs, more cow than fish, settling into stillness among the filthy pebbles.

AT LUNCH-TIME Mandy walks out through the sliding glass doors of the entrance into the bright car park, scanning the cars for Stephen's ute. A white van catches her eye. Two men in red monogrammed shirts stand talking to one another beside the vehicle.

The van explodes. Spinning metal, droplets of wet.

The van has not exploded. She breathes, looks at it again, shining white in the ordinary daylight. The first man turns his back on his friend for a moment, cupping his hands to light a cigarette away from the breeze. The air turns bloody again, spinning and powdery in Baghdad, and then clunks back again into the Rundle morning. And Mandy is suddenly sick to death of the memories. What is the neurological point of these insistent bursts, the exhausting appearances and disappearances, the same images, unchanged every time—the boy in the morgue, the lather turning pink; the old woman watching her son convulsing on the ground? All the years of images: the nurse's shaking hands, the boot with the bone sticking out, the head-height axe notches in a church doorway, the white tilt of a car where it slid down the embankment.

A car down the embankment.

Oh God, her own hands gripping a fire hose, and Tony's thick fingers over her wrist, and then the car down the embankment.

You'll remember.

She stands staring at the ground, seeing nothing but what she now remembers.

At eighteen she had sat in the *Rundle Examiner* office, its blinds closed against the heat, and typed that a man was found burned to death in his car on the old Menindee Road.

She typed that police believed the car had driven off the unsealed road, and down an embankment, some time between four pm and midnight, that it probably caught fire in the early hours of the morning, and was found by the driver of a bushfire brigade truck returning to town at 7.50 am. She transcribed what she had seen typewritten on the blue form at the police station, when she'd stood there with Mike Hake, the pimply twenty-year-old reporter from 2RX. She had scribbled her schoolgirl notes on pieces of paper held together with a bulldog clip.

Back at the office she typed out the story of the fire preceding this discovery, the story she herself had watched develop. She typed out the numbers: how many volunteers attended, how far the fire moved, how many hectares had been lost, and what time it went out of control, burning out towards Gilgardie. She did not type that a young man in a boiler suit had shouted at her *Are you gunna fucken get up here and help?*, and that, too embarrassed for protestations about 'reporting', or 'media', she had braced her knees as she stood on the back of the jostling truck, too shy to ask where she should direct the hose, but had wetted the grass in the general direction the man had pointed, and then the man put his hands over and under hers on the hose, showing her to lift it, where to point it. When she first arrived in the mid-afternoon the fire had looked pitiful to her, a few patches of grass burning towards the truck. There was no roaring or threat—until later, in the early evening after the lazy flames of their few paddocks had been extinguished, when she realised what the men knew all along: theirs was only a little spot fire; the main front was approaching from the east. They heard it coming even though it was still miles away, and standing on the road in the dark—all the cars packed and ready to bolt—they watched the orange line roaring across the distant ridge, speechless, staring, willing the predicted wind change to arrive. And then, like clockwork, it did: the line stopped moving, the sound seemed to drop, and the men and their wives leaned on the bonnets of their cars, straining their eyes with watching, not breathing lest it start again. Over the next hours the mood gradually began to ease; slow conversations began again, and finally somebody snapped open a can of beer.

It was nine o'clock; she was exhausted. There was nothing keeping her there but politeness—she'd taken all the photographs she could, none of them very good. She'd helped wash the dishes in the hall where the women had made sandwiches for the volunteers. She felt her own tired muteness the whole time, but smiled and nodded when they talked to her. Then she had left them calling with relief to one another across the cars and ute-trays, the fire fading for certain now, and she had climbed into the newspaper's pale yellow Renault and driven home. Along the Menindee Road.

Then, the next day, on the blue paper of the police form, a body in a burned car. The fire had changed direction again in the night, and burned along the road she had safely driven a few hours before.

There in the police station, Mandy was swept with a sickening, confused guilt.

Had she seen a car, or a person, through the trees?

She was tired, it was deep night. As she rounded a bend on the dark road she might have registered, through the tree trunks and the light smoke haze in the swipe of her headlights, the tilt of a car down an embankment. She might have. And then a movement—something—may have made her glance into the rear-vision mirror. But she had been tired, she wanted nothing to appear back there in the hazy dark, and she glanced ahead again and kept on driving through the night.

Mandy said nothing to anyone. She typed the story. The young guy from the back of the fire truck had found the burned corpse, called the police, the ambulance. But when the editor made Mandy telephone him he'd said, in his slow, friendly voice, *Lucky it wasn't you.*

She had said, *What?*, and he said, *You went on the Menindee Road, I watched ya.* And she had frozen in the stifling office, her pen in her hand, the only sound the clicks and hisses of the telephone line. And then Tony said, again, *Lucky it wasn't you.* He had paused, and then out of the silence he said, *I found him 'cos of you.* She could only breathe her panic, in and out. Then he said, *You and me're the same.*

She'd put the phone down, her heart slamming.

TWO DAYS later the fire was still burning up into the north, while she sat on a box of brochures in the sweet inky air of the printery for her own farewell party, drinking cheap champagne from plastic cups with the other journalist, the ad sales girl, the printers and compositors. And the morning after that she put a suitcase and three cardboard boxes of belongings into the back seat of her green Gemini and drove along Monarch Street, past the shops and the RSL Club, past the swimming pool, the petrol depot, the skating rink.

On an impulse that day, she had turned in at the short gravel road to the river's swimming hole at the outskirts of town and had gone to stand for a last time at the river's edge, watching the brown water churn. As she turned finally to leave, she noticed, jammed between the rocks at her feet, the half-rotted carcass of a bird, its grey feathers matted and wormy.

She had got back into her car and driven away, back out to the highway, and when she came to the 100 km sign she reached down and turned up her radio, and she could feel the smoky air of Rundle leaving her lungs and her clean future rising up. And relief escaped from her in a long, cool breath.

And if occasionally over the years it has come to her that there might have been something in the rear-vision mirror that night—that the swipe might have been a car, a human movement—she has made the thought dissolve, become only the carcass of a rotted bird back in the past, years and years ago, when she was someone else.

But now she is standing on the hot white concrete of the Rundle hospital car park, and this recognition, this memory finally cannot dissolve, and she is not someone else. She is standing outside the room where her father lies dying, and Stephen's Subaru pulls into the entrance from the main road and the sunlight is very bright, and her heart is hitting and hitting in her chest.

But first Tony is walking down the white path towards her, and he sees her face, and he's grinning in a broad new way, this man who found the corpse, who said, *it's because of you*, and he says, 'You remember now, don't ya.'

'Yes.'

She can't breathe, she can't speak but she doesn't need to; they both know it: his hand over hers on the fire hose, the juddering of a flatbed truck, this same waiting breath near her ear—they both know that she let a man burn and said nothing, and that he has reeled her back through the years to peel away her disguise. Here in her childhood home he alone knows who she is, and he has brought her here to face herself.

She might be sick. She bends over, staring at the soft curve of the gutter. *Breathe.* The dread of his hand gripping her arm. Then his voice, loudly: 'She's a bit crook I think,' and she lifts her head and Stephen is walking across the concrete, tossing the car keys from hand to hand.

He cocks his head to look into her face. 'Are you?'

She inhales, forces breath in, out again, shakes her head. But she walks, fast, towards Stephen's ute and she opens the door and lowers herself in, shuts the glass between herself and Tony.

Stephen is a few paces behind her. He gets in, and looks at her for a second before he starts the vehicle and reverses it out from the parking spot. As they drive away Tony stands watching, hand raised in a serene little wave. 'Seeya, Mandy,' he mouths at her.

She watches the buildings, the town, slide by. Stephen is talking but she cannot hear him. She has entered another, unprotected country and she cannot ever go back. She is in the country with a man curled into a ball inside a car, aflame.

'What's the matter?' Stephen is saying again. His tone says *drama queen*.

'I know who he is,' she says. Her voice thin as water. 'There was a fire. When I was on the paper.'

'Huh,' Stephen says. He looks past her and turns the wheel to enter the traffic on Monarch Street. 'He said something about that. Said you'd remember.'

She wants to look at Stephen, to say *I am terrified*, but she can only stare at the dashboard while the shops and the people of this town glide by, and in her head there is nothing but smoke and chemical burning, and a shrieking flame of a man, and behind it all is Tony, waiting to show her who she is. *We're the same.*

'Fucking *vermin*,' Stephen says with sudden force as the car jerks to a stop.

Mandy looks up. They have pulled into the driveway at home, and Stephen is watching an Indian mynah shooting around the backyard, watching its deft sorties from the fence to the garden bed, back to the fence, then the stone birdbath. Trilling its wings, looking out of its yellow-ringed eye.

Mandy leans down to the floor to gather up her bag. Her body feels stiff and old. 'It's only a bird,' she hears herself murmur.

'Vermin,' says her brother again, as he waits for Mandy to climb out of the car and slam her door, and then he reverses back down the drive, swings out into the road and drives off. She stands in the driveway with her handbag dangling from her wrist, watching the mynah. It flips down to the front verandah and walks in its jerky little stride along the cement. It walks up and down the top step outside the front door. It looks around, distracted by a noise, then turns back to its business and begins walking again, up and down, up and down.

Waiting and walking, stopping and watching, waiting to get in.

TONY WALKS back in through the loading dock, hands in his pockets, jiggling his keys. She's remembered now. He feels his chest filling with it. He knew she could not forget.

More than twenty years, and he's followed her on the television around the world, ever since, and it all started here, and how could she forget. She had been standing at the edge of the paddock like a schoolgirl. He'd yelled at her so she climbed up on the back of the flatbed and he watched her from the corner of his eye, how scared she was, holding the hose out too low in front of her like a dog's leash.

He'd felt bad for yelling at her then. So he'd put his hand over hers to show her how to lift the hose, and she was jumpy and silent, and he'd decided to look out for her. Had stood between her and the perviest of the blokes, and as the truck jolted over the tussocks he'd pushed her camera case to the front so it didn't slide about, had told the driver when to stop so she could get a good picture. He made sure she was all right, got something to eat when they did. He didn't hassle her or anything, just watched her from a little distance, for the rest of the night, until he saw her get in her car and drive off. He'd watched the tail-lights of her car getting smaller like the coals of the grass fire, while the others were watching the ridge, and he saw, way in the distance, that she didn't keep going on the main road but turned off onto Menindee.

He slept in the truck, and next morning when they could see how the fire had gone everywhere, when all the country was just smouldering black, he took the Menindee Road back into town. No reason, just making sure.

And then when he rounded the bend and saw it, the smudged skeleton of the car down the embankment through the tree trunks, his guts lurched like he'd never felt. He stopped on the road, and his feet crunched over that black stubble in the smoking sunlit morning, towards the melted car. He can't remember holding his breath, leaning in, careful not to touch the blistered black metal. He cannot remember the noise of his own bawling breaths going out of him, *Oh no, oh no*, nor putting out his hands to feather in the air around that human shape, his sobs and gasps floating with the smoke, up among the burned stalks of the trees. But he remembers the curled nubs of the hands, the foetal angles of the legs. He cannot ever forget the bubbled black skin, as if a bandaged infant of a woman had been dipped in tar and left to burn, shrieking and alone.

And when the cops said later it was a man, he wept with relief. He had saved her. By seeing what she saw, by it not being her. He knew this was stupid, but also that it was the truth, and when her voice came on the phone that day he was unsurprised, and he didn't have to say *I saved you*. He had saved her, and it was impossible to forget what they both had seen, even with the years and years, and now that he'd found her staring at him in the car park he knew that she did not forget, and that at last she recognises that they are the same.

MARGARET HAS to go and see Bid Grogan about swapping her turn for the flowers at Mass, and her children are to meet her at the RSL Club.

'It's called Ciphers,' she says again before leaving, liking the sound of the word.

At six, Cathy says, 'Why don't we walk? Then Mum can drive us home.'

The four of them speak little as they walk in the warm evening. Near the fire station the air grows electric with cicada noise. The drone of a car approaches; as the black hatchback passes them the rich, melodramatic tones of a local FM radio announcer's voice—*music from the SIXties, SEVENties*—booms briefly out.

Mandy walks ahead with her arms folded, biting the inside of her cheek. She has not spoken to any of them about what she knows can only sound ludicrous, the dread that is seeping, soaking slowly and surely, through her whole being.

Chris hurries to keep pace with her. At the corner he touches her arm, making her wait for the others, almost half a block behind them. They both stand staring across the road, unseeing. A shopping trolley, far from home, angles into the gutter.

Chris says, 'Are you okay?'

Mandy cannot reply, expressionless, still looking at the road, still biting her lip. She shrugs. 'Are you?' she says then.

When she finally looks at him she sees that his eyes are wet.

'Not really,' he breathes. They can hear Cathy and Stephen coming up behind them. Mandy takes Chris's arm and tucks it beneath hers, holding his hand to the warmth of her side.

The others are almost alongside them now, and Chris withdraws his hand and whips it to his face, flicking his tears away, and starts walking again.

At the corner of Massie Street, Stephen yells out in sudden glee. 'Hey!'

They turn to see him grinning at a shop sign: INERTIA HEALTHCARE. The sign is painted with curly text, and another advertises *Reiki—Tarot—Health Foods*. They chortle. Cathy says, 'Do you think we should tell them?'

'Nup,' says Chris.

They walk again, four abreast now.

'Didn't that used to be the barber?' asks Mandy.

'The one that sold ammo!' Stephen says.

'With the bullets right near the kids' chair!' cries Cathy. 'And the shotguns!'

They explain to Chris how it is true, that the barber used to sell ammunition, how there were rifles and shotguns on the walls, how the window was painted with a barber's pole wreathed in a garland of guns.

'Bet Hair-on-Hamilton doesn't sell ammo,' says Stephen.

They walk on, in the blue evening. Mandy has hold of Chris's arm beneath hers again now, skin to skin. As they walk she recalls that their father had a rifle in the house when they were young. None of them knew it was there until one ordinary afternoon when Geoff lifted the rifle down from a high shelf in the hallway cupboard, disassembled it, and took it away. Margaret was out, and the children stood around the kitchen table, thrilled and silent, while their father opened the long wooden box and removed the rifle. He turned dark bits of metal and broke open the gun. Astonishingly he did not speak a word while he carried out this task, which was hot with danger. There were no warnings, no lessons on how the machinery worked. The children—even little Cathy—knew somehow not to break this spell by speaking, or fidgeting. They stood holding their breath. He took the pieces of the gun and ran a grubby cloth over each of them before putting the pieces back into the box. Then he snapped it shut, carried it out of the house to the car, and drove away.

The children had watched the car drive off and then dispersed. They said nothing more about it, not even to each other. Until dinner, when they were eating strawberries and cream, and Stephen said, 'Hey Dad, wheredya take that gun?'

Margaret had inhaled audibly, but kept on eating. Their father cleared his throat and said, 'I took it to the police station and had it destroyed.'

There was a moment of silence, and then Margaret had said quietly, 'We don't want it.' And the moment passed. But years later, when Mandy worked on the paper, she learned from an *In Memoriam* that it was around this time that Rowan Young, the fifteen-year-old son of Geoff's friend Doug, went to a vacant block near his house and shot himself in the head.

They walk along the main street in the falling dusk. Some boys are playing with a football on the pavement outside the club, calling to one another. Mandy wonders if Stephen ever knew about Rowan Young. She thinks about all the things that are never gotten around to, in a family. And she wants to tell him, suddenly, about the gun, about Rowan, and about the frightened, unutterable love that fathers have for sons. Maybe even, somehow, to begin trying to explain what she could not in the car today—Tony, the fire, the unnameable fear spreading through her. But when she catches his eye he only looks away again. And when they reach the club he strides ahead of them all, through the group of boys and up the steps.

Margaret is sitting alone at a long table under the track lighting of the restaurant's vast room. Looping blue neon letters fixed to a far wall spell out *Ciphers*. There are curved blond-wood dividers separating the barn of a room into several areas, and each divider is topped with a curved wave of frosted glass. There are only a few occupied tables, the pairs and quartets of diners seated far from one another. The tables are vaguely surfboard-shaped in outline, and there are turquoise paper serviettes. It is the sort of generic décor that might belong to a small-town coastal resort, but Rundle is a long way from the sea.

As they sit down and a waitress hands out the padded vinyl menus, Mandy watches the four boys kicking the football to one another outside on the street, beyond the tinted window. The boys are enjoying the mild nuisance of their game to passers-by, the ball's unpredictable bouncing, their lurching to catch it, the space their bodies take up. One boy kicks the ball spinning low across the ground to another, and it bounces sideways, just missing a middle-aged woman hurrying towards the steps. The catcher leaps but he has to drop and scuttle in front of the woman, batting the ball away from her step just in time, making her lose her stride. The other boys smirk and lean away with their hands in their pockets, as he calls *Sorry!* to the woman. She has stopped and narrowed her eyes in annoyance, is saying something to the boy. He stands listening to her with the ball held low in his hands while his friends snicker behind the woman. When she has gone, the boy grins widely and shouts to his friends, running to grab one by the arm and punch his shoulder, hard.

Margaret and the others are reading the plastic-coated menus. Mandy looks down the list. She stops herself from remarking on the spelling.

'It's supposed to be very good,' Margaret says. 'The chef is new. From Sydney.'

There is Thai Beef Salad, Oysters Natural or Kilpatrick, Steak with Pepper or Diane or Mushroom Sauce, Filet Mignon, Tuscan Lamb, Bangers and Mash, Beer Battered Fish.

Mandy reads down the list, then mutters in contempt, 'Jesus.'

'What?' asks Cathy, scanning the menu.

Mandy reads it aloud. 'Adriatic Salad: Cajun prawns, sweet potato, snow peas and lime mayonnaise.'

Margaret says, 'Mmm, that sounds nice.'

'Sounds disgusting,' mutters Cathy beneath her breath. 'And where are they getting prawns?'

But Margaret hears, and looks at her hotly. 'We have a man who comes every week. *Fresh* seafood.'

Mandy takes a swig of wine from the too-small glass. 'It's ignorant, is what it is.'

Stephen has been looking on from the end of the table, amused. 'Why?'

'Because they don't even know what it means,' says Mandy.

'It means a salad made out of prawns, sweet potato, snow peas and mayonnaise,' says Stephen. He's leaning back in his chair, the menu open in his hands like a prayer book. Cathy looks at her own menu, trying not to smile. Margaret is confused, looking from the menu to her children and back again.

Mandy looks away, rolling her eyes. She leans down to rummage in her handbag.

'What? What's the matter?' says Margaret. But as soon as she's said it she changes her mind about wanting to know. 'I'm having the Tuscan Lamb,' she says, closing the menu. This mystifying, looming quarrel will be ended. She frowns at Stephen and Cathy.

Cathy begins, helpfully, to explain. ' "Cajun" means Southern American. Louisiana.'

'Oh,' Margaret says, nonplussed. She shakes her head briskly, as if to see off a fly. Then she sees Mandy's hand emerge from her bag with a packet of cigarettes. 'You can't smoke in here, Mandy,' she says, an anxious note in her voice.

'And the Adriatic, obviously, isn't anywhere near Louisiana,' says Mandy, unfurling the clear wrapper from the cigarettes.

'So who cares,' says Stephen.

Mandy stops unwrapping and stares at him. 'I care.'

Stephen is enjoying the predictability of this moment. But he says, widening his eyes as if surprised, 'And why's that, Mandy?'

She knows she's being ridiculed. She has a sudden surge of adrenaline, of spite. She leans forward, looking Stephen in the eye: 'Because it's ignorant. It's just some exotic name they made up. Why don't they just *call* it prawns and whatever? Why do they have to make up some pretentious thing they don't even understand?'

'Maybe they like the sound of it,' Stephen says.

'Maybe the chef is called Adriana,' says Cathy, smirking.

Mandy's hand goes back to her cigarette packet. Margaret cannot stop watching the cigarettes, except to look swiftly about the room to see if anyone else is noticing what Mandy is about to do. Suddenly a large figure looms at her side.

'Hello, Connollys,' says Ken Lewis in a hearty voice.

Their heads swivel.

'Ken!' says Margaret. 'Hello!' She beams; Ken Lewis will save the moment with his big, tanned face, his tennis-champion's confidence.

The others murmur their greetings; Chris stands and shakes his hand. Stephen leans lazily forward, holds Ken Lewis's hand for a moment and drops it, then sits back in his chair. Ken stands with his hand on Margaret's shoulder, listening solemnly while she talks about Geoff, about all the kind cards and things from Geoff's friends from the tennis club, from Rotary. The others sit with tight smiles, waiting for Ken Lewis to go. Eventually he sighs, patting Margaret on the shoulder.

Then he leans over to Mandy and says, 'Next time you're home we would love you to come and talk at Rotary.'

She stares back at him with her arms folded. Ken Lewis looks suddenly nervous, and then he says, 'Not now, obviously. Not a good time, obviously.'

Mandy only nods, unsmiling, arms still folded.

Ken Lewis looks around at the others in an alarmed way. 'So, what's everybody having?'

Stephen grins nastily at Ken and says, 'I'm having the Adriatic Salad.'

'Oh, Genevieve had that last week. Said it was fabulous.'

Mandy stares down the table at Stephen. Margaret, flustered, says goodbye to Ken Lewis. As he walks away, Stephen drains his half-glass of wine, and reaches across Cathy for the bottle, pours himself another to the brim. 'So, Mandy, what *are* you having?'

Mandy whispers, 'Get fucked, Stephen.'

'Mandy!' says Margaret.

Stephen's still smiling, controlled, amused. He won't stop. 'Why do you care what it's called? You've been around. You've seen people who don't have any food. Do you think they would care what it's *called*?'

Their mother looks on the verge of tears; Mandy notices but can't stop.

'Yes, I do. Because that's what's wrong with this fucking country.'

'Mandy,' Margaret calls weakly. The others say nothing.

Then Chris turns to Mandy. 'Come on,' he mutters,

close to her face. She has to stop now. But she won't. She stares past Chris to Stephen.

'Because these people don't even know where the Adriatic *is*, for fucksake. Do you think anyone here even remembers Croatia, or Bosnia, or Kosovo? Do you think they care that bodies are still being found in back*yards* in those towns?'

She reaches back to her cigarettes, rips open the lid.

'You can't smoke in here!' Margaret is pleading.

Stephen isn't smiling anymore. He says coldly, slowly, 'You're so fucking superior, Mandy. Why do you have to despise everyone who doesn't know as much as you do?' He pauses, eyes glittering. 'Why can't you just let them have a *go*? For all you know, naming the fucking salad could be the most adventurous thing they've ever done! Maybe they're reaching for something—' he's snarling now, stumbling over his words—'that might *lead* them towards something—bigger. Some *grander* fucking fate than Rundle can offer! What's wrong with that?'

'It's not *enough*!' Mandy's voice is unsteady, on the edge of tears. 'You know why? These people—' she flings an arm out furiously; Chris puts a hand out to push it down—'have *every* opportunity to know about the rest of the world. But they get cable TV so they can watch fucking *sport*! They *choose ignorance*!'

People two tables away are staring.

Chris begs in a low, desperate voice, 'Shut up, Mandy.'

But she only grows louder. 'All around the world, *right now*, people are being blown to fucking pieces. Kids playing with balls, just like them—' she gestures wildly at the window—'are having their fucking *legs blown off*, or are trying to hold their sisters' *heads* together in their hands, because people in Australia—*people in Rundle*—don't *give a shit!*' She shoves Chris's hand away again, violently. '*Or*, they care a tiny bit, if they've been there. But they've only been to Tuscany, or fucking Bali! And *then* they only care about the fucking restaurants, or the bloody *architecture!*'

Stephen spits out a noise of derision. Margaret is calling, 'Mandy!' and Cathy is murmuring fiercely through her teeth, 'Both of you just *shut up, shut up.*'

Chris has given up. He stares at the table, his chin jutting.

But Stephen is aflame. 'You just hate ordinary people, Mandy. You hate *ordinariness*. But the poor bloody people overseas you are always going on about, that you make your famous living out of? You know what they want? Ordinariness. They want *exactly* what it is about this place that you despise!'

Mandy is silenced. She puts a cigarette to her lips, staring at her brother. She has never hated anyone so much in her life.

'*You can't smoke in here!*' Margaret cries.

Mandy wrenches the cigarette from her mouth, turns to her mother and shouts into her face, 'I *know*, Mum!'

And five tables of people watch the violence of her shoving out her chair and walking through the blond wood and the coastal glass waves, out of the restaurant, through the over-lit foyer, past the staring people on the desk and through the big glass doors out into the street.

She walks to the end of the building, flicking her cigarette lighter. She hurls herself back against the bricks and drags deeply on the cigarette, and then exhales a coughing sob of tears and smoke.

Across the road the boys are still playing with their ball on the wide footpath outside the old Muswell & Co department store, now Best & Less. The sun has gone, and the light is low, the air warm. The boys' long limbs move through space slowly, their baggy shorts and surfwear t-shirts loose on their bodies. The boys' reflections ripple across the closed glass doors, patterned with stickers and sale signs, and their shouts are counterpointed notes falling into the quiet air. They are a jostling ballet with a football in the fading, uneventful evening of an Australian country town.

THE FAMILY sits staring at their menus. Except for Margaret, breathless, who cannot understand what has just happened. She looks wildly around the table, and then around the restaurant at the other families turning back to their meals, eating quietly, the men with glasses of beer and the women with wine. They murmur to one another, nobody looking at the Connollys' table. Even Ken Lewis is talking in a studied way to Genevieve. But they have all watched the scene. Grown adults fighting like children. She is still red with bewilderment and shame, and opens her mouth to speak when a waitress appears at her side.

'Are you ready to order, Mrs Connolly?'

Margaret rears back to look at the waitress, and realises it is Patsy Hackett's granddaughter. Elissa, or Alisha, something like that. Margaret has seen her photo in the paper to do with school, or girls' cricket.

She flops her menu onto the table and gathers herself. 'I'll have the Tuscan Lamb, please, love. Thank you, love.'

The others are tightlipped, but take their cue, ordering quietly, handing their menus gently to the girl. Except Stephen, who says clearly, 'Adriatic Salad, thanks,' clapping the pages of his menu together and smiling as he hands it to the waitress. She flicks a confused glance around the table, then lowers her eyes.

Cathy shakes her head at Stephen in disgust.

He leans towards her, whispering deliberately, 'It's just *food*.'

'I'm not fucking interested,' Cathy mutters, not looking at him but along the table to her mother.

Margaret says nothing, but breathes out a long, weary sigh. Then she asks woodenly for another glass of wine, which Chris pours. She sips it, and puts the glass down. Then she gives Stephen a long, sorrowful stare.

'Thank you very much, Stephen.'

'Mum—' he begins, but she puts up a hand.

'*Enough*!' She feels the rage flaring inside her. 'I am Sick. And. Tired—' she hears her loud voice, its shrillness—'of being *sidewinded* by you all.'

There is a silence. She stares around the table, a little shocked at her command, finally. Then Cathy mumbles, picking at a coaster, 'Do you mean blindsided, Mum?'

at exactly the same moment Chris says, 'Sidelined?' She stares at them, breathing in the strange, humid air of the restaurant. Beyond the piped music she can hear the poker machines' carnival burbling. What did she mean? She no longer has any idea how to communicate with her children. She is not the same person she was, cannot recognise them, herself.

Across the room studded with its spangly lights, Alisha Hackett is walking unsteadily towards her, concentrating on the huge white plate she carries in her two hands. She reaches the table and with an uneven knocking sound, dumps the plateful of orange-coloured meat down in front of Margaret.

Margaret stares at the thick sauce sludging its way down the hillock of meat and thinks, *I am no longer the mother of this family*. She is no longer a wife either, not adult, even. She is a strange and lost, unformed person. She thinks of the woman with the terrier face all those years ago, birthmarked and tufted, walking across the road as if everything was normal. Margaret lifts her head to see these people: Cathy, Stephen, Chris; and Mandy's empty chair.

And it comes to her finally. Their father, her husband, has fallen off the roof. He is going to die. And it has cast the whole of their lives in an unfamiliar, new and dreadful light.

CHAPTER THIRTEEN

Day five

MANDY WALKS, Leia panting beside her, along the Rundle footpaths in the early morning.

She has been awake most of the night, lying silent in bed when the others came home. Chris came into the dark room and got into the bed without a sound; she knew he could tell she was awake, but they both pretended otherwise.

She walks faster, beginning to sweat under her arms and her breasts. After a while Leia drops behind, and when Mandy turns around she sees the old dog, her head dropped low, padding slowly back towards the house. Mandy keeps walking, breathing deeply in and out. She is sorry, and not sorry. She hates Stephen, is filled with shame for upsetting her mother.

The town is blank this early in the morning. She wants coffee, but does not want to speak to anyone. And anyway, it seems nothing is open. She walks the few blocks of the silent main street. The footpath paving is new, appears swept clean. The guttering is pale and new, and also clean. She looks ahead, down the street at the horizontal rows of modest signs hanging beneath the awnings; their fading, hand-painted lettering. Rundle Workwear, The Book Nook. Even though it is early, the sun is bright, and without the clutter of cars the street is wide and bare.

From the trees beyond the shops on either side of the street come the irregular squawkings and chirrupings of morning birds—currawongs, lorikeets, magpies, noisy miners. Somewhere else a dog barks, once, twice. Mandy walks more slowly now, breathing deeply. She feels cried out, her face dried and parchy.

She will apologise to her mother. She will not apologise to Stephen. She will leave. But she can't leave. She walks, watching her feet come and go on the footpath before her. She passes the Sea Bream Café; it alone among the shops is open, and the coloured plastic fly strips of its doorway flap lazily into the street. She hesitates, tilts her head to look through the strips. There's no coffee machine; it would be watery instant. She keeps walking, seeing but not looking at her hunched reflection in the windows. Rundle

Real Estate, Vera's Fashion, Uncle Joe's Pizza N Pasta with its painted red and white chequered window-panes. Then she hears a noise and looks up. Ahead of her outside the Commonwealth Bank, two older men are strolling along towards her, chatting. Each of the men holds a nylon leash, and at the end of each leash a tiny white dog patters along the street. One is a Jack Russell and the other a Scotty, the dogs' equanimity mirroring their owners'. The four walk slowly, but with ease, in the sunny morning.

Mandy rubs her face quickly with one hand. Compared to these upright men she feels dishevelled. She takes a deep breath, straightens a little.

'Morning!' one of the men calls as they approach. Both men smile broadly. 'Beautiful, isn't it?' says the other to Mandy, gesturing at the summer air. She smiles back, nods.

Then a hearty shout comes from behind her.

'Ah, Gawd save us!'

The men grin more broadly now, and Mandy turns to see another man approaching from a few doors behind her. He strides along, meets Mandy's eye and smiles a big, knowing grin at her. 'Look at these poor old buggers with their seein' eye dogs!' he cries, winking at her as he stops to talk to the men. Mandy smiles back, and goes on past.

The sun shines down on the empty street, and as she walks, the shopfronts become a coloured mosaic in her peripheral vision. She listens to the men's low, jovial chatter until she's too far away and it fades beneath all the ordinary beauty and the squeaks and peeps and carolling of the high noisy birds.

It's after nine when she gets home. She pulls the back door closed behind her, entering the warm grey chaos of the laundry. Then, through the kitchen doorway she sees Stephen bent over the table, the painted white table of their childhood, and it is stained with bright swathes of coloured tissue paper.

And Mandy is somehow suddenly released, in this instant, from everything that has gone wrong between them. What she sees is Stephen making a kite in the colours of childhood, and there is something insistent and primary in it, and this moment is the gap through which she might reach out at last to her brother, through all their mistakes and the torn years behind them. She steps through the doorway into the kitchen, saying his name—and then she sees that hunched at the table over the kite, that brilliant, patterned possibility, is a second person.

It is Tony.

HER FACE is white, stricken.

'You know Tony,' Stephen says, reaching for a Stanley knife. He watches Mandy's drained face with interest—a knife-pleat appears between her brows and then disappears, replaced so instantly by her usual cool neutrality that he wonders if he saw it at all. It occurs to him that for a long time, seeing Mandy on television, and now in these last days, he has wondered how any man—even Chris—could find her attractive. She's like a corpse.

'Yeah,' she says now, blank-faced. 'Hi.'

And she turns and leaves the room.

Stephen looks at Tony to see if he's insulted, but he's sitting exactly as before, pressing the dowel beneath his fingers, waiting for the glue to dry over the fishing line. He does not concentrate, but scans the room around him, looking intently at the fridge, the cupboards.

'She's nice,' Tony says then, nodding at the empty doorway.

Stephen snorts. 'She's scary,' he mutters, more to himself, as he bends to concentrate on cutting a notch into a piece of the wood. The notches he made earlier were not deep enough, and the fishing line skidded off the end of the dowel when he pulled it taut. He lowers himself over the stick. His neck aches.

'I think she's nice,' Tony says, seeming to focus suddenly. 'Smart.'

Stephen breathes out through his nose, hunched over, going at the dowel with fierce little nicks of the knife. 'Yep. She's very smart.'

It was Tony's idea to help with the kite. In the corridor of the hospital he'd asked Stephen about the book, about what he was going to do. Stephen had talked about going up to the transmitter tower on the outskirts of town, said that he had to talk Cathy into helping him.

'I'll helpya,' Tony had said then, and asked Stephen about the kite, about aerodynamics and weight and lift.

Now they are trying to make the kite's diamond outline, running the nylon line through the notches in the ends of the crossed spokes. Cathy would have been more useful,

Stephen thinks, in this knotting and then gluing of line and dowel, but she still has the shits with him from last night.

He's trying once again to tie the tiny, accurately spaced knots with his too-big fingers, and Tony's not a good listener, staring around the kitchen while he fails to pin the cross of the dowel firmly enough to the table for Stephen to tighten the line.

'Is that Port Arthur?' Tony says.

Stephen grimaces; he's got the line taut now, but has to tie off the knot at the last notched end to keep it that way. He pulls the line tight. And the entire length goes loose; the loop has slipped off the other end of the stick.

'Sh*it*!' He stands up straight again and stretches his neck before bending back to the kite. 'Can you just press down a bit harder?'

But Tony is squinting at a postcard, from one of Margaret's friends, held to the fridge door with a magnet. Elegant stone ruins in a sweep of Tasmanian green. Stephen turns his head to answer Tony's question. 'Yeah, I think so. So mate, if you can just hold that really firm for a second?' He waits for Tony's focus to return to the kite; to nod, to do as he's asked.

Then Tony says, lowering his voice, 'You know Bryant didn't do it.'

Stephen frowns, his face very close to the end of the stick, dragging the end of the loop over the slit with his fingernails. He glances back to the centre of the kite, and Tony obediently pushes harder to keep it still. It works.

'Excellent,' Stephen says, straightening and sighing. 'You can let go now. What d'you mean, he didn't do it?'

'Couldn't have,' says Tony, flexing his fingers. He folds his arms and leans forward, his voice taking on a self-important tone. 'Explain this. Sixty-four bullets to kill thirty-five people, wound twenty-two others and cripple two cars.'

He pauses, looking stern. 'And Bryant had no military experience at all, and yet he kills nineteen of them with a single five-point-six millimetre bullet to each head.'

Stephen snorts in surprise, eyebrows raised, as he holds up the skeleton of the kite, two fingers at each end of its elegant spine. He thinks of the white-haired boy, loping through the ruins. 'That's a lot of numbers, mate.'

Tony is undeterred; this is a point he has made before. 'Some of the best fast-moving combat shooters in the world couldn't be so precise. And he's supposed to be *just some loony kid* wandering around.' He rears back in scorn, as if the idea is impossible.

Stephen shakes his head, amused at this new, borrowed voice of Tony's. 'Right,' he says, setting the kite back down on the table. 'Who did it then?'

Tony's face grows very serious. 'The government.'

Stephen hoots. 'The government! Of course!' He reaches for the big swatch of red tissue paper, then looks at Tony. 'Mate, where did you get this stuff? First of all, all those people *saw* Bryant—'

Tony cuts him off, his voice louder than before. 'The government needed a reason to bring in laws to disarm the populace. Simple. Bryant was a patsy.' He glares at Stephen. Then he folds his arms and looks upward, shaking his head in resignation. 'The evidence is out there if you want to find it,' he says.

Stephen begins clearing the table, making space for the sheet of red paper, sweeping bits of cut fishing line and shreds of masking tape into a clump. He can no longer be bothered with the argument.

'Right,' he says, and puts the kite skeleton down on top of the paper, then reaches for scissors. 'We have to cut this into the shape, the diamond.'

But Tony has left the table, is walking around the room with his hands in his pockets. He strolls over to a shelf next to the microwave. 'That your sister's wedding?' he asks, nodding at the framed photograph of Mandy and Chris.

'Mmm.'

'How come she doesn't wear her wedding ring anymore?'

Stephen stops cutting. 'I haven't noticed, mate, if she does or not. Can you pass me that glue?'

Tony's staring now at another photo, one of Mandy with Geoff when Mandy was eight. She holds a kite under her arm, a huge bright bundle. Geoff squints into the camera, his thinning hair blowing against a pale sky.

An hour later they gather up the kite. Stephen carries it, and Tony walks behind, lifting the loops of its long tail, the row of torn-fabric ribbons tied in short, frayed bows, trailing through the house behind Stephen like a bridesmaid.

Stephen holds open the front door for Tony; as he waits, he kicks out a foot towards something on the verandah.

'Fucking vermin,' he says to the mynah as it scoots out of his way across the porch.

Tony says, coming out of the doorway, 'What's vermin?'

Stephen slams the door. 'Them,' he says, nodding at the bird, which has been joined by another. 'They're always trying to get in the bloody house. Piss off!'

He kicks his running shoe in the air at them again. But the birds only take a few sidesteps, cock their heads and look at the men. They stand on their spindly, angled yellow legs, unafraid, and watch Tony and Stephen stepping down the stairs.

Tony grunts as he passes them, 'They're only mynahs.'

Stephen lifts the kite, opening the back door of the Subaru. '*Indian* mynahs. Bloody pests. They don't belong here.'

Tony looks over his shoulder at the two birds.

'They mate for life,' he says mildly, lifting the tail for Stephen to begin looping it into a plastic bag. Stephen snorts, but says no more. Tony looks up at the birds stepping over the cement of the verandah, striding out. One shits on the cement, and then jumps up to join its mate, staring into the frosted glass door of the family's house.

INTO THE darkened living room Cathy calls warningly: 'Don't forget Celia is in that thing at the park at four.' Mandy doesn't reply, engrossed by the television.

Cathy says, slowly and louder, 'Do you know where Stephen is?'

Mandy shakes her head but still does not speak. Cathy comes into the room and drops into the empty armchair. She has just returned from the hospital with Margaret, and she is heartily sick of her brother and sister but has an iron resolve about them today. They will both come to Margaret's friend Celia's dicky little concert in the park, and both of them will be bloody nice about it.

She turns her gaze to the television to see that Mandy is watching a documentary about the Beslan massacre.

'Oh, Christ.'

On the screen flash images of the parents; women dressed in cardigans and headscarves standing in the Russian street through those dreadful waiting days, their arms folded across their stomachs. Now and then a shot is heard, a bang. A woman puts up both hands, cupping them over her nose and mouth. Another holds the fat wad of a handkerchief, pads her eyes with it, then clenches it in her fist, then puts it to her eyes again. When she turns to look past the camera her eye sockets are carved hollow from crying.

Another scene flashes: a grassed area, stretchers, a sea of near-naked, bloodstained children lying dazed and expressionless, or standing, guzzling water from bottles tipped toward the sky. Their bodies are thin and white and streaked against the dark of the shrubs. The shreds of their underpants hang off them. It is a painting of hell.

Mandy stares at the screen, her arms crossed over her chest; she hasn't looked at Cathy. The voiceover goes on and on. Cathy reaches for the remote control on the coffee table. She waits, glances at Mandy, and then says flatly, 'I can't watch this.'

Still Mandy ignores her. Now a Russian police officer stands looking at a stack of bloodied stretchers, a pile of large, crumpled, clear plastic bags fluttering at his feet, and then there's a wide shot: of rows and rows of naked young corpses in the plastic bags; a trail of ghastly, cellophaned bouquets lining the street.

Cathy breathes deeply. The kitchen door opens, and their mother's footfall enters the room, there's a pause and then her whispered, 'Oh dear God,' and the sound of the door closing again.

The television screen is suddenly a luminous, flat green. A cricket field somewhere in Australia appears; the players mill about in their coloured uniforms. A seagull flaps; the soft wash of crowd noise laps over it all.

'For fuck*sake*.' Mandy swings around to glare at Cathy, who is slouched back in the chair with one ankle resting on her knee. She stares at the screen, the remote control in one hand, pointed toward the ceiling like a fired weapon. Her mouth is a tight, defiant knot.

She says, her voice barely controlled, but not looking at her sister, 'I can't watch that.' Her face is bloodless. 'What good does it do those people, for us to see that . . . It's over a year ago,' she finishes weakly, turning at last to face Mandy. 'It's just—*upsetting*.'

Mandy throws back her head in a nasty laugh. 'It's upsetting!' she repeats, in a high, sarcastic baby voice. 'What if everyone just said, *it's upsetting*! Try living in it! What if *everyone* was like you—'

But Cathy bolts to her feet, and Mandy sees that she's begun to cry. She comes around the coffee table to Mandy, pointing the remote control at her, and then lurches forward, her face close to her sister's.

'You know what, Mandy? Everyone *is* like me.' She spits the words. 'Nobody wants to live in it. And *nobody wants to watch it.*' She hurls the remote into Mandy's lap, leans even closer. '*You're* the fucking weird one. *You're* the ghoul.'

Mandy stays sitting in her chair, hears the kitchen door slam, then the back door, her own heart slamming in echo in her chest.

The house is silent again. It is the same as last night. She has turned them all away.

She looks at the remote control in her lap. It is true. She is the weird one; she has always known it. But *ghoul*.

She picks up the remote, flicks the channel back. The screen shows another series of Beslan body bags, these ones black plastic. A ghoul would savour this—that here and there a zipper is opened to reveal the charred, curled body of a child.

CATHY RUNS down the back steps, almost tripping with rage. She shouts towards the empty kitchen window, to no-one, 'I'm going back to the hospital.'

She hurries across the street, past the houses of her

childhood; the old red brick bungalows, then the blond- and brown-brick Jennings houses built here and there across the town in the seventies. She passes the houses of families they knew all through her childhood—the McElvogues, the Colmans, the van Kools—with her head down, arms folded.

She hates Mandy. Hates her.

She passes the windblown play park with its globular, early eighties play equipment—the blue spinning space-ship, the red and yellow tubular climbing frames. Once when she was twelve she had sat smoking with Sean McElvogue on the cold metal seat inside the little blue space-ship. She strides down to the corner of Monarch Street with her hands jammed in her jeans pockets, and her adolescence comes swelling up. Mandy's scathing glances, her bored raising of eyebrows if Cathy ever plucked up the courage to voice a newly minted opinion. She is flooded with righteous rage now, thinking of all the more recent times she has defended Mandy—against Stephen, against other people's hinting that she is weird. *She's just gutsy*, Cathy has often said, fierce in defence of her older sister. *People can't take that in women.* But they all are right: Mandy is just a cold, horrible bitch. Cathy walks faster, wiping her eyes and trying at the same time to slow and deepen her breathing, to stop the rising pain of a huge sob in her chest.

A car drives past. Cathy remembers her driving lessons on this road with Dad, driving too fast; he shouted at her to slow down. She had decided to eat an apple as she drove, because that way she wouldn't look so serious, so frightened. She had seen kids from school in their driving lessons around the car park of the Corroboree Room and was appalled—they looked so desperate, their concentration and fear and dependence so clear on their faces. But when she fumbled the apple out of her windcheater pocket Geoff had shouted—and she'd dropped it clunking down onto the floor to roll about beneath the pedals, while the car swerved into the middle of the road and Geoff cried out.

At the thought of her father Cathy breaks into bitter, self-pitying tears. Her father is not going to wake up. He's going to *die*. She stops, and then squats on the side of the road, sobbing and sobbing into her hands.

BY THE time she reaches the blue hospital sign on the corner Cathy has stopped crying. She trudges along, the gravel of the road's shoulder rhythmic and noisy beneath her feet. She sniffs. Her face is taut and grimy from crying. From here the town has its own special desolation: she can see all the way down the wide road towards the hospital: the petrol depot with its huge gas bottles and its barbed-wire-topped fence; and beyond, the old railway keeper's house, the matted dry grass growing through the disused railway tracks. She can see the drab telegraph poles studded along the road like grave markers. The awful cellophaned bodies in Beslan come back to her mind, and she's struck by a fresh wave of rage and hatred for her sister.

She passes the Ford dealership, where the divorced father of a girl she went to school with used to live, in a little cabin behind the building. The girl's father ran the car yard and when the yard was closed they were allowed to play in the cool quiet of the showroom, between the shining, silent cars. Cathy remembers going into the cabin with the girl once, and the father sat watching football in his underpants, and Cathy suddenly wanted to go home.

She reaches the long, ugly Moonraker Motel, its sign unchanged since her childhood. Once, the son of a family who ran the motel was badly burned by oil in the kitchen, and he had to wear a thick foam suit over his whole body for years and years. Mandy had to take a photograph of him wearing it, for the paper. She had told Cathy it was awful, seeing the boy, who was eleven and ashamed. He had been naked except for his flesh-coloured suit, with its one long and one short leg, and she had to photograph him in his family's living room so they could raise money for the hospital to get him another suit. The parents told the boy to stand this way and that, and lift his arms, and Mandy had been able to say nothing much but tried to smile at him. *His penis was completely deformed*, the boy's father said in front of him.

Mandy had told Cathy it was awful. But now she watches other children being deformed, over and over again, and she makes other people watch it with her, even while their mother covers her eyes and ears, while their father lies dying. Cathy sees now finally that something has gone deeply wrong with her sister, something is irretrievably, horribly broken in her.

A semi-trailer grinds by, whipping Cathy with grit and dust. Up on the hill the sunlight makes a silhouette of the Lutheran Church against the sky, and a leaf blower begins its lurching, repeated moan.

STEPHEN DRIVES out onto the highway, towards the bare, windy hills where Geoff used to fly the kites. Stephen is quiet, listening to Tony talking about the soccer game he played last Saturday, how the ref was one-eyed, how there is a bye today. They drive up the track to the transmission tower, the ute buffeted now and then by the wind.

When Stephen unlatches his door it's instantly yanked open wide, bouncing on its hinges. The men get out and the wind is dry and cold in their faces despite the heat of the day down in the town. Their t-shirts flap.

'Jesus Christ,' says Stephen into the wind. It shoves at him even as he leans inside the vehicle, and the plastic shopping bag and the paper of the kite begin to riffle and flap from the space behind his seat.

He looks around for Tony, but can't see him. Turning, he sees then that Tony has walked over to the cyclone wire fence around the grey transmission tower, and is holding to the wire with the fingers of both hands, the toe of his boot resting in one of the holes. He leans into the fence, peering up into the centre of the tower above him.

'Bet you could see everything up there,' Tony yells.

Stephen squints, then turns back to the bag, which he now has pinned to the seat with his knee. He lifts out the red paper kite, clutching it at the centre where the wooden sticks cross. The wind takes it immediately, and he has to lift his arm with the gust of air so the kite is not ripped from his hand.

He yells over his shoulder, 'Can you gimme a hand?'

Tony saunters across the cobbly tussocks, hands in his pockets.

'I reckon you could see everything up there. Out to the coast even, I reckon. Right at the top, I mean.'

Stephen concentrates on the kite. 'I have to fix the bow,' he says. 'Can you hold this?'

Tony leans in and steadies the kite while Stephen carefully pushes the cross-beam into a slight arc, and manages to hook the looped end of fishing wire over one nicked end of the dowel.

'Okay!' he says, and looks up at Tony, grinning. 'Let's see if this thing'll fly. Do you wanna hold the line or the kite?'

But still Tony stares, across the car roof, at the tower. 'I could climb that, I reckon,' he says in a soft voice.

Stephen looks at the tower. He snorts. 'You couldn't get to the ladder.'

Inside the tower's frame is a narrow, caged ladder going all the way to the top. But a round steel plate has been padlocked across the opening at the ladder's base. Stephen doesn't say anything about the problem of first climbing the barbed-wire-topped fence; he has the feeling Tony has gotten over such fences before.

Tony sniffs. 'I'd go up the outside.'

The tower is made of diagonally crossed steel bars. Climbing up the outside would mean hanging your body over each diagonal, straddling it without sliding down, and then reaching through the high space for the next bar above you. Stephen has a vision of Tony dangling from one of the crossbars near the top.

'I suppose. But what for?'

Tony juts his chin. 'Just to see.'

Stephen squats and holds the kite on his knee, tugging at the line to test the strength of its fastening to each end of the dowel. Seeing Tony standing there, staring upward with his mouth open, hands in his pockets and with his feet planted wide on the ground, Stephen remembers that for a time when he was a kid the worst insult was *Piney*. The Pine Lodge school was for Down syndrome or retarded kids.

'I could,' Tony says defiantly, as if Stephen has challenged him.

'Whatever you reckon, mate,' Stephen says. 'But you'd be an idiot.'

Too late, he hears the dull contempt of his own voice.

Tony drops down suddenly, comes face to face with Stephen.

'I don't give a flying fuck what *you* think of me.'

He hisses it. His face is flushed, his eyes moist with anger. Stephen is suddenly conscious of Tony's potential wiry strength, of the close grey stubble of his face.

'Hey!' Stephen says, forcing a smile. 'Joke, Joyce! Take this?'

Tony snatches the kite from Stephen's hands and stalks off across the hill. Stephen watches him moving away. What *you* think of me. Who's he talking about then?

'Okay,' yells Stephen, and Tony stops, turns around. 'Just hold it up,' Stephen shouts.

Tony raises up the kite in two hands, and the wind immediately wrenches it from him, whisks it sideways and up. Both men yelp with delight. Stephen lets the line whirr out from the spool, then holds it steady in one hand, above his head.

The kite is up. It climbs higher. Stephen holds his breath as the kite lifts. And now it's a punch of red in the blue sky, lurching and tilting sideways on each tiny calibration of the wind, and in those shifting coloured movements against the sky it is a flickery animation, a bird's moving eye, one marvellous moment, again and again and again. Stephen lets out more line, feels its steady pull, taut as a slid raindrop now, and the kite climbs further still, sailing out into the spare blue distance. It is escape and beauty, it's the tether and the leaving home. Him and his father, before the fall.

Then out of nowhere the line slackens, the kite dips and swings.

Stephen catches his breath. *Don't fall*. He starts running backwards, all breath and begging, yanking on the line with both hands to tighten it, gathering it in. But faster than he can pull it in the kite sinks—a slow, beautiful stone—then goes taut again, zigzags a moment—then plummets point-first into the ground.

Stephen stops running, lets the spool fall to the ground. He leans forward to catch his breath, panting, hands on his thighs, his pulse jittery. '*Fuck*it.'

He sees Tony coming towards him and wishes suddenly that he hadn't let him come. He walks away across the grass until he reaches the kite. He bends to it, picks it up. Tony has followed him; stands there with his hands on his hips.

'Maybe the tail's too long,' Stephen says.

'It didn't work,' says Tony, grinning.

'You have to get the tail the right length.'

Stephen trudges back across the hill to the car, takes the scissors from the plastic bag, cuts the tail a few inches from the end, letting the bright fabric bows fall. Tony looks on with his arms folded, bored now.

'You dunno what you're doing.'

Stephen doesn't reply. He hands Tony the kite, and he walks off again across the grass, head down.

This time the kite does not rise as high, and the swinging gets worse; it speeds around in a spiral twice, three times, before hitting the ground again, harder this time. When Stephen picks it up, one of the paper edges, despite the reinforcement with masking tape, has begun to tear.

They move to a more sheltered side of the hill. Stephen tightens the bow-line, then loosens it. They take turns holding the line and the kite. But each time the result is the same, or worse. The kite lifts thirty feet and then plummets. And with each attempt, the men's exchanges become tenser, more exasperated.

'Hold it *up*, for Christ's sake,' Stephen yells. Tony glares at him, muttering something, and when the kite plunges again and breaks its spine he laughs.

'I'll have to have another look at the book,' Stephen says eventually, running his finger along the kite's battered edges. 'Maybe it's the bridling.'

Tony stands apart with his arms folded, sulking. Then a nasty smile comes on his face. 'Shoulda got your sister to do it. She's better than you.'

Stephen feels sweat at his hairline, on his back. He meets Tony's eyes.

'Let's go,' he mutters.

He shoves the broken kite and the plastic bag of stuff behind the driver's seat, and then gets in and slams the door. The ute's interior is quiet and still; it is a relief to be out of the wind. He turns on the ignition, waits for Tony to open the passenger door. But then, in the rear-vision mirror, he sees that Tony is at the tower—and is inside the fence. He stands there on the ground beneath the tower, looking straight above him.

'Jesus,' breathes Stephen. He waits for Tony to begin climbing. He swallows.

But Tony only stands there, hands in his pockets again, his thin, tilted body unsteadied now and then by the wind, staring up above him as if it's the sky, not the tower, he's interested in. As if the tower is only stairs into the sky, as if he's thinking, *up, up and away.*

CHAPTER FOURTEEN

'WHERE IS everyone?' Stephen has come home to the silent house.

Mandy looks up. 'I don't know.' It is the first time Stephen has noticed how dark are the circles beneath her eyes, how her cheeks sag.

The living room seems dark. He wants to say something to her, about last night, about Tony.

Then she says, 'Oh, shit. Celia's thing is on, at the park.'

Stephen looks at his watch. 'Come on.'

As Stephen's Subaru pulls into a parking spot half a block from the park they can hear the thumps of an electric bass, a guitar grinding out the chorus of 'Addicted to Love'. A woman singer is missing the higher notes.

They don't speak, but Stephen raises his eyebrows at Mandy. They each allow the beginning of a smile.

A sagging banner at the entrance to the park says *Rundle Festival of Art and Living*. 'Oh yeah,' murmurs Stephen, spotting the sausage sizzle, where women from the Lions Club push sweaty hair away from their foreheads, attending to a line of customers.

They eat the sausage sandwiches as they walk between the stalls, in the cool shade of the park. Another stall has a handwritten sign, *Turkish gozleme*, and two women wearing small white headscarves work industriously over a grill and large mixing bowls. The next stall is stacked with ugly, polished wooden carvings in vague bulbous shapes suggesting yin and yang, or Buddha. There's a second-hand CD stall, and Stephen wanders to it, lingering while he chews.

Mandy stands apart, watching a gaggle of women dancing in front of the stage, their arms waving above their heads. One wears a grey jersey dress, which clings to the small rolls of fat around her bra and underpants as she twirls slowly one way, then the other. Middle aged, Mandy thinks, then realises straightaway the woman is her own age, has her body. Stephen is beside her again, shaking his head.

'Twenty-two dollars for fucking Rod Stewart!'

They keep walking, past a small collection of native plants being sold by a tall, anorexic-looking girl with violent black hair, buzz-cut short. She has a pierced eyebrow and wears a black t-shirt, tiny, bright green boy's football shorts and a pair of enormous black motorbike boots. Her t-shirt says, in small white capitals, *I SWALLOW*. 'The only punk in the village,' says Stephen into Mandy's ear, making her laugh.

Next along, a tired-looking woman is sitting on a stool with a brown suede bum-bag in her lap, holding a fistful of sticks with coloured ribbons folded into loops at the ends. All around the park children have these ribbon-sticks, twirling and swirling them in graceful arcs.

'How was the kite?' Mandy says, staring at the children.

Stephen sniffs. 'Didn't work.'

Mandy turns to him then, sees his boy's disappointed face. He glances at her, then blinks, shrugging away her sympathy. But she thinks it is possible he is grateful anyway.

They keep walking.

They pass the Volunteer Bush Fire Brigade display, small boards on easels, dotted with blurry snapshots of fire and smoke with typewritten labels beneath each one. Two women sit beside the pictures, rocking back on their director's chairs, wearing thick orange overalls with reflective arm-bands and big black boots. One has a long blonde ponytail sticking out from her black baseball cap, and reflective sunglasses. Further along is a woman at a table piled high with carrots, demonstrating a vegetable peeler, little streamers of carrot skin a flurry in the air around her.

Mandy and Stephen walk in silence in the slow, cool chaos, glancing around the park for their mother and the others. Once they realise there is no sign yet of the choir, they do not hurry. Stephen thinks he can sense Mandy's mood shifting, lightening. They come to a stall which has a framed sign in painstaking, curlicued gold lettering: *Baby Memories*. Beneath it a display board is hung with other framed things, dark little blobby sculptures behind glass. As they move closer the sculptures become plaster casts of babies' hands and feet, spray-painted gold, mounted on white boards and framed with thick gold wood.

'Bloody hell,' says Stephen at their ugliness.

Some frames contain a set each of both hands and feet, with a soft-focus picture of a sleeping baby between them. Mandy and Stephen move along the line, stopping here and there to read a mawkish poem stuck between the casts. But some frames contain a single hand or foot, painted a dark, faintly glistening greenish colour meant to look like bronze. The hands are curled into little blackened fists, severed at the wrists.

'Jesus,' Stephen says beneath his breath. He leans in, staring, and then turns to Mandy to say something.

But she's not smiling anymore. She is breathing deeply, and Stephen sees her bloodless face.

'I have to go,' Mandy whispers, wheeling away, walking fast through the park, away from the severed hands, the wailing and the smell of burning meat.

'Wait,' Stephen calls. He jogs after her as she strides off

through the green light. He catches her, puts a hand out to her arm. 'Wait, Mandy.'

She tries to shrug off his hand, breathing hard, but he grips her arm, turns her, and says, 'Just wait, okay.' She stops, staring at the ground.

'I can't—' she says, tears in her eyes. She is dragging in broken breaths. 'I can't—*explain—*'

But Stephen holds her arm tight, won't let her go. 'It's okay,' he says then, kindly, softly. Then adds, 'Look.'

Near the children's playground a large group of women has gathered in an arc around a little brass band, sitting in two rows of plastic chairs on the grass. The women are almost all grey-haired, dumpily dressed in dark elastic-waisted trousers and electrically bright cotton blouses—hot pink, yellow, orange, purple. Along with a small audience, the women look on, silent, while the band creaks along in a sluggish version of 'You Are My Sunshine'. A crumpled cotton banner hanging from a music stand says *Rundle Town Band* in blue lettering beneath a blue treble clef. The band has two clarinets, two trumpets, a tuba, a pair of trombones. Most of the players are old men, except for two teenage boys—one with a trumpet and the other the tuba—and a young girl, hair pulled back in a thin plait, her pink lips gripping the mouthpiece of a clarinet.

Stephen holds Mandy close beside him, pulling her closer to the band, squeezing her arm; she stares at the musicians without looking at him, still breathing deeply but a little more easily now. She watches the men, intent on their music books as they play. A couple of them are purple in the face, yet still they don't have the collective breath to raise the volume of the music above the onlookers' conversation. At the end of the song the men drop their instruments into their laps, panting. The crowd claps without enthusiasm. The band heaves into life again, starting 'Oh What a Beautiful Morning'. All the while, the electric-bloused ladies wait their turn, some staring with glazed expressions at the ground, songbooks closed flat over their chests. A small clutch of them bops along in an exaggerated way to the music.

At the end of the song, a thick-set, hearty man—the choirmaster—moves to take up his position. The women stand to attention; they clearly love this man, their faces alight with excitement. Mandy looks around and sees her mother in the little crowd, beaming. Margaret's friend Celia is in the middle of the women, frizzy dark hair above her pink face. There is a large collective intake of breath then, and the women begin to sing. Mandy doesn't recognise the tune until the chorus. The choirmaster turns to the audience, swinging his arm wildly to encourage them to join in. Stephen sings along with gusto, raising his eyebrows at Mandy as he bellows out, grinning all the while, '*I am, you are, we are Austray-liunn.*'

Mandy rolls her eyes, but Stephen makes her stay, through 'Waltzing Matilda' and 'What About Me'. Mandy watches the women, all singing in their high, whiny voices, jubilant with the occasion, with pride. Despite the size of the choir—they must have come from all around the district—there has been no attempt to separate the voices into parts, or to do anything clever or original with the songs' structure or lyrics. Occasionally an individual's vibrato is noticeable, but mostly the voices are of ordinary pitch, trying to hit the same notes; it reminds Mandy of mumbling out the national anthem at school assemblies on November the eleventh.

She looks around the audience to identify the women's family members, to search for pride on the onlookers' faces. But apart from her mother—who has seen Mandy and Stephen now and is beaming even more—the other watchers stand back, expressionless, their arms folded across their chests, or squinting unsmiling into the sun. Mandy begins to feel embarrassed for the singers, plugging on in the face of this blank boredom.

'It's so lame,' she says into Stephen's ear. 'Let's go.'

But he is smiling ear to ear as he turns to her; apart from their mother, he appears to be the only one in the crowd having a good time. 'One more,' he whispers back during the applause, now no more than a few bored claps.

The choirmaster turns to the audience. 'And now we're going to sing about something that is very close to all our hearts,' he says, smiling broadly. 'It's in our hearts and our minds, on our shores and across the distant seas.'

He's enjoying this chance for oration; Mandy wonders if he is a priest. The women jostle and giggle. Mandy can't bear to look at them anymore, with their lunatic smiling. She is shamed to her boots for them all. The little blackened knobs of the hands come back to her, won't leave her. She forces an exhalation, closes her eyes, trying to listen to the choir, but she can't make out the words.

But when she opens her eyes again she sees that the women have stopped their clowning and smiling. Some of them seem to have caught a glimpse of something important, and dignity begins to fill their expressions, rippling through the choir. They are singing, a hymn she doesn't recognise, slow and languorous, *Blessed be the hungry and the thirsty*,' they sing. A few people around Mandy are humming along, and she thinks of what the choirmaster said. And then as the women sing, with their backs straight and their gazes clear, Mandy's shame and the little fists fall away and the boy, Ahmer, comes back. *Blessed be the reviled and the harmed*, and there he is, sitting in the grit and the dirt with his blood soaking the ground; *the pure of heart*, and the morgue attendant turns his body again and again.

Blessed be the peacemakers.

The song finishes with a long, perfectly held note suspended in the air.

Stephen turns to Mandy—and she's standing there with tears running down her chin. 'Oh, Mand,' he says. He puts both his arms around her and pulls her to his side, shielding her from the stares of the other people, from their mother's concerned face craning through the crowd.

He guides her body, jolting with silent sobs, back through the park. He does not understand his sister, has never understood her, but he knows now that he loves her, whatever she has become, whatever the world has done. Tears of his own are stinging as they walk, and now he must bend his head close to hers, to try to hear what

Mandy is saying through her tears into her hands.

'What?' he says, bending to her.

'Why are you hanging around with Tony?'

Sadness surges over him. 'I dunno,' he says simply. His voice is kind, soft. After a moment he says, gently, 'But why do you hate him so much?'

Mandy inhales deeply, her breath catching again in the high final gasp of a sob. She shakes her head, sniffing. 'I don't hate him,' she says, in the quietest voice Stephen has ever heard.

She cannot say it. Even now, here, with her brother's warm arm firm around her shoulders, she can't say, I am terrified. She cannot say, *I'm coming undone*.

'I don't hate him,' is all she can whisper, again.

CHRIS FINISHES his beer and puts the empty glass on the bar. It's five o'clock. He has been here for four hours.

The taste of the beer is thick in his mouth; his movements are glazed as he reaches to the bar, feels the damp red bar cloth beneath his fingers.

He watches the screen above him, waits for the end of the over. When the list of detailed scores appears on the screen he stands up, and walks slowly out of the bar.

He walks across the park. Only a few people are left, taking down banners, packing up microphone leads. He walks past the deflating jumping castle, folding in on itself, its orange turrets sagging inwards. Somewhere a kid is shrieking; the high, hysterical liquid screaming of too many lollies.

He follows the path past the duck pond, smells its rank

sewery stink. He goes to the fence and leans on it, hitching his armpits over the wire, watching the ducks sliding across the water. He likes their sudden direction changes, the seamless gliding. He should go back to the house. But the idea of Mandy, of going back, the hospital, all of it, fills him with an enormous weariness. He imagines instead getting in the car, driving up the main street, ignoring the turn towards Aurora Street, just keeping on driving out along the highway. If he kept going, where would he end up? Broken Hill, maybe. Or Lake Eyre. It fills with rain sometimes and comes alive. Little creatures slurping out of the mud. He hears a clang from the park, a van door sliding shut. He stands up, untangles himself from the fence, pushes himself off.

He thinks of the dead lake, wonders how a person might know when it would come to life again.

MARGARET COMES in the back door at six-thirty, as Stephen and Mandy are setting the table in the dining room. They greet her in low voices. Chris is slumped asleep on the couch in the living room; the cricket drones from the television.

Margaret has been at the hospital. She puts her things down on the sideboard, then walks stiffly across the room.

'How is he?' Stephen says, dropping knives and forks in a heap on the table, plonking the pepper grinder down.

Margaret doesn't answer for a moment. She says, 'Where's Cathy?' There is a croak in her voice that makes Mandy and Stephen look up.

'In her room.'

Margaret says, 'Oh,' and looks toward the hallway, as if she is not sure what to do next.

'What's happening, Mum?' Stephen says slowly, as Margaret steps to the table, putting out a hand to its surface. Cathy has heard her come in and now appears at the living-room door. All three wait for the words to come out of their mother's mouth. She looks about the room, dazed, eyes bright in her pale face.

'They said that in the morning,' she says, staring around at her children's faces, 'they want to turn him off.'

CHAPTER FIFTEEN

OUT ON the farm night is falling and there are bats wheeling against the sky between the big trees behind the machinery shed. Tony hears the bats squealing up there while the dogs hurl themselves at their dinner bowls.

He goes out and stands beneath the trees, his head craned back to watch them crossing back and forth between the branches, circling and whirling, maybe fifty of them. The bats swoop and swish and you can hear their wings like a dog's panting breath. Squeaking too, making little *chikkuting* noises to each other while they fly, back and forth, around and around, as if they're on strings. And all about him the bats' piss falls in a quiet patter on the dirt, in little raindrops on the leaves above. A sprinkle hits his shoulder and he jumps, says 'Fuck.' His voice is loud in the twilight.

He brushes at his shoulder as he walks back to the house, sniffs his fingers. It stinks. You can get diseases from bats. From bat piss, maybe, from bat shit. Or maybe it's that sort of lice you get, like from birds. *Vermin*, her brother said this afternoon. You could get diseases from vermin.

He thinks of the mynahs strutting around the verandah at her mum's place; thinks of Stephen's violent kick at the birds. But they were only birds. An Indian bloke in the hospital told him once that mynahs mate for life. And that the name came from some word for 'girl'.

He trudges in the back door and crosses the kitchen to wash his hands at the sink, craning to inspect the bat piss on his shirt. Filthy, fuck it.

He hears the television news theme from the bedroom as he gets changed, and comes out in his socks, pulling on a t-shirt.

'*More Cronulla rioters turn themselves in,*' says the woman with the news headlines, over the pictures of a kid walking up some steps to a cop shop, or courthouse. The news music still underneath the pictures, the kid turning his face from the camera. And then the picture changes, to a dusty street, a blasted shopfront with people yelling and wailing. '*And yet another attack in Iraq: officially the most dangerous place on the planet.*'

Tony stands in his socks, feet apart, watching. The newsreader's talking about some politician now, about roads in Sydney, so he goes and gets a beer from the fridge and twists off the lid. He sits down to peel the spuds at the table, where he can still watch the TV through the doorway.

A couple more riot kids have turned themselves in after the cops put their photos on the Internet. He looks at the kids walking in and then out of the cop shop. Ordinary kids with their dad or some other bloke, shame-faced and downcast, trying not to look at the cameras.

They didn't care in December, cameras or not. Tony watched it all, every bulletin, read every paper he could on those hot long days before Christmas when Sydney went ballistic. He takes a big gulp of the cold beer, and then another, waiting for it to slip cold over his brain like a sigh.

That week before Christmas he watched the Cronulla days unfolding, unrolling like a threat, like the fizzing rumour of a schoolyard fight. He watched how it spread, with the same hungry crowd always standing around, wanting it like a circus. On the television he saw how they chased for it, running in their thongs on the bitumen, the noise of their panting breath in the sound recordist's gear. He watched them gulping down their need of it with the beer and the sun, the moment growing and growing. He saw them sweating and red-faced, bawling, *Fuck off Lebs! Fuck off kebabs!* Screaming, *Go home you fuckin' filthy cunts*, and he saw WE GREW HERE YOU FLEW HERE, and he knew their need of it, the longing like their balls would break, and then they burst through the roof of the moment and it was all exploding relief—everywhere, even on a train, all the arms and legs and the jackhammer speed of punching.

He gets up from his chair and pulls some chops out of the freezer, tosses them in a dish and puts it in the microwave.

Watching it all, Tony had wished he was there, for the warm relief of being swept along in the human need of others, of belonging to it, to the running and the panting and all that hot revenge. And he wanted to be driving through the dark with them, with bats and nails and knives, smashing every window you could for the almighty fucking magnificent release of it all.

The microwave pings and he takes out the chops. They've started to cook at the edges but are still frozen in the middle. He bends the lump of them with his fingers, back and forth, to soften the frozen part, and then he breaks them apart and throws them on the grill tray and pushes it in. He puts the peeled potatoes into the water and sticks the lid back on.

Afterwards, on the TV he had watched the ones that did it, the Lebs and the Aussies. He watched them, surly and sulky, saying none of them done anything wrong of course, all the guts and glory gone with the new black eyes and the cops on the warpath. But in the middle of all the *we done nothin'* and the backsliding there was something Tony understood like a stone dropped into water. It was about the women. When they said what if it was *your* mum, your sister, who couldn't walk around without nobody to protect them. And when they said that about their women they straightened themselves up, sharp and hard and proud again, and Tony understood the power of their rightness.

He goes back to stand in the lounge-room doorway now, swigging from his beer while the Arabs on the screen wade through rubble and glass and broken window-frames from another bomb blast in Baghdad. It's a bloke reporter there now, and he's listing casualties. Then at the end, he says, '*Sixty-seven journalists have now been killed in Iraq since the US-led invasion in 2003.*'

Tony licks his lips, goes back to the stove.

And suddenly he knows something new, staring into the bubbling, milky potato water. It is Mandy, walking around without nobody protecting her—from Baghdad, from terror, from the old man's gunna die. Nobody else knows her; not the useless brother, the poofter husband.

Iraq officially the most dangerous place.

Understanding arches over Tony like a clear night sky. He has saved her once before, and he feels like a soldier for it. They're the same, they both recognise it now: only *he* knows her gruesome language, only they know what witnessing is. And only he protects her—this is the purpose of his life, he knows it now. She's come back, and it's an omen, and it's so simple it circles round and round him, graceful as a dark bat against the night.

THAT NIGHT they all come into the room as Chris sleeps heavily beside her. The old woman with the deformed back, the nurse shaking, the oiled and perfumed Kosovar girl. The earth full of faces, the boy Ahmer, the bushfire and the burned corpse.

Mandy sits up, breath hurting against her ribs. She tries to breathe quietly as panic dries her skin. Her ribs will crack.

She drives through the dark streets. The hospital car park is almost empty. Mandy walks the long fluorescent corridors and pushes the buzzer at the door of the ward. Through the door's small glass window she sees the nurses look up, and they let her in. As she enters the ward they take in her tangled bed hair, her tracksuit, give the briefest of sympathetic smiles and look away again, saying nothing as she walks past them to her father's bed in the gloom.

She sits down beside him. A light glows somewhere a few beds away. She can see the outline of his head and his face. The machines still blip and peep; she hears the same slow mechanical rise and fall of his chest. She hunches there in the chair, her hands around her knees. His slack jaw, the tape over his skin. She reaches out and draws one of his fish-limp hands from beneath the tight sheet, holds it in hers. She knows he can't feel anything, but she pulls down the pyjama sleeve where it has rucked up, in case he is cold.

She holds his hand to her own dry lips, and whispers to it, *Hello Dad.* And now all the days and years of swallowed fear and sorrow are merging into a single river, of grief, of never again being able to hold her father's hand in the night. She puts her forehead to the cool back of his hand, and with her free hand she fingers the lumps of a balled-up tissue from her pocket, wipes her dripping nose. A nurse's feet squeak towards her then, and a handful of clean tissues falls silent into her lap and the footsteps squeak away, and this kindness is the breaking of a final, cobwebbed thread, and in the near dark of her father's finishing life Mandy begins to cry, at first trying to stop and then letting it take her, her whole body croupy with the noise and breath of it. She cries that she can neither run from this nor save him, and her tears and snot run down the birdleg bones of her father's hand, her own two hands open beneath his like a beggar's, and she cries and cries and cries.

'WHEN ARE you going back?'

Her mouth is dry, her neck aching when she hears the voice. It wakes her, this question nobody has asked. She stares at him, stares around her. She can see no-one else awake in the ward now; the two nurses are somewhere else. It's just her and him, and the motionless bodies in the beds. She closes her mouth, bites down on the dry air, swallows. It must be nearly morning. Grime in the corners of her mouth.

She shakes her head a fraction, moves her lips but makes no sound.

Tony clears his throat. 'It's just. I've got something to say.' His voice quiet and steady, all eagerness gone, a shy, new certainty in its place.

She looks around for the nurses again, but the station is empty. She folds her arms across herself, draws her legs beneath her chair. Her sickened pulse begins, and time spreads out thin as gas, and her mind reels across years to a boy she sat next to in fourth class. Robert Cox, the boy she shared a desk with for a term. At nine years old she had the capacity to despise this boy for his hands with their blisters and warts. Robert Cox fought with other boys in the playground and he could not read, but lumbered over syllables, pointing at each one with his stubby finger. She was made to sit next to him as punishment because she once laughed to herself when he stumbled over a simple word. It was punishment for knowing she was better than him, with his spitting and fighting and swearing. And she knew he hated her, everything about her. For weeks they sat as far apart on their shared bench as the space would allow, not a sound passing between them. She did her silent reading from the Scholastic comprehension cards: she was up to olive, just one away from gold, while Robert Cox was still on blue. She read and read, hating the way he breathed through his mouth, hating his filthy hands. And then, over the weeks, something happened. Once he was rummaging in his bag for a pen and couldn't find one. The teacher scowled across at him and she could feel his body, across the space of the bench, could feel his fear. She pushed a pen across the desk to him. They didn't speak, but he grabbed the pen and she knew, without looking at him, his gratitude and his surprise. Another time she had a runny nose, but no tissue or hanky, and as the panic rose—she had to sniff, her nose dripped once—Robert Cox produced for her a handkerchief, perfectly blue, perfectly clean. In the playground they would never look at one another, nor speak, but if they saw one another in the street, outside school, their eyes might meet and they might exchange a glance. And there in the classroom, the space of their shared desk took on the air of a marriage, of sorts. A mistaken one, to be sure, but not without kindness, not without dignity.

Robert Cox and the intimacy of a school desk pass through her mind in an instant, but now she is an adult and alone, and Tony Warren has something to say. He turns, and she turns too, to see her father, to listen to the ventilator's low motorised noise. Then she turns back to face him, standing there with his hands in his pockets beside the bed in which her father lies dying, and she waits for him to open his mouth to destroy her.

'Have you got an iPod?' Tony asks.

And Mandy's breath comes rushing back.

She almost faints with it, this rushing familiar elation of survival—that Tony Warren is only a fool, that he is nothing at all. She breaks free of this moment and his beautiful, stupid question.

'No,' she says, in a voice cold as death, and she stands up to finish him. But Tony cuts in, nodding, eyes shining.

'I thought I could get one. For us to listen to when—' he pauses, eerie with his knowing, certain smile: 'I'm coming with you when you go back. To look after ya.'

She cannot believe what he has said.

And now he's standing so close to her with his horrific smile, and the stale waft of his breath and his waiting life enters her nostrils, throat, lungs. There is no escape. Dread surges up through every limb, seizes her, thrusts her backwards and she hears her own shouting, she is tripping and shoving chairs, trolleys, there is the tinkle of drip stands. '. . . get AWAY FROM ME,' she is shrieking, raising her hands before her. And all the while through her raised arms she can see his face—the shock, the disbelief—and he's grasping at her, as if trying to fathom his way through her dread that is unfathomable, and he's calling 'but *I know you*' and '*protection*' even while the nurses and a security man appear to clamp down his flailing arms.

WHEN THEY have led him away with their calm, loud voices a nurse returns to Mandy, puts a hand on her shoulder.

'I'm sorry. He's a bit—you know.' She tilts her head. 'He doesn't mean anything bad, he's just sort of . . . ' She looks at Mandy's shaking hands. 'But he's been told about harassing people.'

Mandy blows her nose again, shaking her head. 'I'm just so *tired*,' she says, as the breath catches at her ribs, sending her voice up into the start of another cry.

'Don't worry,' the nurse says, rubbing her shoulder.

When she has gone Mandy tries to stop her jittering hands, sitting with her father, and the burned man, and Tony, and the thudding of her heart that will not stop.

CAST OUT in the car park in the near-dawn Tony can think of nothing. He is all breath and his brain is panicked, drowning in not understanding, in *her* not understanding.

He cannot grasp it, the meaning of her looking at him with that face, the horror in it.

He stands there alone in the electric light of the car park, sweat all over him, his legs shaking. The doors have been locked behind him. They called *security*. He shakes his head hard, quick, for a second. He's gotta try to understand. He walks to his ute, gets in and drives through the dark streets. Keeps driving, licking his lips, trying to figure his way through. The floundering of his mind. *Slow down*, but his thinking sloshes and flails. Driving and driving, grinding the gears. When he finds himself at home it's like he's never left it, like none of it happened. But something happened. He turns off the ignition, hears his own panting breath. He wants a drink.

In the back of the kitchen cupboard there is one half-empty and one full bottle of rum. He grabs them, clinking, and goes back out to the ute, throws the bottles onto the passenger seat. He goes into the dark shed and comes out again, knowing only faintly what he is doing as he moves in the grey light. The dogs shift in surprise and one barks once, soft, at his approach, and then they shake themselves awake, confused and whining, at the sound of the feed hitting their bowls. He cannot think but his body knows where he's going, knows what to do.

When he comes back to the ute he falls into the seat, starts the ignition again and drives back down the rutted road, shuddering the vehicle along the track, driving and driving and grinding the gears.

When he finally gets there he stops the ute, turns off the ignition. With the lid off the first bottle, its sickly sweet stink fills the cabin. He swigs a big, long drink, and tries, again, to think. But all he can see is her backing away with her arms up, dragging things, a chair, a trolley, between them. He drinks again, and now the alcohol prickles warmly at his brain, in his sinuses and his chest. His breathing begins to slow down. Something begins to emerge out of the dreadful spangling noise in his head.

He shoves the car seat back as he drinks some more, staring out at the grey diagonal bars of the transmission tower. The tower is cool, taut and elegant in the moonlight. Something gets clearer, and then a word crystallises out of these last few days with a final, throttling shock.

She thinks that he is *vermin.*

He cries out in the dark.

CHAPTER SIXTEEN

Day six

THEY SIT and stand, a still life gathered around Geoff's bed. Margaret is in the chair nearest the head of the bed, leaning forward, her legs crossed beneath the chair. Her palms are open in her lap, and she turns her wedding ring around and around with the third finger and thumb of the other hand. She's not ever looked at it this closely; the thin gold band is scuffed with the tiny marks and scratches of all the years.

Cathy stands next to her, one knee resting on the padded mauve arm of the chair, and her hand lies along the squashy vinyl of its headrest. Now and then she squeezes the soft pad of it beneath her fingers, watching it compress and slowly expand. Stephen is at the foot of the bed, rocking back and forth on his long legs, hands in the pockets of his jacket. Mandy and Chris are on the other side, Mandy leaning with her elbows on the bed's rails, Chris standing behind her, a hand on her back.

They are all watching the battered body of their father, as they have watched him for a week. A minute ago they stood outside the curtain while the nurses pulled away the tubes, removed the sticking plaster. They heard the sound, then. A switch, and then the stopping of the ventilator's breath that has muttered beneath all their moments in this room for the long last days.

Then the curtains drew back and now here he is, unburdened, breathing his own breaths, asleep. It is as though he is, suddenly, going to live. As though this moment is the beginning of his life.

'You know,' says the young nurse, her face serious, 'that this can take a long time. Days, possibly.'

They nod; their glances skitter around the bed at each other. The nurse moves away, wrapping the tubing in a quick, graceful figure of eight and then with a single practised movement she shucks off the latex gloves which now contain the tubes, and she lets the white rubber bundle fall with an arc into a yellow bag as she passes.

They stand and sit for an hour, shifting their weight, absorbing the silence, watching their father's oxygen come and go. The sounds of work and life take place behind them, rising and falling. The sound of working footsteps, of telephones, the hydraulic door opening slowly, *pshhhh*. There is a nurse's murmured greeting. Then there is the sound of the same voice risen in shock. There are high drawn breaths, and something dropped, and to Mandy these are old, old sounds, and even before she turns around she recognises them, in the passing of that long slow second, as the sounds of death.

All their faces turn and then there he is, and all the days, all the years have been gathering towards this moment of Tony standing in the room, naked but for the blue tracksuit pants hanging off his skinny hips, barefoot. He stands on the cool linoleum with his face collapsed into drunkenness and some terrible grief, and he's rocking on his feet, cradling a shotgun in his arms, his skin goosefleshed with the cold and what he has come here to do.

Stephen speaks. 'Tony.' His voice all breath.

Tony raises the gun with one hand, and points it straight at Stephen.

'You can *fuck* off,' Tony mumbles, slurring, and he's looking past all of them, to Mandy. The smell of the rum, his voice sticky with it.

Stephen's voice goes lower still, he whispers, '*Stay calm, mate,*' he is praying it, '*please mate, please mate,*' but the shotgun stays up and they are all suspended in the silent exploding of their heartbeats and breath. The only sound is their father breathing aloud in the unconscious air, and now of Tony beginning to cry, in liquid, nasal sobs. Then he starts to mutter, staring at Mandy, and the open mouth of the gun moves through the white air, a weathervane slowing to stop at her, and his voice is crackled with its own disbelief, sobbing out to her, 'I . . . am not . . . *vermin.*'

Mandy hears her own cool clear voice.

'Tony.'

She is surprised at how easily she has slipped from Chris's grip and propelled herself past the others. They are making noises but she cannot hear them, she has straightened her arms behind her to shed them and now the weathervane follows her as she steps out of her family and into the open centre of the room, into the last seconds of her life.

She says, 'I know why we're the same.' She has never felt so calm. 'I know what you meant. I understand now.'

And as she speaks the crisp, dark openings of the shotgun barrels are opening up to her, and she stares into the blooming shadows and thinks, *okay.* She has left her life behind, and she and Tony are together again in the suspended dark space, the fire burning towards them. She stares into it. *I'm ready.*

And Tony starts to move, a violent shaking takes his body and he's sobbing out incomprehensible things, the snot running down into his mouth, and the rhythm of his shouted words is the rhythm of his body as he lifts his other hand to steady the shotgun's aim at her. All she can see is that dark approaching centre, and she hears her sister inhaling great breaths, hears running and shouting coming from far away down the corridor but it is like listening to the soft beat of bird wings. Tony steps towards her with one swoop and sound, and then she shouts out '*NO!*' and there is a single unstoppable *crack*.

He has shot his own throat and face away.

The screaming breaks open the sealed moment then, as the bright bloody mess of him falls to the floor. One nurse stands screaming and screaming with her two hands clamped over her mouth, and another hurls herself to Tony on the floor, pulling sheets with her, and Chris is holding Mandy rigid by the arms and Stephen is open-mouthed and crying with a hacking sound, and Cathy and Margaret are cleaved to each other heaving, and everywhere there are people running in their rubber shoes and shouting.

But Mandy pulls free once again to kneel with the nurses at the side of Tony there on the floor in the blood and the flailing, as they tear his clothes away and shout and hold the drenched sheets to his shattered head.

She kneels, all sound gone quiet in her head, paying attention to the petals of his flesh torn open, the black and red and charcoal mess of him, and in the mess she finds an eye, entire and watchful, and people are screaming and shoving and someone is vomiting and it is only Mandy who can be still, who can stay with him, watching him through the clear brown iris of his eye, and as it solidifies and goes pale she sees all the years, all the miserable story of Tony's life falling away from him and he is only a man, naked and stained and mistaken, and with his last few paltry breaths he sheds his life.

# CHAPTER SEVENTEEN

IT IS a Sunday afternoon. Mandy and Stephen slouch on the back steps in the sun. Next to each of them, on the counterpointed stairs, is a half-drunk glass of wine. Lunch is long over; they all sat at the outdoor table, picking over the dishes of reheated lasagne and curry and the plates of slumped cheeses left over from the funeral.

Margaret potters around the garden, dazed from the wine, stepping across the beds to inspect a leaf or nip off the dead head of a flower with her fingertips. Cathy and Chris are washing up in the kitchen, and the sounds of dishes and running water and their talking waft out through the window above Stephen and Mandy on the steps. From far off, across the town, come the lost chimes of a church bell. Mandy and Stephen stare at nothing, across the space of the garden. They are both thinking of Tony.

THREE DAYS ago Stephen sat on a cushioned chair in one of the town's three funeral homes. The rest of the family waited in a row outside, each sitting on the reproduction antique chairs in the plush red-carpeted waiting room. On the smoked-glass table were some brochures for a video production service, a bowl of promotional chocolates, and a vase of nylon flowers on vivid green stalks.

The room in which Stephen sat was set up to suggest a chapel, with thick velvet curtains, a subdued wooden cross and low lighting. It was cocooned in quiet. The coffin was shiny and black atop its folding metal trolley.

They had chosen the coffin from a catalogue, sitting dumbly around the dining room table. The photographs floated in nothingness on the page, set in soft blurs of manipulated mist or rainforest frond. Margaret's finger had hovered over something elaborate and deep mahogany, murmuring, 'That one's lovely.' The others had looked at one another over her head, shrugged.

Mandy had smoothed her mother's back with her hand in long, firm strokes, and then Margaret had lifted her face, eyes full of tears, confusion. She'd said, her fingertip pressing on the same picture, 'It's horrible, isn't it?'

And they had all begun to cry then, nodding, blowing their noses. The plain black, it was decided, with silver handles.

A little later, as the man from the funeral directors' sat with Margaret and Chris on the couch, filling out forms, Stephen flipped through the catalogue on the table. He stopped on a page near the back full of short, stumpy coffins. *Bow side style*, *Tulip*. Kids. How terrible. *The White Pearl*, in Polished White, Decorative Floral Handles. Stephen felt the tears coming again. Then another line at the bottom of the page caught his eye. *The Bow-sided Pet Coffin is an elegant variation on the toe-pincher style. Small, medium and large sizes.* He let out a gasp, and at the same instant Mandy had seen it, and they seized each other's arms in silent, tearful chortling.

At the funeral home the next day Stephen sat beside the coffin for long minutes, not lifting his head to see over its lip. After a while he heaved himself up and stepped across the carpet. His father lay there, perfectly straight, dressed in the old black dinner suit he wore to Mandy's wedding so long ago. There was some white silky fabric wispy over his lower half. Stephen moved the fabric to find his hands; they were there, a strange, pale yellow, crossed at his stomach. His face was yellowish too, smooth and hard and faintly gleaming. *Waxen* the only possible word, Stephen thought.

Geoff's hair was combed back, the dreadful wound cleaned and drained of colour, covered now with only a small white dressing.

Stephen reached out and gently, gently touched a smooth grey wave of hair. Then he stepped back and bent to a plastic shopping bag on the floor, pulled out the battered red paper kite. He held it for a moment and then flexed his fingers and bent it, snapping the remaining thin crossbar of the dowel in two. It was a gentle snapping, the final breaking of an old bone. He folded the kite carefully and then pushed the narrow triangle of it down into the space between the satiny pleats of the coffin and his father's gauze-wrapped thigh.

He did not know what to do then, in that last long moment. He leaned over, patted his father's chest. He said, in a whisper, 'Bye-bye, Dad.' It was not enough, but it was everything he had, and then he walked, tears streaming, from the room.

MANDY PICKS up the glass from the step next to her, twists its stem in her fingers. Across town Tony is being lowered into the ground, the same ground into which they let their father go. Into which, perhaps, they all will go. She wonders whose job it was, to patch poor Tony up, arrange his shattered remains back into human shape.

The hospital is organising a trauma counsellor from Sydney for the staff, for all of them. For her mother's sake, Mandy has agreed to go.

She watches Margaret now in the garden where she reaches gingerly to grasp a thorny rose stem between two careful fingers, leaning to peer into the flower's browning petals.

I know why we're the same, Mandy had said to him in the raining terrible air of that moment. And she does know; too late, she knows. She and Tony are the ruined. They are each that trapped long-ago bird, wedged rotting between its river rocks, both stained with decay from too much death, from too much misery too closely watched.

Mandy notices, across the garden, how her mother's aching hip has given her a lopsided lean as she walks. Then she brings her attention to Stephen's calloused toes in his blue rubber thongs on the step beside her. She listens to the chink and dunk of the dishes in the kitchen sink behind them. Then Stephen's feet disappear, she hears him pull himself upright and now he passes her, flip-flipping down the steps in his thongs, walking over the grass to their mother. The screen door bangs above her and she turns to see Cathy holding it open, calling out, 'Anyone want tea?' From behind Cathy in the gloom Chris meets Mandy's eyes, his gaze tender. She tips back the glass to drink the last of her wine, listening to these murmuring voices, watching Stephen's hand on his mother's shoulder as they frown together at the spotted rose.

When everything is useless, when there is nothing to be done, all we can do is pay attention, keep watch. In his boy's-own innocent's fucked-up vigil, Tony knew this, and it was all he had. Her remorse will never leave her.

She leans forward, stands up, collecting the glass to go inside and help with the dishes. Because it is enough. And her purpose now, she knows more certainly than anything, is to keep watch over these small things, these ordinary decencies. To pay attention to her mother's walk, to Chris's voice. Her sister's, brother's eyes.

As she turns to go inside, there in the bright backyard something catches her eye. An Indian mynah is arcing up to the roof of the house, carrying in its beak one end of a white streamer of nylon packing tape. Mandy watches the bird as it settles for a few seconds on the crossbar of the television aerial, the long, long white strand trailing down over the guttering.

And then it's gone, the aerial quivering, and the bird shoots up in a sharp swoop over all the roofs and yards, up and up, its white kite-tail streaming behind it, up into the wide blue sky.

 ACKNOWLEDGEMENTS

MY GREATEST gratitude is to Kylie Morris—for reading, generous advice, and above all, her encouragement.

The book was partly written in Hobart, Tasmania, as part of the Tasmanian Writers' Centre's Island of Residencies program, which was supported by the City of Hobart and Arts Tasmania. The writing was also supported by a grant from the Literature Board of the Australia Council and by Varuna, The Writers' House.

Among a great many helpful books, the writings of Janine di Giovanni—especially *Madness Visible: A Memoir of War*, from which I adapted the incident on page 171—were essential, as was Denise Leith's *Bearing Witness: The Lives of War Correspondents and Photojournalists*.

For their generosity in myriad ways, my thanks to the Farey and McElvogue families; Jane Doepel; my colleagues, especially Graham Smith; the Clifford-Smiths; Russell Daylight; Caroline Baum and David Roach; Beck Hazel; Anna Funder; Jane Johnson and Brian Murphy; Henry Simmons; Jenny Darling; Siobhán Cantrill; Judith Lukin-Amundsen; and Jane Palfreyman. And enormous thanks to Tegan Bennett Daylight, Peter Bishop, Vicki Hastrich, Lucinda Holdforth and Eileen Naseby for early reading and insightful comments.

As always, I thank my brother and sisters and their families for their loving support. And to my husband Sean, always encouraging through the daily grind, my love and gratitude.

Greatest American Hero (Theme) 'Believe It Or Not'
Words and music by Mike Post/Stephen Geyer
© 1981 Dar-Jen Music Inc, Darla Music
For Australia and New Zealand:
EMI Songs Australia Pty Limited
(ABN 85 000 063 267)
PO Box 35, Pyrmont, NSW 2009, Australia
International copyright secured.
All rights reserved. Used by permission.
© 1981 SJC Music administered by Universal Music Publishing Pty Ltd
All rights reserved. International copyright secured.
Reprinted with permission.

'I Am Australian'
Words and music by Bruce Woodley/Dobe Newton
© 1987 Pocketful of Tunes Pty Ltd
For Australia and New Zealand:
Alfred Publishing (Australia) Pty Ltd
(ABN 15 003 954 247)
PO Box 2355, Taren Point, NSW 2229, Australia
International copyright secured. All rights reserved.
Unauthorised reproduction is illegal.
Reproduced with kind permission of Origin Music Group.